Measure of Vengeance

A Mystery

by

Jerry Jellison

A Write Way Publishing Book

Write Way Publishing
PO Box 441278
Aurora, CO 80044

First Edition; 2000

ISBN 1-885173-72-5

1 2 3 4 5 6 7 8 9

Chapter 1

Megan Roarke gazed down on the agitation of Fifth Avenue, twelve floors below. The morning sun scattered intense reflection and deep shadow across the tall buildings of Manhattan. It was still fairly cool, but those on the street would be sweltering in the soggy afternoon heat before long.

"Ah, summer in New York."

She turned and sank into the foamy chair at her desk. The editorial meeting was an hour away, and she expected to take some heat from Harmon Jarvis. It had required four months to plow through the pile of manuscripts left by her predecessor, and there wasn't a decent novel in the heap.

Her eyes fell upon a black envelope neatly centered on the desk. She slid the dozen pages out, coming wearily to rest on her elbows as her head drooped forward in a gesture more resignation than interest.

Delicious Pain — Chapter 1

The first woman, I killed for practice—mainly to see if I could. We have been taught from birth that murder is wrong, and it is difficult to override social conditioning.

I do not know why life exists here. From dark and swirling gases, amino acids formed. Then living cells, each cell bearing the right and responsibility to reproduce itself to benefit the greater organism. When this copy is made, it must form the same ilk. Otherwise, a

mutation will occur and the hapless result will experience rejection or reproduce itself into a nonessential and destructive cancer.

These troublesome issues lead me to contemplate our origins and ultimate destiny. There are those who would call me atheist, but not so. Random probability is no more believable than divine direction, leading to perfection of the female form. But had an omniscient God created us, would he not define relationships between men and women? Regrettably, these were left to chance on this planet.

Megan reached for the phone. "Heather, what is this thing on my desk?"

The soft voice of her assistant floated back. "It's an unsolicited submission. I thought you'd want to see it."

"Why? It sucks."

"Have you gotten past the philosophy yet?"

"No."

"I think you should finish it."

"If you say so, but I need some coffee to get my heart started."

Heather brightened. "I'll bring it in if you'll keep reading."

"Deal."

Megan hung up and turned back to the manuscript, tempted to sweep it into the wastebasket. But her eyes fell on the next line.

So I killed her ... elimination of one destructive cell for the good of the whole. I was in the Air Force at the time, maintaining the vast pipeline system that carried fuel to our bases in Morocco. There, I met my first love.

My partner in crime was named Ben Brouhagh. We had a flourishing black-market operation, and we spent our off-duty time whoring in ports along the Atlantic Coast—even kept a mattress in the back of our truck.

We went out that Saturday night and drank ourselves into oblivion. In the half-light of dawn, we climbed into the truck and managed to find the ignition. Then I saw her. Even in my condition, her sexuality called out. It sprang across the void between us like a powerful radio wave. Her name, I would soon learn, was Najia.

She was gloriously beautiful, and the flowing garments provided no concealment for her supple body. They enhanced her fluid lines, causing the breasts to well up, her pelvis more round and perfect than seemed possible in a real woman. She carried a water pot on her hip and turned her head away as we approached, appearing to ignore our attention.

Of course, I understood the ploy—no better way to attract men than flout advances. With coyness, she clung to the wall and remained silent. Silence is a great attribute in women most of the time, but in this case I found it infuriating. Ben cut her off by lodging the truck's bumper against the wall and we hauled her into the back.

I pinned her to the mattress as Ben drove into the desert. She was clever, this one. She knew how to entice a man ... bring him to the edge of passion by feigning resistance. Suddenly, I sensed the evil in her, and bound her wrists and ankles with wire.

Minutes later, Ben turned off the road and came back to join us. The bitch turned to him, pleading that we had misunderstood—that she was not that kind. For a moment I thought he might believe her lies, but he too sensed the evil in her and walked away into the sunrise, lest he be infected.

She stared up at me with the pleading brown eyes of a wounded doe. But I was not to be fooled. I knew she would destroy me if I let her go. Never directly, no! With those wide eyes and façade of innocence, she would beguile other men to harm me in the name of the law or social outrage.

In the early morning light, I unsheathed my knife to cut away her clothes, exposing the radiant brown skin. How many men had she teased into sexual frenzy, only to drive them away after making them crawl? Now, it was

my turn—my responsibility to exact a measure of vengeance for my own kind. Before I was done ...

Megan threw her head back as Heather entered the room. "If you ever get another submission like this, burn it."

"I had the same reaction, Meg, but I think it might sell."

"Why?"

Heather set down the coffee and settled into a guest chair. "A few years ago, I saw an interview with a young woman who had been abducted by a rapist. She told some things he did to her, how he controlled her, but stopped short of the visceral detail—understandable since she was on a major network and there were legal considerations. But it left me hungry to know more. Have you ever experienced something like that?"

"I suppose."

"Well, this guy gives the detail, the perceptions of a whacko—in first person."

Megan smiled. "Who's the author?"

"I don't know. It came with a typed note. No name. No signature. He says he'll identify himself after he submits a few more chapters. Claims he's published in another genre and wants to try his hand at horror."

"You're joking."

"No."

"Is it agented?"

"No mention of it."

"How did it get in the door?"

"Came in the mail, addressed to you."

Megan stretched her long legs and rocked gently. "So this hotshot submitted an incomplete fiction manuscript, unagented, with no mention of credentials ... not even the decency to identify himself."

"Um-hmm. He's broken just about every rule in the book."

"And you still want me to read it?"

Heather considered her for a moment. "Did you get to the actual rape?"

"Ahhh, no."

"Then you won't believe what he does to her ... what he thinks while he's doing it. You have to finish it, Meg."

Megan shook her head slowly. "I'm not sure I can. His writing is pretentious and the concept is disgusting."

"You aren't curious to see where he's going with it?"

"Well, I do hope the one who kills him is a woman."

"That sounds like an emotional reaction." She scanned Megan's face. "Isn't that what a writer's supposed to do? Evoke emotion? If it gets to the reader's gut, it will probably sell."

Megan regarded Heather Bounton. With the natural beauty of youth, and long blond hair in large looping curls, she looked like she'd just dropped her pom-poms and walked off the field. But she had confidence beyond her years and an instinct for what the buying public wanted.

"All right. I'll read it later." Megan slipped the pages into the envelope and tossed it into her briefcase. "Right now, I have to prepare for a meeting."

"I'll bet you're not looking forward to it."

"I wouldn't take that bet, even with odds. If I don't come up with some decent projects soon ..."

Heather slumped, clasping her hands in her lap. "What are you going to do, Meg?"

"Several things to look for new talent, but the top priority is to steal some of the authors I worked with before."

"Do you think you can lure them away?"

Megan leaned forward and lowered her voice. "Actually, two or three have expressed interest."

"Why? Everyone knows we're on shaky ground."

"True, but you build up a bond of trust when you work together for a number of years."

Heather shook her head solemnly. "I think there would have to be some financial incentive."

"You may be right, but there's always room for negotiation in this game."

"Good luck." Heather rose and headed for the door. "Don't forget you're having lunch with Irv Miller today. Wolfe's at eleven-thirty."

"I couldn't possibly forget that."

Megan extracted a mirror from her purse. Dark green eyes smiled back, framed by thick lashes above sculptured cheek bones, the delicate nose and sensuous lips that had brought her within a heartbeat of the Miss Nebraska title in a former life.

"I hope it's enough. God knows I don't have a story." She ran her fingers through her rich auburn hair, feeling the weight of swirling curls that settled onto the shoulder pads of her dark blue jacket, then reached for the warbling phone.

"Meg, this is Janet. Please hold for Harmon Jarvis."

She shuddered. Why would the editor-in-chief call her only minutes before the impending meeting?

Jarvis had preceded her to Gladiator Press by a mere two weeks. His pale blue eyes, framed by short graying hair, tended to peer over half-height reading glasses, an effect both quizzical and reproving. He was six feet tall with a barrel chest which forced a sharp wrinkle in the lapels of his tweed coats. Somehow he didn't look the part, but his marketing flair was the greatest hope for turning Gladiator's fortunes around.

"Megan?"

"Yes?"

"Harmon here. I was wondering if you have some solid projects for this morning's meeting."

"Well, I've got several manuscripts with potential."

"Potential won't make it. We need some winners here." He paused. "That's why I wanted to speak to you privately ... no use to make a scene in front of the others."

"I appreciate that, Harmon." She glanced at her case. "I should have something in a couple of weeks."

"I'll take your word for it. But we need results, Meg, and we don't have a lot of time."

Megan dropped the receiver and sat for some time as if she'd been slapped. Slowly, she pivoted and stared at the table by the wall—a hundred manuscripts stacked on top, and two hundred more underneath. Had she missed something? Could there be one or two strong novels in there? Did she have the time to go through them again?

She sensed a presence, and her head snapped around. Achal Bedi was standing in the doorway. Originally from New Delhi, his features were remarkably Caucasian except for thick black hair and dark skin that stood in stark contrast to the snow white of massive teeth and large brown eyes. His athletic frame was accentuated by a very deep chest, and the spring in his step belied his forty-some years. He was quite possibly the most handsome man she had ever seen in person ... an Indian version of Omar Sharif.

"Sorry, Meg. I didn't mean to startle you."

"Well, that doesn't take much nowadays."

He smiled. "Are you ready for the meeting?"

She whined like a little girl. "Oooh, could I pass on this one?"

"I don't think Harmon would like that."

"Believe me, he won't like it any better if I'm there." She dropped her head forward to sink her fingers into the thick tresses, then pulled hard and let out a muted scream. "Go on, Achal. Save yourself!"

"All right." He backed out and turned down the hallway.

She blew at a lock of hair that was covering her right eye. *But we need results, Meg. And we don't have a lot of time.* Through a dreamlike haze, Megan watched the long red nails of her right hand slip across the rim of her briefcase and settle in vivid contrast on the black envelope.

Chapter 2

Megan flowed out of the crowd on the sidewalk and ducked into the doorway of Wolfe's on Sixth Avenue. The long room was comforting with its dark wood paneling and smell of cooking spices. An array of liquor bottles gleamed behind the antique bar that ran nearly the length of the room on her left, and under the high tiled ceiling people sat at tables or stood drinking in clusters, embroiled in the din of competing human speech.

She climbed the dark staircase along the right wall and rounded the corner to see the approaching maitre d'.

"How are you today, Miss Roarke?"

"Fine, Armand. Has Mr. Miller arrived?"

"Yes. I put him at your table up front."

He turned to escort her, but she touched his arm. "Never mind, I know the way." She strode toward the windows, aware of the eyes that scanned her. Conversation was suspended as men stared openly at full flashing calves, flowing hair, or the wide V of her back. She nodded to several colleagues from the publishing community and smiled as the room resumed its normal buzz in her wake.

Irv Miller sat reading the menu, his profile strikingly outlined by intense sunlight streaming through the large windows. Very trim, and three or four inches over six feet tall, his three-piece suit and distinguished silver hair reminded her of a politician.

Megan dumped her purse onto the floor. "Good afternoon, Irv." She glanced at her watch. "Almost afternoon. Sorry I'm late."

"No problem. So was I." He stood up and moved around to hold her chair.

She settled in and gazed down at the street. Sunlight glinted from the endless sea of Medallion cabs, interspersed with private cars and delivery trucks, all creeping erratically northward in the eternal gridlock that was Manhattan.

"This town depresses me, Irv. So many people with so many places to go. Half of them going one way and the other half coming back, and every one of them on some urgent mission."

"Like bees. Many disconnected parts that make up some greater whole." He eyed her across the table. "But there's also great energy here—commerce, big money, and cosmopolitan atmosphere. Don't you feel a twinge of pride in being a part of it?"

"I don't know if I belong. I'm still a naive little girl sitting on a tractor in Nebraska with a stalk of hay between her teeth."

He gave her a bemused look. "So, what tortuous path *did* bring you to New York? You've never told me, you know."

"You want the long version or the short?"

"We have an hour."

"Then, let's not waste it on the long version. I escaped from a farming community in a place you never heard of. Women were supposed to get married and spawn children to work the fields. We had scintillating conversations at the Sunday dinner table about uncle Carl's gout or the Andersons' tragic divorce ... a crashing bore.

"The boys shunned me because I would rather read Voltaire than pooch around behind the barn. My girlfriends couldn't understand why I wasn't into animal husbandry and home economics. I knew there was a world beyond the south forty, and I wanted to get out there."

Miller smiled. "So you rebelled against your origins."

"No. I just refused to live my life according to their constraints." She paused in thought. "It's hard to explain. Except for my mother, nobody believed I could make it on the outside. But it wasn't just a passive doubt. It was aggressive derision, like they would be somehow diminished if I succeeded."

"And in the end, you showed them all."

"Who knows? It did result in a scholarship to Wellesley, and this—wonderful career." She lowered her head for several seconds, then looked up with misty eyes. "How about that? Maudlin at noon and I haven't even had a drink."

Irv leaned forward. "Most people would give their eye teeth to have your job."

"Well, one of them may get a shot at it before long." She picked up her menu and made a face. "Same old stuff."

He gave her a wry glance. "Why do you bother to look at the menu? You'll order shrimp curry."

She looked up. "That predictable, huh?"

"That consistent." Irv sat back as the waiter approached. When the attentive young man departed, he grinned at her. "See?"

Megan tossed her head. "Why take a risk, when you know it's the best thing in the house?"

"Indeed." He tore open a roll and scooped butter into it. "Are you ready to talk about your novel?"

"I guess."

"I'd like you to make a few changes before we take it to market." He extracted a folded sheet of paper from his inside coat pocket and laid it on the table in front of her. "Look this over at your leisure, and call me if you have any questions."

"How about a quick look now?"

"If you'd like."

She opened it and scanned. "There are some serious problems here, especially this paragraph on characterization."

"You want to discuss them now?"

"No." She slipped the page into her purse. "You're right. I should do my homework first."

He dipped his head in agreement. "I hope you don't mind me making suggestions."

"Not at all. Show me how to improve profit potential, and consider it done." Megan sagged onto her elbows. "Know what does bother me though? I would peg these problems in a heartbeat in another writer's work. Why can't I see them in my own?"

"At the risk of being obvious, you're too close to it. You've been living with these characters and events for some time. They are crystal clear in your mind, but you can't be sure those wondrous images have been transferred to the page until someone else reads it." Miller sat back and thumbed his shirt into his belt. "Every writer needs an editor, Meg. And believe me, it gets easier to critique yourself as time goes by. Just keep writing."

She turned away and stared at the people sitting on the fountain across the street—some eating brown-bag lunches or deli sandwiches, while others read the daily newspaper or talked in pairs. For a moment, she sensed that she had adapted to Manhattan. The scene was almost pastoral in spite of the horns and raised voices that wafted on the still, hot air and penetrated the thick windows from time to time.

So what if her book wasn't perfect? She would never live to see a perfect novel. At least it was a good story. Irv had no complaints about the plot, and the other problems could be solved with relatively little effort. But she had seen some great novels shot down because she could not get corporate approval. And she'd seen trash published, occasionally with great financial success. Megan shuddered as she remembered the black envelope in her case.

Irv studied her face. "Is something wrong?"

"Oh, it's been a rough day."

"You want to talk about it?"

"Well, I got chewed out by Harmon Jarvis this morning." Her eyes narrowed and she leaned forward conspiratorially. "You better get me published quick. I may need a new job."

"That serious?"

"It might be. Jarvis has a specific mission, and he can't afford to mess around with people who aren't producing. Probably the smart move would be to jump ship and let Gladiator sink by itself. But I can't."

"Why not?"

"It's how I was raised." She stared into space for a few seconds. "I remember a cold autumn day, overcast and dreary ... my father trudging home along the dirt road with his lunch pail in hand. He'd worked his fingers to the bone to build a feed and grain business in town. Then, just when it was turning the corner, the owner built a big house, bought the boat, and started taking off for weeks at a time. When the cash flow caught up with him, he neglected to pay his taxes."

"And the government shut him down."

"Yeah." Megan chewed her lip. "It wasn't my father's fault, but he was never the same. Now he works harvests or paving crews ... anything to keep him out of town. I think he's embarrassed to be around people he used to deal with."

"Will you leave town if Jarvis fires you?"

"No, but it wouldn't be easy to live with." Megan shook her head. "I can't even allow myself to think of that possibility. I have to make this work."

"What are you doing about it?"

"Well, I'm courting some of my old authors. I've contacted every agent I ever worked with, stepped up trips to writer's conventions, and asked a number of writer's clubs to put a blurb in their newsletters."

Irv nodded. "That should bring in a ton of material."

"Yes, but I don't have great expectations about quality of the stuff out there. In the meantime, I'm clutching at straws." The dark hair quivered as Megan shook her head. "Like this strange piece that came in the mail, ostensibly the first chapter of a novel. In normal times I wouldn't have gone past page one. Today, I read the whole thing."

"What's it about?"

"It reads like the memoirs of a serial killer."

"Might work well in today's market." He grinned. "Does he have an agent?"

Megan stared at him, the green irises framed by white. "Irv, you don't know what it's like."

"Graphic violence? Sexual perversion?"

"In the extreme."

"Scary?"

"Sick. He writes like a misogynist. I think he truly hates women."

"The character or the author?"

"I'm not sure."

Irv drifted off for a few seconds. "You know, I always wanted to write a dark novel."

"Why didn't you?"

"I was afraid people would think those crazy, evil thoughts were my own." He eyed her with friendly concern. "Believe me, I've worked with some goofy writers over the years. Who cares, as long as it sells?"

"I have a bad feeling about this one."

"Why?"

"Because it's abnormal. Nobody submits one chapter at a time. Why did he use a black envelope? And since it isn't my genre, why did he send it to me?"

"I'd guess he doesn't know the rules of submission." Irv laughed. "He probably sprayed it out to every editor in town. I wouldn't take it personally."

Chapter 3

A Mexican with blue eyes was rare, even in his native New Mexico. Here the anomaly frequently drew open stares. Oscar Colunga squinted into bright sunlight as he gazed down on the streets of Hartford from the Office of Special Investigation, the research and analysis section of the Connecticut State Police.

Sensing that everyone was seated around the large conference table, he turned to the three people expectantly gazing at him. Hank Oliphant and Earl Hoffman were detectives he'd met on previous cases. The woman was a slender young brunette who worked in his department, one of the best data analysts he'd ever come across.

His gravelly voice rose from a stocky frame and bounced off the walls like a growling bear. "Gentlemen, do you both know Kathy Huntsinger?"

"I don't believe I've had the pleasure." Earl Hoffman rose from his chair and extended his hand across the table.

Colunga waited for them to settle. "We are opening an investigation into a series of unsolved murders in the state, and I requested a task force to include officers with eyes and ears on the street."

"And they stuck you with us?"

"Welcome aboard, Hank." Colunga smiled and moved to

a six-foot map of Connecticut on the wall. He picked up a wooden pointer from the tray.

"While doing some routine demographic analysis, Kathy came across a surprising fact. Over the past decade, a statistically high number of female corpses have been discovered in this northwest quadrant above Waterbury—most of them buried in shallow graves. Are you familiar with the region?"

Oliphant lifted his pudgy hand. "I live in Torrington, just about dead-center."

"What's the area like?"

"Oh, basically a bedroom community with a bunch of little towns and private estates. By that, I mean single-family homes set off on a piece of land in the woods—locals who've been there for generations and more recent émigrés from New York. The terrain is basically forested hills with lots of rivers and reservoirs."

"And lots of murders?"

"God, no. Murder is rare, and almost always solved."

"Hence the reason for our investigation. We have eight bodies with one thing in common. All of them were killed elsewhere and dumped in this area after the fact. I'd like for Kathy to brief you."

The two detectives nodded, and Oscar moved to a seat by the windows.

Kathy opened the three-ring binder on the table in front of her. "As Lieutenant Colunga said, we are dealing with bodies that have been dumped. This excludes victims of felonies, domestic violence, and other cases where the murder location is known. We also limited the scope to bodies which show no sign of invasive injury. While this does not rule out the possibility, there is no indication of a piercing instrument or gunshot wound from the skeletal or tissue remains.

"Three of these women have not been identified because they don't match missing persons reports from Connecticut.

We've requested reports from adjacent states, but they haven't come in yet. So let's look at the ones we do know about."

Kathy produced a photo. "Caryn Kendall was only sixteen when abducted from a shopping center in Hartford eight years ago. She was found in a shallow grave above Colebrook a year later."

Oliphant grunted. "Do we know the cause of death?"

She glanced at the report. "Unfortunately, we didn't use archaeological forensics on this one, so we're short on information."

Kathy held up the next photo. "This one was unearthed about twelve months ago ..."

As Colunga stared at the soft brown eyes of the dead girl, another image superimposed itself like a double exposure. He shifted sideways and sat head in hand to obscure his eyes from the rest, while the vision fixed itself in his mind—Julia.

Daddy, my dress won't stay up. You need to pin it. Tommy's coming for me in ten minutes, and I don't want to be late for the prom.

Ever-present memories flooded his mind once more. His wife's funeral and the many years of raising a daughter as a single parent. Night shifts in his patrol car, worrying about her alone in the house. And a father's helpless attempts to teach things a daughter needs to know ... to be warned about.

What if something had caused him to change jobs or towns? Would it have made a difference? Yes. She might have gone to another college, or come home that weekend. Any slight variation in her life would have been enough to save her. His failure. His shame.

With a slight shudder, Colunga pried his mind from the emotion washing over him and tuned in to Kathy's voice.

"She was found only one month ago, and the State Medical Examiner is working to ID her. Preliminary indications point to Sybil Morrison from Amesville.

"And this last woman is a minor exception to our criteria." Kathy held up her photograph. "Faye Tucker was found in a cave near Riverton by a party of spelunkers about four years ago. They literally stumbled over her because she was weighted down in a pool of water. Missing for three years, she was single, living in Hartford, trying to make it as a model in New York. We speculate that the killer might have been a local since he knew about the cave."

Kathy closed her binder. "In studying these known cases, I began to see other common factors among the victims. All of them were pretty, if not beautiful. They were fairly young, ranging in age from sixteen to twenty-six. They all disappeared within the past ten years, and were never heard from again ... not typical in the case of missing persons such as runaways. I applied these criteria to our database of dead and missing persons, and found fourteen women who fit the profile."

Hank Oliphant gazed at her. "Are you saying that we have a serial killer operating in Connecticut?"

"There is a finite probability."

Colunga turned his chair to face them. "Have you guys been involved in any of these cases?"

Earl Hoffman nodded. "Most of these girls lived between Hartford and the eastern border—pretty much my turf. I was in on the search for one girl that Kathy discussed, and several more who haven't been found."

"Did you suspect a serial killer?"

"You always consider that possibility, but we weren't certain all of them were dead."

"I think you should assume that now."

Oliphant rubbed his eyes, as if shutting out a bad vision. "And I was on the scene for the exhumation last month, but I've only been on the force one year. I had no idea there were so many bodies with similar characteristics."

"Well, there are." Oscar regarded the detectives. "Kathy has set up a jacket for each of you. Reports, maps—everything we have. Commit them to memory. I'm hoping, when you see it all in one pile, you'll uncover some avenue that the original investigators missed."

Oliphant pressed his hands together, fingertips against his lips. "One thing occurs to me already: If some of these girls were not from Connecticut, what is the range of this guy's operation?"

"An excellent question, Hank." Colunga hauled himself up and moved to the windows. "It's not unusual for murderers to bury their victims, so we can't be sure these were all killed by the same man." He put his hands on the sill and leaned heavily, his voice reverberating from the glass. "But if we do have a madman running loose out there, I want him."

Chapter 4

Achal Bedi sat at Wolfe's bar, staring blankly at his reflection in the mirror. It was a long road from New Delhi to New York, and the years as science fiction editor for Gladiator were taking their toll. Days were an empty blur of thankless work, the nights an endless stream of nondescript faces and bodies. Too many years alone. Too many women who offered no more than satisfaction for one night.

It was some giant con game for both sexes. Millions of people held jobs, operated successfully in polite society, and passed themselves off as normal ... until the second date when they confided that they loved their cat like a child or believed the world's problems could be solved by enslavement of hermaphrodites.

Young women were naive and self-involved. Mature women always carried some baggage—difficult children, hostile ex-husband, or a deep-seated mistrust of men based on disastrous decisions of their own making. He smiled, remembering the woman in Seattle. He had fallen in love the moment he laid eyes on her—breathed her in like a gift from Vishnu. Now he couldn't remember her name.

He shuddered and turned as Megan stretched onto the barstool at his left and jostled against his shoulder.

"Hiya, handsome. Can I buy you a drink?"

"Hey, I wouldn't want you to think I'm easy."

"I don't. But I'll bet you can be tricked." Megan glanced at Ralph behind the bar. "Johnny Walker Red, and another round for my friend."

She turned back to Achal. "Are you ready for the editor's meeting tomorrow? Did you read Bernie's latest project?"

"Yes, and I was a little surprised. I'm not big on mystery, but it was better than I expected. Didn't you think?"

"I suppose." She gazed into his soft eyes. "How long has Bernie been at Gladiator?"

"Well, he was here when I came aboard about ten years ago."

"Do you know him very well?"

"Nobody knows him very well. He keeps to himself. All I know about his personal life is that he married the same woman three times."

"Decisive thinker, huh?"

"Actually, no. And I'm afraid it's hurting him professionally. He doesn't trust his instincts anymore ... won't take a risk. I know of a dozen books he rejected that made a fortune for our competition. And there may be dozens more I don't know about."

"So the rumors are true."

"What rumors?"

"That Bernie's days are numbered."

"I think it's beyond the rumor stage. Jarvis is openly hostile at this point."

"Big deal. He's openly hostile with me." She flashed a weak smile as Ralph delivered their drinks, then leaned toward Achal. "Does that mean my days are numbered?"

"You've only been here a few months. It takes time."

"I don't have time. What I do have is an office full of schlock manuscripts, and Harmon Jarvis on my back."

Achal smiled broadly. "You have the experience, and you have the contacts. You'll pull it together."

"Right, but I'm looking to hedge my bets." Megan glanced around. "That reminds me. Have you seen Irv Miller?"

"No. You expecting him?"

"He said he might drop by to talk about rewrites."

"Oh yeah. How's your book coming?"

"A most difficult question. Irv requested some changes that looked fairly simple at first, but it's turning into a major effort."

Achal nodded. "Rewrite is far more difficult than the original creation."

"I'll say. It looks like this may take a month or two, and I wrote the whole book in six months."

"Interesting. Now you're getting a glimpse of what you put your writers through."

"Unfortunately." She lifted her glass and daubed at the condensed water with her napkin. "But it helps me understand why novels come in with such glaring errors. It's so much easier to judge work you're not familiar with."

"This is true." His voice developed a slight lilt. "The hardest thing in life is to evaluate oneself."

"Hindu philosophy?"

"School of hard knocks."

"I just enrolled." She sipped the Scotch and made a face. "I don't know if my book will sell. Or when. Or how much it will earn. This town is starting to get to me. Work is a nightmare. Jarvis makes me feel like a guilty child. And I never know if I'll have a job tomorrow."

"Is that all?"

"Give me a minute. I can probably think up one or two more."

"Hmm. Now it's time for Hindu philosophy. Life is a precious gift and we should revel in every moment. What matters your position on the Earth, or the nature of your current employment? As long as you have your health and creative mind, you can always live in peace."

She reached for his tie and pulled him closer until their foreheads touched. "You're full of it, Achal."

"No doubt. But I do know what you need."

"You do?"

His accent thickened dramatically. "Oh, jes. Vot jou need, is veddy fine vacation."

"Sure." She pushed him away with feigned irritation. "I took a cruise last year. While I was gone for six days, four weeks of work piled up on my desk. I'm not falling for that, the way things are going now."

His flawless English returned. "You don't have to go away for a week. It could be a weekend ... a day."

She shrugged. "Where would I want to go for a day?"

"How about Atlantic City? Maybe catch a show, and shell out a few shekels at the tables. You wouldn't even have to stay overnight."

Megan stirred her drink. "That might be a good idea, but I don't have anyone to go with. My friend left town last March."

"Your friend? You have only one friend?"

"Only one I would travel with."

"How about someone from work?"

She dipped her head, looking up at him like Scarlett O'Hara. "You, for instance?"

Achal grinned. "I might make the sacrifice, if you can assure me you're not after my body."

"In that case, forget it." She pulled a bill from her purse and laid it on the bar. "Right now, I must go home to prepare my own defense for tomorrow's meeting."

He gripped her arm. "Are you going to present your mysterious submission?"

She stood up tentatively. "How did you know about that?"

"The grapevine."

"You mean Heather."

"She thinks it shows promise. Do you?"

"I don't have enough to determine that." Megan gathered up her purse. "I'll let you know after I digest a few more chapters ... assuming any others come in."

Chapter 5

Staff meeting had not gone well. The tension between Harmon Jarvis and Bernie Yellanik was palpable.

Megan closed her office door and dropped her briefcase on the desk, then froze at the sight of a package centered neatly on its surface. She slumped into the chair and pulled the pages from the black envelope.

Delicious Pain — Chapter 2

The second woman, I selected for money. You should not find this surprising, since it parallels the path of many women. The first husband is for love—the second for security.

I have always been puzzled by young women's naiveté in selecting their mates. The most beautiful women usually end up with bastards who cheat on them or beat them. While this seems absurd, there is a valid reason. Most beautiful girls rely on their looks for social acceptance from the time they are born. Boys have fawned over them all their lives, and they find decent men boring because they can be led around by the proverbial ring in the nose. When a guy stands up to them, even for the wrong reasons, these women find him irresistible.

This is why it comes so easy for me. I could never kill a mother, a good woman struggling to raise her children against the odds of this perverted world. It is the parasites who must be eliminated—those who wield their beauty like a sword to force men into subjugation ... who lie and cheat and tease for the sake of their own greed and lust for power. God never intended men to be victims of these Satanic takers, but victims we are.

So like women, my second love was selected for money. It was in a bar near the air base in Morocco. Ironically, I was about to be mustered out. Five days later, we would not have met.

Her name was Ilona—Countess Ilona, in fact. She was the last of a line of European royalty dating back to the breakup of power caused by World War One. Rumanian I believe, she was roughly fifteen years older than I, very handsome with silky blond hair, classic European features, and full breasts displayed by the plunging line of her gold lamé gown.

She was holding court with three important locals and a weasel who worked for the American State Department. Even at this distance, I saw the light in her eyes. She loved having these men grovel at her feet.

I sat around for a long time and got very drunk, stealing glances at her in the mirror behind the bar. Eventually, all the men left except for the weasel. He had been assigned to escort her. I think he hoped to score, but I could tell he had no chance by the way she looked at him, the way she kept looking in my direction.

Suddenly, she appeared at my elbow. "Have you room for one more?"

I hadn't seen her approach and wheeled around, genuinely surprised. "Always room for one more." I stood up and helped her onto the barstool next to me, trying to find the right words. Finally, I blurted out the only thing that came to mind.

"Can I buy you a drink?"

"Amaretto and soda, if you please."

The bartender was staring at us with open mouth. I nodded to him and turned back to gaze at her. She oozed wealth and breeding, and she moved like a queen. As I stared into those smoldering eyes, I understood why men were so easily taken in, a condition I was to suffer many times over the next few weeks.

I paced the parlor of her suite while she changed in

the dressing room. I did not understand her interest in me and had no idea where it might lead, but a plan was forming in my mind.

The profits from our black-marketeering seemed to pale in the light of her wealth.

When she came through the door, I was stricken. She wore a lilac dress that came halfway up her thigh, and plunged to her waist. Soft pleats enfolded her slender hips, and her nipples protruded through the gossamer material, looking hard enough to cut glass.

I stammered, "I expected a bathing suit."

"It will be adequate for the night," she said. "We will need nothing to swim."

We rode down on the elevator and turned to the back of the hotel, emerging on a beach with rippled sand. Moonlight reflected from the water and cast an outline of her astonishing form as we walked along hand-in-hand.

I was young again, a kid picking up his high school date. We headed south along the beach, leaving the hotel lights behind us. She turned to me and held both of my hands in hers.

"And what will you do when you leave the Air Force?"

"I have no plans."

Pulling her to me, I forced her arms behind her back and kissed her hard on the mouth, reveling in the sweet scent and the soft tongue that found its way between my teeth. Pinning her hands with one of mine, I brought the other up to interweave my fingers in the golden locks and tilted her head back to bury my lips in the soft vulnerability of her throat.

She moaned, heart pounding against my chest. Her gray eyes were barely open, matched by the narrow gash of her full lips and white teeth gleaming in the moon- light. I released her and held her at arm's length. I too knew how to play the game. Bring them to the edge of passion, then push them away. To grasp is a sign of weakness that will always be rejected.

"Let's swim!"

Her eyes opened wide, and she shook visibly. Then, with most subtle movements, she dropped her dress and kicked off her sandals.

"Last one in is a ... how do you say in America? Rotten egg?"

She sprinted toward the waves, diving in at the moment they reached sufficient depth. I was impressed. Years of holiday at San Trope and Hawaii had taught her well, but I had learned to swim in the stiff currents of Tennessee rivers.

I followed her into the untamed power of the Atlantic. At that instant in time, it was not me. Or should I say it was not I? For a brief moment, I was a child again. Not the bad times. Not the pain of physical abuse or the feeling of impotence, but the good times. I began to forget who I was ... what I had suffered.

Upon my discharge, she showed me wondrous things. We flew to Egypt and took a boat along the Nile—a strange craft, half cruise ship, half trawler. We toured the Valley of the Kings and Giza. At night, when we were making love, singing wafted across the water from towns along the bank.

From there, we went to Greece on our way to her villa in Florence. It was more of a palace than villa, with tall, ancient trees lining the half mile driveway. The massive stucco structure rose from the green fields, and people looked up from their toils and shouted greetings. I will never forget the color of light at sunset.

Megan shook her head. "Let's skip the travel log." She skimmed several pages.

That night, Ilona told me that she loved me. I told her the same, for it had been true since our first night in Morocco. Then she proposed marriage. I was stunned. How could she marry so far below her station? Would her family accept an American sergeant?

I laid awake most of the night. Was it possible to settle down in Italy? To check the harvest, sample the wine, and walk the grounds of an Italian villa like an aristocrat? It seemed absurd. And yet, what would I do if I returned to the States? I had no plans or holdings there. My instinct was to lay back and let the answers come.

The following night, Countess Ilona threw a party to announce our engagement. I stood by her side to greet the guests, trying to suppress my awe. I was out of place, having nothing in common with these people. I couldn't speak their language, figuratively or literally. The party was a miserable and awkward experience, and I began to doubt that moving into her world was a workable idea.

After the guests had gone, we talked about our wedding plans. When and where seemed very important to her. Then, she dropped something in passing that shook my very soul—something about becoming an American citizen.

I stopped her in mid-sentence. "You don't want to live in this beautiful villa?"

A tear trickled down her cheek. "It is not possible, my love. Since the new regime came to power, my family is *non grata* in Italy. My father and brother have already been deported, and my time here is limited. That is why I went to Morocco ... why I met with your State Department. I was evaluating my options."

I told her I was going for a stroll, and smoked a pack as I paced the darkened grounds in tears. Now it was all clear. I was her ticket to the States. Once she had citizenship, she would dump me like a used milk carton and go back to her fancy friends. Strangely, I took solace in the fact that my instincts had been right about her. She was a taker and user of men.

The next few weeks were the hardest of my life. I married her and was forced to pretend with everyone who filtered through my life that I was her adoring mate. Even our lovemaking was strained, in spite of her constant inventiveness.

Fortunately, our time together was limited. She was extremely paranoid that the Italian government would rip off her assets, and I played on this fear. We worked furiously to convert everything to cash, deposited in an American bank under the name of a Delaware corporation. Of course, I was the president of this corporation.

At last, everything was done and we flew to England en route to the States. I took stock of the situation. The money was banked in my name. But I have been remiss on this point. It was actually an alias I used for black-market operations in Morocco—a friend of mine who died in the fifth grade. I had complete papers for this name, even a passport.

I was sure her alleged friends would never worry if they did not hear from her again. By the time her family became concerned, the money would be withdrawn. And if her body was ever discovered, the likelihood of identification was slim without knowing where she came from. I felt safe in executing her.

The time had come, and I will not dwell on her demise. Suffice it to say that she rests on the bottom of a very deep lake in Scotland. There was nothing sexy or intriguing in this act. It was a necessary thing, one I did not enjoy because of the good times we had shared.

There is only one thing I remember clearly. Her surprise. Countess Ilona thought she had fooled me completely, and was astonished when she realized that I was too smart for her.

"Too smart for her?" Megan reread the last paragraph carefully. "You crazy, arrogant bastard!"

Chapter 6

Harmon Jarvis took advantage of the lull in their conversation to look around the room. Rodney's was woody and masculine, with dark paneling and equally dark blue ceiling. Tiny lights in the chrome-and-glass chandeliers sparkled like miniature galaxies, reflecting from the large windows that overlooked the Brooklyn Bridge. For a moment his eyes danced across two attractive women who graced the bar.

He cradled the snifter in his open palm and sipped the Grand Marnier, glancing at Guenther Rombach, the crisp German businessman across the table. Even on a Saturday night it would take the better part of an hour to get home, and it was nearly ten o'clock ... time to talk turkey.

"So, Guenther, have you spent much time in the US?"

Rombach nodded affably. "I have made a point for many years to work for companies with interests here. I very much like this country."

"And I like yours."

"You have been to Germany?"

"It's been a while. All I remember is the people. I found them to be *lustig*. Is that the word?"

Rombach grinned. "This means full of spirit ... love of life."

Jarvis nodded. "When I was a lad, a wise man said that Americans work to live, but Germans live to work." He took a sip and screwed up his face. "I think that's basically true, but the German people are capable of cutting loose when the work is done."

"I think Americans are even more *lustig*. There is vitality here, from your relative youth as a country I suspect. Like your music, your language draws from all other cultures, making your literature rich and beautiful."

Jarvis suppressed a sneer and waved at the waiter for another round. "I hope your praise is deserved. As in all things, I see nothing outstanding about us. In fact, I see much degradation in the quality of American society since I was young."

"But you have so much more now."

"Yeah. More drugs. More divorce. More poverty. Kids carrying guns to school. Even a stock market that rallies when people are thrown out of work."

"I think there is still much fire in the American spirit."

Jarvis eyed him and took some time to respond. Guenther Rombach was the consummate German with ruddy face and wavy blond hair. Roughly forty-five, his frame was solid and powerful under the three-piece suit. He sat relaxed with hands folded comfortably on the table and returned Jarvis' gaze through sky-blue eyes.

"Tell me why your company wants to buy Gladiator."

"Please. The word 'buy' does not convey our intent. A publishing house cannot be purchased like a sack of potatoes. We wish to enter into an association with your fine staff and excellent reputation."

Jarvis paused while the waiter delivered fresh drinks. He held up his snifter and bobbed his head once. "Well spoken. Have you considered a career in the diplomatic corps?"

Guenther lifted his glass in response. "No, I have not. Why do you ask?"

"Oh, I just wondered what GBF intends to do if this goes through."

The German set down his glass and leaned forward. "I am happy you asked that question. I was told you were a man of directness, and I want you to know exactly what we would expect."

"Go on."

"We do not want to make any major changes in your operation."

"Why not? Before I came to Gladiator it was losing money hand over fist. Now we're barely holding our own and we're deeply in debt. Sounds like something that should be changed."

"I agree with your analysis, but you must realize that a combined operation would be more efficient. We will infuse capital and marketing expertise to increase your market here, and we have the capability of translating into other languages to increase the yield on many of the books you print. We already have European distribution in place, and we are rapidly expanding into new markets like Japan and Russia."

"Would you expect us to print works from other languages?"

"Only the best. Of course, we would perform the translation for you. It is a symbiotic relationship. You see?"

"Hmmm. Sounds logical." Jarvis swirled his drink. "Almost too simple. You don't want to make any personnel changes?"

"If your concern is losing people, no. We may however loan you experienced people in certain areas, to ease the transition."

"And when would this merger be effective?"

"After the end of our fiscal year—within a month or two from now." Rombach threw down his schnapps and smiled. "I know you have many questions, Harmon. I have taken the liberty of preparing a written proposal that will answer most of them. If it is acceptable to you, I will have several copies delivered to your office. You may pass them out to your key people if you think it appropriate."

"That might be very helpful, but what happens if this merger doesn't go through?"

"Then you will be taken over by somebody else. With your current debt structure, I see no alternative. You cannot pull out on your own, and no company of this size just closes its doors. Your only choice is to select the buyer you prefer to work with. If you wait too long, you may not have that option. I have come to convince you that it should be GBF."

Jarvis rubbed his eyes. "A very pretty speech. Now, let's cut to the chase. You know, as well as I do, what will happen. Whatever you pay for us, you will expect us to pay back. Since we're unprofitable now, the only way that can happen is to cut expenses—staff. That means you will expect more productivity out of fewer people. Then, we'll start to produce inferior books and our best authors will jump ship. Nobody can win from this, Guenther."

The German nodded. "That is how it usually works. But we have very powerful backers who are committed to the establishment of a global publishing entity. I assure you our returns will come only from future profits, which will develop as a result of our joint operations."

"What makes you guys think you'll be more successful than we have?"

"Sometimes, you can only see from the outside." A smile flitted over his face. "I remember once, somebody suggested that your President Bush trade places with Gorbachev, since they were both better at dealing with problems outside their own country."

Jarvis' eyes flashed. "Not very funny when you have to live with the results." He swirled his drink. "Can you give me one solid example of what you would do differently?"

"Yes. One of your biggest problems is that advances have gotten out of hand—six or seven figures in many cases. Unfortunately, this has occurred in parallel with increasing time to bring a book to market. The result is that you have a fortune tied up for two years before income occurs. And that's assuming the book makes a profit. If it's a bomb, you will lose the entire advance."

Jarvis eyed him. "And your solution?"

Rombach extracted a Gauloises cigarette and lit up. "Change your practice. Offer lower advances."

"We can't!"

"Why not?"

"Because other publishers have tried it, and lost some of their best authors."

"What if we can prove to the authors that a huge advance is not in their best interest?"

"How?"

"One of the best ways for a publisher to destroy a writer's career is to offer an excessive advance. If the book does not sell well enough to cover it, the publisher eats the difference. He is unlikely to want the author's next book. And, if word gets around, other houses may follow suit. Better to give a reasonable advance and allow the book to earn what it can, based on the quality of the author's product."

"They'll never buy it."

Rombach smiled. "There may be things we can do to make this more attractive for the writer—perhaps offer a percentage more in royalties in return for the lower advance. If it is a good book, everyone wins. The author nets more overall, and the interest we save on advance money will probably offset his good fortune. Even if it costs us more, the outlay would come after we experienced income from sales. By coupling such ideas with appropriate cost consolidation and international distribution, I think we can make it worth their while to stay with us."

Jarvis shook his head. "Now I know how the Indians felt when the government commission arrived to negotiate."

"This means?"

"What you say makes sense, and I believe you have good intentions. But do you have enough clout to ensure that your Great White Father will honor this treaty?"

The German nodded gravely. "I have put it in writing—to preclude any misunderstanding at a later date. And I am assigned as your liaison when the merger goes through."

Jarvis nodded. "I appreciate your conviction, Guenther. And I must say, if it's inevitable, I would rather work with you than some of the assholes who are sniffing around. Give me a week to grease the skids with my people."

Rombach extended his hand across the table and they shook firmly. "Enough business for tonight. Are you a married man, Harmon?"

"No."

"Where does one go in this great city to find companionship?"

"You mean hookers?"

The German smiled broadly. "When this merger is completed, I will be spending a great deal of time in Manhattan. There are many advantages in having a ... local friend."

Jarvis tossed his head toward the pair of women at the bar. "Well, this ain't a bad place to start."

Chapter 7

"Yeah, I never did well with women. One time I asked a girl if she'd like to come up to my place for a good time. She gave me the look. 'I don't know. You going to be there?'"

The standup comic paused for a mild round of laughter. "And it got worse with age. The other night I asked this girl if we went to the same high school. She gave me the look. 'I doubt it. Your high school burned down in nineteen forty-two.'"

He cocked his head. "Maybe I just never met the right woman. Like this one girlfriend of mine. You could eat off her kitchen floor." He grimaced. "There was enough down there to keep you alive for a week!"

Achal appeared to be having a good time. But then, Achal always had a good time. He was at peace anywhere.

Megan sighed and scanned the sea of heads sloping away to the giant stage. Why had she let him talk her into Atlantic City? It was a longer trip than she remembered, and it was after midnight now. If they stayed for the rest of the show and gambled awhile, it would be a horrible time to start driving back. Her only solace was that tomorrow was Sunday, giving her time to recover. But she wasn't sure she had the strength to go on tonight.

She reached across and touched Achal on the arm. "How long does this show last?"

He glanced at his watch. "Another hour or so. Why? Do you want to leave?"

"If you don't mind."

"No problem. I'm funnier than he is, and I have no sense of humor at all." Achal smiled and sucked up the dregs of his drink. "Let's do it."

She followed him out, ignoring the inquisitive eyes that tracked them. Passing through the wide door, the world seemed more spacious. It smelled better and the panoply of flashing lights revived her spirits somewhat.

He scanned the tables. "Feel like trying your luck?"

"Oh, Achal." She stopped and turned to him. "If you could find it in your heart to forgive me, I'm dead tired and these three-inch heels are killing me. Could we call it a night?"

"No problem. Let's head for home."

"Actually, I'm not sure I have the stamina for that. Any chance we could get some rooms at this hotel? I'll gladly pay for them."

They walked to the hotel lobby and Megan leaned heavily against the counter, feeling like she couldn't support her own weight.

Achal glanced over. "They have one no-show that they'll sell us. You want to try somewhere else?"

She dropped her forehead onto his shoulder. "I can't move another step. Could we share?"

"Fine with me." He turned back and nodded to the desk clerk.

Megan's eyes drifted toward the casino. The strange electronic boops of the new slot machines were obnoxious, not like the reassuring clank and bells of the old one-arm bandits. In the last few minutes, some sort of night shift had descended upon the place. Now there wasn't a vacant seat at a Blackjack table, and people were huddled two or three deep around the croupiers. The din was deafening.

Achal jangled the key in her ear and she followed him to
the elevators, holding his arm tightly for support against the
upward rush to the fourteenth floor. They walked in silence
through waves of light and dark that ringed the long hallway, like high school conspirators creeping to some illicit
rendezvous. Megan followed him inside and sensed a wave of
relief as the door closed behind her, shutting off the strange
and unnatural world beyond.

Achal walked the room, noting the sitting arrangement
with a large couch and two overstuffed chairs, king-size bed,
and cabineted television set with its pay-me movie box intended to suck a few more dollars from the weary traveler.

"Anything you want?"

She kicked off her shoes. "A hot shower. A stiff drink.
And clean sheets."

"Sounds marvelous! You hit the shower, and I'll call room
service."

Megan wandered toward the bathroom. In the dressing
area, she shed her green satin gown and slid one of the
mirrored doors aside to hang it up. She turned the water on
to heat, slipped out of her lingerie, and donned the gaudy
purple shower cap from the counter. Her head came up and
she gazed at her reflection.

"You know how these things work, Meg. Why didn't you
pack an emergency bag?"

Ten minutes later she emerged, clad in a large beach towel,
to find Achal twirling a bottle of champagne in a silver
bucket on the glass table in front of the couch. She hesitated,
making sure that the towel was securely tucked in, and fluffed
her hair with a hand towel.

"Champagne okay?"

"Lovely." She stashed her underwear in a drawer and
turned to behold him. Usually he appeared quite stiff and
serious in his workplace garb. Sans coat and shoes, he looked

like a normal man—sitting with his feet up on the coffee table, his collar unbuttoned and thick black hair protruding through the open V of his shirt.

She sat down across from him and draped the hand towel over her long thighs with a show of propriety, then took the tulip glass from his outstretched hand. "To you, Achal. A good friend in spite of your gender."

He gave her a bemused smile. "Men can't be good friends?"

"Rarely. They usually want ..." Her brow knitted in a puzzled look. "What was that we used to do?"

Achal laughed. "Sex?"

"That's it!" She stabbed the air with an arched forefinger and nodded with great satisfaction. "Sex."

He leaned across to refill her glass. "Better take it easy on this stuff. As tired as you are, it may put you away."

"I don't care. I'd like to sleep 'til Monday." She took a sip with a mischievous grin. "Could we do that, Achal? Play hooky and walk in late on Monday?"

He sat back and glanced at the ceiling. "I suppose we could get away with it, but what would we do in the meantime?"

"Oh, we could lay in the sun or paddle around that mammoth pool."

Achal smiled, his great white teeth glowing like pearls. "Why don't we see how you feel about it in the morning?"

"Good idea. I'm not thinking very clearly right now."

"Me too. You take the bed and I'll sleep on the couch."

"Nonsense. A big strong man like you would be all cramped up. I'll take the couch. It's about the same size as the bed in my apartment."

Achal wagged his finger. "In my culture, a gentleman would never be so inconsiderate."

"In your culture I would walk two steps behind and throw myself on your funeral pyre." She arose, the small towel on her lap falling to the floor. The damp embracing beach towel bulged precariously at her breast and barely covered the point where her legs met. "You're in my culture now, and I say we should share." Megan leaned across the table and held out her hand. "Come on, Mamma will tuck her tired boy in."

He took her hand and gained his feet. "Do you think you can trust me?"

She drew him around the table and kissed him softly on the mouth. "I hope not."

Megan awoke with a start. A rainy morning light forced its way through the slightly parted drapes. For a few seconds she surveyed the alien scene. Then her mind snapped into focus, and she whirled around to gaze upon the sleeping Indian whose placid features radiated an angelic aura.

"God. That beautiful, and good in bed?"

Achal stirred. His large brown eyes opened slowly. "Good morning. Sleep well?"

She pouted. "Hmmm. After the third time, I slept like a baby."

"Bad analogy." His lips curled up. "Most babies don't sleep very well."

She placed her hand on his shoulder and gave a gentle push. "What would you know about babies?"

"Had one once."

"No." She stared in surprise. "You were married?"

"You don't have to be married to have a kid, Meg."

"So, you weren't married ..."

"Didn't say that."

"I think you better tell me about it."

"Not much to tell. She was a cheerleader at Wazoo."

"Wazoo?"

"That's what the locals call Washington State University in Pullman ... where the students rioted a few years back."

"What were you doing there?"

"Studying media."

"Did you love her?"

"In that era, I loved all beautiful women madly. She was just the one who caught my seed." He had a pained expression. "I was too young then. I thought you wanted a woman for her body."

"You don't?"

"Not if you're smart." He arched his back and stretched. "When my grandparents were married, life expectancy was shorter. Their wedding vows constituted a contract good for two or three decades. But when you say 'I do' today, you may be serving time with the same woman for fifty or sixty years. You better like her."

Megan nestled her face against his cheek. "Do you like me?"

"Very much." Achal stroked her hair and gazed at the ceiling. "Were you ever married?"

"I never found a man who loved me for my mind."

"Then, I presume there are no kids."

"Fortunately."

"You want kids some day?"

Megan tilted her head and gazed at the wall. "When I graduated from Wellesley, I decided not to have children. I didn't believe that I had any wonderful qualities or knowledge to pass on, and I don't deal well with irrational beings. I wanted the freedom to go anywhere life might lead me. Rome. Hong Kong. Whatever."

"You still feel that way?"

"So far, life has led me nowhere. Also, I realized something a few years ago. My grandmother suffered internal injuries when my father was born ... her only child. My parents had two of us, and my brother passed away when he was fifteen. If I don't have children, this entire branch of the family tree will die with me." She turned to him and smiled. "What say, Achal? Do we humans have some social obligation to calve out?"

He raised his hand to play his fingers across the shadowed line below her cheek. Megan blinked her long thick lashes at his touch. Achal caressed her full sensuous lips with his thumb, smiling as he reached the subtle upturn at the corner. He slipped his fingers into her flaming tresses and pulled her down to kiss her nose and brow.

"My God, you are beautiful."

"So are you." Megan found his mouth, shivering at the energy of his tongue and the click of his massive teeth against hers. She had never responded to a man like this. It wasn't sex as she had known it, more like a marriage of souls. She wanted to devour him. For the first time she understood cannibalism, the merging of flesh with flesh to assimilate the power of a revered friend.

Megan pulled away in feigned resistance. "Oh, Mr. Bedi, don't you think we should be on our way?"

He lifted his head to view the dismal world outside. "To do what? No fun in the sun today."

"I guess that's out." She feigned a pout. "Any other ideas for killing a free morning?"

He pulled the sheet aside and caressed the long arc of her silken thigh. "Something will come up."

Chapter 8

Megan scanned the place they had fallen into at Cape May, the old fishing village on the peninsula south of Atlantic City. She surveyed the room, trying to decide how she would describe it in a book. Maybe "quaint" or "local color," with wooden walls and floor aged by decades of salt air and intentional neglect. The interior was lighted only by candles, and by streaked shafts of midday sun that forced their way through skylights in the roof. A dusty swordfish hung over the grimy mirror behind a pretty young bartender who slopped beer to regulars who embraced the bar in silent adulation.

Achal was seated with his back against the wall, legs stretched out along the bench of the large booth. She reached out and scratched the back of his hand with her long nails.

"You look comfortable."

He turned and gazed in her direction, resting his head on the seat back. "I can't remember when I felt so comfortable, but I can tell you it's been a long time." He turned his hand over to hold hers. "Thank you for a wonderful weekend."

"The pleasure was all mine."

"The pleasure was not all yours."

"Maybe not, but the pleasure was unexpected."

"No shit." He slipped his hand away and lifted the schooner of beer. "Being here makes me wonder about my life.

Have I gotten so caught up in the rat race that there's nothing to live for outside the job?"

"I know I have. That's why I want a place in the country.
And that's why I hope to get a decent advance on my book."
Her eyes went vacant. "You know, it seems like I've lived my
whole life anticipating some major event that will bring peace
of mind. Meanwhile, I'm stumbling through life uptight and
afraid at every turn in the road."

Achal swung his feet to the floor and leaned forward.
"You've hit on something important. I think most of us live
like that. Everything will be okay when I graduate, or get
married, or become filthy rich. Whether those things happen
or not, time passes us by, and then we realize that we've
sacrificed all the happiness we might have had during those
waiting years."

"Yeah. I came to the same conclusion awhile back. But I
don't know what to do about it." She bit her lip. "It's hard
to change your perspective. What we are has been ingrained
into us for a lifetime. I've even thought about changing
jobs ... maybe moving to a different city."

"No, Meg! The company needs you."

"They don't seem to be aware of that."

"Well, I am. And I don't want you to bail out on us."

"Does it matter? There may not be a company when we
get back. That concern certainly doesn't do anything for my
state of mind."

"I wouldn't worry about that. Companies like this never
really go under. They flounder around for a while and get
purchased by somebody."

"I know. But how will they be to work for? And which of
us will still be here after a takeover?"

Achal shrugged. "Nobody could answer that. But don't
give up now."

Megan leaned back. "Don't worry. It's not my style. If

the building comes crashing down around our ears, I'll be sitting amidst the rubble yelling at people to get cracking."

He smiled. "Very commendable."

"Or very stupid." She considered his noble face. "And what about us? Where do we go from here?"

"What do you want?"

"I want to be friends."

"Friends like we were last week, or friends like we were last night?"

"Whatever works. Maybe friendship could bring some of that peace of mind we were talking about."

"I couldn't agree more. Let's give it a shot, and see where it leads."

She nodded, gazing at him through green eyes that looked smoky in the dim light.

Achal checked his watch. "Right now, I think we better hit the road. There are a couple of things I need to do today."

Megan hoisted her bag from the floor and followed him to the bar, half leaning against him as he peeled off several bills and laid them down on the check. He turned and put his arm around her, guiding her out the door to the car. Achal fired up the engine in the Mercedes sedan and made a U-turn to head north.

She sat in silence, rummaging through the maelstrom of thoughts that assaulted her mind. Could there be something permanent with Achal? Would it be good for either of them? She recognized the depression she was suffering, fueled by uncertainty about her grandmother, the company, and her book. She also realized that she must not latch onto Achal as some sort of magic cure and spoil their chances.

She dropped her head back against the rest, lulled by the gentle whine and subtle thumps from the tires, talking to herself. "Best thing since pneumatic tires." Megan stole a glance at Achal. "Best thing since pneumatic sex." Then Megan Roarke slept.

***

Megan's head jerked forward as the driver on her right laid on his horn, complaining at the slow-moving car ahead.

Achal's eyes flitted in her direction. "Good sleep?"

"The sleep of the dead."

He grinned. "Something keep you up last night?"

She reached across and dropped her hand between his legs. "The same thing that kept you up all night."

Achal gripped the wheel with both hands to correct for the slight wobble she created, coming uncomfortably close to the cars on either side. He gave her a mock glare. "Can't you wait until we get home?"

Megan sighed and sat back. "If I must."

For several minutes she stared out at the sea of lanes and endless chains of vehicles that were the New Jersey Turnpike. "How far are we from home?"

"About an hour."

She smiled. "Back home, distance is measured in miles. In New York, it's measured in time."

"Distance doesn't mean much here. Given the time of day, tollbooths, and traffic, it can take two hours to go ten miles."

"Well, if we have an hour ..." Megan leaned forward to the large purse on the floor and unzipped a side pouch, extracting a sheaf of papers that had been folded once.

Achal glanced over. "What's that? Work?"

"Yes. I thought I could read it on the way down, but you were so entertaining." Her nose wrinkled. "Do you mind if I do it now? It'll only take a few minutes."

"What is it?"

"It's that damned manuscript. A new chapter arrives every Friday, and I haven't read this week's edition."

"Every Friday? How does he manage that?"

"I wonder. It seems there should be more variation. When

people mail things from California, it can take anywhere from two days to a week. He must be local."

"Or he doesn't mail it at all. Maybe he hand-delivers it."

"No. They're always stamped and postmarked."

"Then you can tell where he mails it from."

Megan shook her head. "Nice try, Achal. But so far, the postmark's been blotted out by the black envelopes he uses."

"Why is he going to so much trouble to remain anonymous?"

"Beats me. But it's starting to bother me." She gazed out at the passing countryside for a few seconds. "I don't know if there really is a book, or if someone's messing with me personally."

Achal's eyes narrowed. "You're not sure there is a book?"

She expelled a long sigh. "If he'd sent the entire manuscript, or even a synopsis, I'd know a lot more than I do now—trivial things like the length, or plot, or where he's going with it. Does he get caught in the end? Is there a theme? A moral message? But I've only seen two chapters."

"What are they like?"

Megan paused. "Graphic, but not like pornography. None of this 'thrust your throbbing rod between my lusting loins' stuff."

Achal grinned. "That's only pornography if a man's reading it. If it's a woman, it's called romance."

"True, but this is different from anything I've ever seen. I just don't know how to describe it."

"Read it to me."

"Out loud? I haven't done that since I was in school."

"I'll forgive you if you stumble. I'm no good at it either."

"If you insist." Megan opened the pages. "This is labeled Chapter Three." She read aloud:

With Ilona's money squirreled away in three Florida banks, I took up residence in Key West. I purchased a

sizable boat and set up a nice little business taking tourists and businessmen out on fishing junkets.

For several years, things were fairly quiet and I felt no compulsion to ply my trade, probably because the women I met were harmless. Most of them were widowed, or divorced, wives and mothers. Nor did I find fault with the sexy young things who willingly bartered their bodies to wealthy men in exchange for high living, because I felt they were themselves being used. And I rather enjoyed their firm, virtually nude forms adorning my decks.

I even dated a few women from the area—good women, trying to hold house and home together while raising children against all odds. One I saw, off and on, for several years and I was like a father to her two boys. As in Italy, I had flashes of settling in, and began to wonder if a wife and home were practical. I hadn't felt the urge for some time, but I couldn't be sure it would not return. Perhaps this was because of my wife's death. The performance of that duty had not set well, and I suffered bad dreams from time to time.

Those were good years. I worked hard most of the time, but there were the occasional open days and brief seasons when I had some slack. That's when I began to write again. I bought a good typewriter with an erasing ribbon, and started in on the novel I always wanted to write. Since I lived on my boat, my writing environment was always with me. Even when customers were aboard I could plan, make notes, or rough out scenes on paper. As a result, I finished my first novel in a year and sent it off to an agent in New York with great expectations.

This was the beginning of my reality period. The agent returned the manuscript with a note saying that the writing was amateurish and lacked imagination. Crushed, I paid for a critique by a woman in Missouri who confirmed the agent's response. For the next two years I studied day and night to learn the art of writing. Once I knew my craft, the first novel was a total loss. It would be far easier to build a good one from ground up, than attempt to save the mess I had already made.

Strangely, it was during the process of writing this second book that I came across Jane. More accurately, she

came across me. It was on a Friday. I had just returned
from a day's work and was policing up the boat for the
following Sunday when she showed up on the pier. It was
dusk, and I remember being stricken by her outline in
the subdued light. I dropped my rag when she called out.
  "Ahoy. This your boat?"
  I saw no reason to lie.
  "May I come aboard?"
  I saw no reason to forbid it. I helped her onto the
starboard cushion and offered her champagne, which
she willingly accepted. As I held out the glass, I got my
first good look. She was a raving beauty with clear blue
eyes and thick blond hair pulled back at the sides and
cascading halfway down her back. I estimated her to be
in her late twenties. Her body was firm and her skin
supple and taught. For a moment I remembered Najia's
radiant skin, the same in a different color.
  This girl wore a black one-piece swimsuit which both
supported and took form from her enormous breasts.
Three round straps arose from the top of each cup to a
wide collar around her throat, and similar straps came
around her back to pull the clinging material tight
against her midriff. From there, the outline tapered
downward to a white wraparound skirt that did not fully
obscure the narrow black V plunging between her legs.

Achal glanced over. "This is a crazed killer? It sounds
more like a swish doing color at a fashion show."

Megan gave him a lingering look. "You see? He'll lull you
into a sense of normality, then hit you between the eyes. Let's
see where he goes with it." She continued reading:

There was no use lying to myself. I wanted her, but I
also wondered if she wanted me. I sat down across from
her and raised my glass in a toast.
  She took a sip and smiled. "Do you live around here?"
  "On the boat." Again, no reason to lie. "And yourself?"
  "I just flew in from Long Island ... needed to get away
for the weekend."

"Well, you picked a good place to do that." I looked around the marina. It was nearly devoid of tourists at this hour and none of my immediate neighbors were aboard their boats. "What do you intend to do while you're here?"

"I'd like to try my hand at deep sea fishing."

"Ah. You have come to the right place. My boat is free tomorrow."

"Free? Like kiddies day at the zoo?"

"No. Available."

"I see. What do you charge?"

As they say, her face fell when I told her the price. She clutched her purse. "Too bad. I couldn't afford anything like that."

Then, dear reader, is when I had my first twinge of doubt. Was she trying to wheedle a free trip? She was certainly beautiful enough to take a great deal from unsuspecting men. Of that, I was certain. I was also certain that she would not take advantage of me.

We talked for some time. When the champagne ran out, I made up a pitcher of martinis and kept her glass filled. It was much like playing a fish. I would not be used, but I was loathe to drive this stunning woman away before I knew her intent.

At last, she played her cards. "Do you ever take people out? Just for a ride?"

"Oh, once in a blue moon."

She leaned over and touched my knee, a dark V forming where her breasts were pressed together by the uplifting suit. "Is the moon blue tonight?"

You may think me an incurable romantic, but I still had hopes that her intentions were honorable. As a test, I covered her hand with mine and leaned across to kiss her gently on the lips. She pulled away at first, then kissed me back a little harder.

I glanced at the sky. "I believe the moon is blue to-night. Why don't we motor out a ways. I'll fix dinner and we'll drink some wine. In the morning, you can try your hand at fishing." This, of course, was a test. If she went along now, she was accepting my invitation to spend the night. To my surprise, she did.

We set out westward into the Gulf as the sun gave up
and darkness took complete control. One thing I love is
the sight of lights across water. As I prepared our meal, I
watched the lights of Key West dance and sparkle in the
distance. After dinner and two bottles of wine, she
seemed to be in a dreamy state. I was on a natural high,
myself, and certain that she was now ready for me. I
dowsed the interior lights, removed her skirt, and
guided her to my spacious berth.

She was as impressive going away as from the front.
By the time she fell face down onto the bed, I was in a
lather. I turned her over and tried to undo the thong that
secured the lower part of the suit.

She looked up at me with glassy eyes. "What are you
doing?"

I doubt that I covered my surprise. "I'm putting you
to bed."

"No." She pushed my hands away and securely retied
the straps.

"What do you mean, no?" I could hear my voice
echoing off the close walls.

She became a little more alert. "Is that why you
brought me out here? Did you think you were going to
fuck me?"

The mocking in her voice stabbed at my heart. I felt
anger rising in myself—anger at my eternal stupidity.

She had seemed different. She had talked to me for
over an hour and returned my kiss before we left the
dock. We had shared a lovely conversation during dinner. But now I knew what she was. A taker. A scavenger
of men's souls who had unhappily found her way to walk
among human beings.

I lashed out and stripped the black suit from her
body, noting how her breasts reacted as the shiny material pulled away. For what seemed like an eternity, I
gazed upon her misbegotten gifts. Her stomach was firm
and flat, the discernible line of her rib cage etched in
shadow.

When I tore my eyes away to look at her face, I reeled
at the mixed emotions of fear and hatred. She dug her
heels into the mattress and pushed herself away from me

like a baby trying to move on its back, holding her long
sharp fingernails out in a gesture of defense.

There was no longer any doubt. I brought my fist
down hard into her stomach and she doubled over in a
fetal position, gasping for air. I pulled some rope, a
length of chain, and two small locks from a cabinet. She
struggled and fought as I chained her hands behind her
back and tied her feet with rope. Then I sat her up and
wrapped the remaining chain three times around her
waist and locked it into place.

She tried to kick and bite me. She called me terrible
names, but I knew it would not last for long. Soon she
would be docile and loving as a puppy.

Megan dropped the pages to her lap. "You see how he is?
How he thinks?"

Achal nodded. "Yes. But I've seen worse. I remember one
case where a woman was bound and gagged and tied to a
barstool with a motion sensor that would blow her to bits if
she moved a muscle. And *that* was on prime-time television."

"It will get worse."

"Then, read on."

Megan found her place.

... docile and loving as a puppy.

Like a great concert pianist or master painter, I was
learning my craft as I went along. My first two loves
provided good experience and I had found much time to
reflect on those events. I had been brutish with Najia. It
was nothing more than animal joining, like a bull and
cow. No love. No caress. No affection. I had come to
understand how wrong that was. My beloved mother had
taught me that women are to be revered—that the act of
physical love can only be sanctified by the presence of
emotional love.

I lifted Jane from the bed and carried her up onto the
afterdeck. There I stood her up on the stern cushion, my
hand looped through the chain around her waist. She

swayed, struggling to keep her balance, as the boat rocked on the gentle waves. I watched her eyes as she came to understand the danger of her situation. She could not have avoided plunging into the sea without my stabilizing force. And if she fell overboard, she would sink like a rock because of the chain's weight. I could not have saved her if I wanted to. When she looked into my eyes, I saw stark terror.

I smiled to reassure her. "Now, would you rather sleep with me than stand here?"

The lovely head turned to the murky water. "You wouldn't really push me over ..."

"We keep you alive to serve this ship." I was proud of that line on the spur of the moment. But as a writer, I was guilty of plagiarism. It came from Ben Hur, I believe.

She slumped as the arrogance drained from her proud body. "Yes, I'll sleep with you."

I spoke sternly. "Not enough. You must love me."

She stared at me in confusion. "You must be crazy!"

"Perhaps, but the price of your life is to make love to me as if I were the greatest love of it. Can you do that?"

"I don't know."

I felt it was a fair answer. I pushed gently on the chain and felt her body tense in momentary panic. The boat rolled slightly and she fell. I was able to pull her back and down quickly enough to keep her from going over, and she came to rest hanging over the rail from the waist up.

"Yes!" She screamed it into the still night. "Yes, I'll fuck you." She began to cry—the last bastion of an evil woman.

I pulled her back aboard and sat her up. "Please do not use that word again."

She stared at me with open disbelief. "What word?"

"Fuck. It is most unbecoming for a woman." I smiled. "Invite me to lay with you as a lady would. Darling, please make love to me."

Her hair had come undone in the struggle, and now fell across her face. I brushed it back from her supple cheek and lifted her face to mine. "Darling, please make love to me. Say it!"

She focused on me, her eyes dull and staring. "Darling, please make love to me."

What joy! I carried her back to the bed. There, I removed the part of her suit that still clung around her neck and replaced it with a rope that I tied to the bedposts.

Megan folded the papers and jammed them into her bag. Achal ventured a long look. "Had enough?"

"That's all I can stand for one day."

"But I don't know how graphic it gets."

"You can read it at home. It gives me the chills." She rubbed her hands over her arms. "You see what I mean? Would we publish this? Could anyone publish it?"

Achal checked the mirrors and changed lanes. "Have you ever seen a newscast where they warn you that the next scene may be too violent or too gory for some viewers?"

"Sure."

"How many viewers actually avert their eyes?"

Megan considered it. "None?"

"From the moment we're born, society starts conditioning us ... what we're supposed to believe, and how we're supposed to act. This may be the basis for 'the dark side.' When we are being observed by others, we must react as society dictates. But in the privacy of our darkened room, when nobody else will ever know, is there any limit to what we hunger to experience?"

"Heather said something like that when the first chapter came in." Megan gazed at a puffball cloud. "I don't want to acknowledge that I have a dark side."

"Then why are you so fascinated with this book?"

"Who says I'm fascinated?"

"I do."

Megan slouched in the seat with arms folded and looked around. "Where are we?"

"Thirty minutes south of Newark. We still have a bit of a hike."

"A bit of a hike? Where did you pick that up?"

"From an Australian bloke I used to know."

"Bloke? Did you go to school in England?"

"No. But my grandfather was English, and I was bilingual from birth." He paused, mulling over old memories. "I knew I was going to leave India by the age of ten. So I read every English book I could get my hands on."

"Is that why you became an editor?"

"Could be."

"And your family is still in India?"

"Except for my brother, Anil—one of the finest cooks India ever produced, in spite of the fact that he's an engineer."

"Where does he live?"

"Boston." Achal glanced over. "Maybe we could get together with him next weekend."

"I would like nothing better, but I have to go home to see my grandmother."

"Why?"

"They tell me her mind is failing, and I've been away so long."

"How long?"

"Christmas before last."

"Sounds like you're feeling guilty."

"I am."

"Distance is a reality of adult life, Meg. I see my grandmother once a decade."

"I know, but this woman practically raised me." Her head fell back against the cushion. "My mother worked when I was little, and I went to Gramma's house after school. I'd load the paper rolls onto her player piano and pump away on the pedals, singing at the top of my lungs. 'Blue Moon.' 'Sentimental Journey.' 'Stardust.' I still remember the words to some of those old songs.

"And I can't imagine how many cold winter afternoons

we passed playing chess or Chinese checkers. I never won a game." Megan rolled her head to look at him. "She was a dynamo, Achal ... unquestioned family matriarch. It may be very hard for me to see her now."

"I doubt it. Personality and affection seem to survive, even when other faculties fade."

Megan closed her eyes. "I hope you're right."

Chapter 9

The night was pitch black and humid. Too humid. Winding through the gentle turns on Route 69 north of Wolcott, Oscar Colunga switched on the windshield wipers and strained to penetrate the reflection of headlights from light fog.

He rounded a bend and slowed, pulling up behind two patrol cruisers and a State forensic van. Their red, blue, and yellow flashers stabbed into the mist with the pulsating intensity of a carnival midway. Across the road two vehicles sat darkly, a pickup truck and the unmarked sedan of a state detective.

Colunga stood beside his car and gazed into the forest. A hundred yards from the road, intense lights projected vertical shafts between the trees like rays of sunlight through a cloud. He skirted the patrol cars and turned up the gentle slope, picking his way carefully as the unmistakable sound of a motor generator came up against the stillness of the night.

Breaking into a clearing, he took root. A half dozen men stood or moved across the scene, barking over the generator's noise. Backlit by four spotlights mounted at shoulder height, the most subtle gestures were exaggerated, casting elongated shadows across the broken ground.

A police tape had been strung through the trees on the far side, then wrapped around steel poles driven into the ground in a line that roughly bisected the clearing. A hulking silhouette stood with chest against the tape, observing the operation. Six foot two, he was wide at the shoulder and wider at the hip–light brown hair glowing like a halo.

Oscar pulled up beside him. "Evening, Hank."

"Evening, Lieutenant." Oliphant turned to him. "Sorry to drag you out on Sunday night."

"No problem. I'm sure the Queen Mother will forgive me for leaving her party early."

Oliphant grinned. "I hope so."

"Your message was rather brief ... something about a shallow grave?"

"We're not sure it's a grave yet, but there is a patch of freshly turned earth."

"How fresh?"

"No more than a few days."

"God, it would be amazing to find a body that quickly."

"Damn lucky, to say the least."

"Did the forensic boys turn up anything?"

"Yeah. They lifted footprints and tire tracks before it got dark. And they've cordoned off several areas for detailed examination in the morning."

"So, what are you doing tonight?"

"We're going into the hole."

"What?" Oscar wheeled around and shaded his eyes. Two men with shovels were carefully lifting small bites of dirt from a shallow pit about fifteen feet away. "Shouldn't we call in an archaeological team?"

"You want to do that before we confirm there's a body down there?"

"Good question, Hank. But I'm afraid it's too late to worry about it now." He turned back to the big man. "Have you seen a recent missing persons report that fits our pattern?"

"No."

"Maybe something came in over the weekend."

"Not unless it was in the last few hours. I called in to check on my way down here."

Oscar zipped his coat against the evening chill. "You don't suppose we've discovered a victim before she was reported."

"Well, stranger things have happened, but I—"

"Hey, Hank!"

Oliphant spun around as one of the men threw down his shovel and fell to his knees.

"We hit something."

"What?"

"Can't be sure yet."

The second man joined him and they clawed at the ground with gloved hands.

"Looks like fur."

Oscar gazed at them. "Fur?"

The man on the right pulled a flashlight from his belt and stared into the hole for several seconds. "Ah, geez. Some idiot buried his dog up here."

Chapter 10

"It was nice of you to bring me to the airport." Megan smiled at Achal across the small table in the concourse bar. "I know it's a lot of trouble."

"Nonsense. I live for the chance to drive to Newark on Friday night." He reached out and took her hand. "After last weekend in Atlantic City, I'm disappointed that we can't spend this weekend together. But I truly do understand your need to see your grandmother."

She gazed out the windows at the darkening sky. "I only hope it's not too late."

"Is something wrong?"

"Gramma fell in her garden two days ago. She's in the hospital."

"I'm so sorry. Why didn't you tell me?"

"I didn't want to burden you with it." Megan shook her head. "I should have followed my instincts ... gone to see her months ago."

"Don't blame yourself. ESP is usually wrong."

"I do blame myself. And I know better, because I did the same thing once before."

"What do you mean?"

She pulled away and sat back in a morose slump. "My father brought home this mongrel puppy when I was little. We named him Pudgy because he was roly-poly, but he turned out to be a magnificent animal. He never lost a fight with another dog, and he never attacked a person.

"He protected me, and he loved me—the best friend I ever had. But we drifted apart when I got older. With high school and church and Four-H activities, I was never home. Then, one cold winter day, we noticed he was sick. He had contracted some respiratory disease and was almost dead by the time we realized it." She pulled a tissue from her purse and daubed her eyes. "I felt terrible."

"I understand."

"No. You don't! I abandoned him and moved on with my life." Megan threw her head back and stared at the ceiling as tears flowed down. "Now I've abandoned my grandmother the same way."

Achal felt the helplessness that only a man knows when a woman cries, wanting to say something brilliant to console her. But nothing came. He glanced around to see several heads turned in their direction. Moving his chair closer, he brushed a strand of wet hair from her cheek and tentatively laid his hand on hers. She did not resist, and he raised it to his lips.

"Give me your pain. Let it flow into me."

"Oh, Achal." She buried her face in the back of his hand. "I didn't mean to do this."

"I'm glad you did." He pulled her closer to kiss away the tears. "I want to share everything with you from now on."

The airliner reached altitude and the engine whine cut back. Megan pressed her right temple to the window, grateful that her row was empty. From time to time her chest would spasm, drawing in a loud stuttered breath.

"Get a hold on yourself, Meg." She glanced over as two attendants jostled a drink cart up the aisle. Then her eyes fell to the black leather briefcase at her feet. She bent forward and struggled to hoist it onto the seat beside her.

With a sigh, she opened the top and lifted out the glossy white binder. Harmon Jarvis had thrust it into her hands as she was making her escape from the office, with an admonishment to read it before Monday morning. It was the plan for the merger between Gladiator and a German company, GBF Media, which had already sucked up four publishing houses around the globe. She picked up the heavy tome and thumbed through it.

No changes in personnel. She shook her head. "Uh-huh." *GBF will provide marketing specialists to advise on direction and stimulation of sales.* "Terrific."

Megan looked up as the stewardess leaned across the seat. "What would you like to drink?"

"Coffee."

"Cream or sugar?"

Megan dropped the food tray from the center seat. "Please."

As the cart moved down the aisle, the weight of the heavy report on her lap became suddenly oppressive. She tossed it into her case, and it came to rest atop the black envelope which had arrived in the morning mail.

She took a sip of hot coffee and wrestled the envelope out, then lowered the tray in front of her to hold the pages.

Delicious Pain — Chapter 4

I suffered greatly after Jane's unfortunate demise. I had hoped for one brief moment that she would be a companion, since I certainly would never expect to find another woman as beautiful. But her head was not right and our joining all too brief. I fell into a period of depression over the possibility that I might be undone because of my impromptu actions.

I was certain no one had noted our departure from the marina, and there would be no investigation since her body was under a thousand feet of salt water. Still, I worried. Perhaps it was the similarity with my wife's

death that so unsettled me. I vowed never to use that
method of disposition again. It's unfair to the family to
live throughout life without knowing, and I may someday
notify Jane's father, a prominent lawyer on Long Island,
of her death.

One year later I had completed a novel worthy of
publication. At that, I spent more than two years trying to
entice agents and editors to take on the book. This,
combined with my fears of discovery, convinced me to
move to New York. Relocation was a good move. As I had
suspected all along, I just needed the personal contact to
sell it—not to imply that the job was easy.

It was no best-seller, but it did fairly well for a first
novel and established my name, making future sales
much more profitable. When the next book sold, I decided it was time to put down roots once again and found
a house in New England that was ideal for my purposes.
The former owner was a wealthy industrialist who collected rare cars. What looked like a four-car garage from
the front was deep enough to house eight cars. Built into
a hill, the rear of the garage was underground.

I instantly recognized the potential and signed papers
the following day. Then the difficult phase began. I
couldn't allow local contractors to do the work ... too
easily traced. So I called on people from Jersey and did it
in phases to prevent anyone from seeing the whole
picture. First I had a man subdivide the garage by a thick
concrete wall with a heavy steel door in the center. I had a
plumber install a bathroom in the northwest corner.
Then I built shelves from floor to ceiling on the garage
side with a movable section that completely secreted the
door.

I greatly enjoyed furnishing the place. I bought a bed
with many tie points at the head and foot. I procured a
TV set and hundreds of volumes from used book stores
and garage sales, knowing that boredom would be a big
problem for my visitors when I was away.

Megan groaned and shifted her weight. "Damn consid-
erate."

Of course, I had set up TV cameras in two corners and arranged for cable transmission to my bedroom. I also bolted a sturdy chain to the wall, terminated at the other end with a locking collar that would allow my guests access to the bed, a small writing desk, and bathroom facilities. The entry door and entertainment center were out of reach, the latter being activated by remote controls modified to prevent excessive volume. I had taken great care to soundproof the room so that I could go about my life without concern.

Why did I go to all this trouble? As I said before, I was learning my craft. With both Najia and Jane, our time together had been much too short. Now I had a little nest where I could keep my loves until they learned to love me.

For the next several weeks I traveled New England, frequenting bowling alleys and taverns well off my beaten path. There were plenty of evil women around, but not with the characteristics I required. I finally found Sandra, quite by accident, working in a sandwich shop near a small college in Massachusetts.

As I came in, her back was to me and I stared in wonder. She had the most beautiful legs I've ever seen. Below her short uniform, the thighs were perfectly formed with an enticing line etched by her taut muscles. Her calves were full and firm, nearly balanced inside and out, and they flowed gracefully down to trim ankles embraced by wide straps of her high-heel pumps. She had the tiny waist that I so love, and her streaked golden hair fell halfway down her back.

I held my breath in those seconds while I waited for her to turn around, expecting her to have a face that would stop a clock. When she did turn, it was my heart that stopped. She was beautiful, with full red lips, a pert nose with delicate nares, and clear hazel eyes surrounded by thick lashes. She was in her early twenties, but conveyed the bearing of an older woman. I broke into a sweat when she smiled and asked for my order.

I truly wanted to believe she was a good woman, but I overheard her conversation with a young waiter who wanted to get into her pants. She teased him and led him on. She smiled and looked innocent ... said she would go with him to the Caribbean if he would not expect "favors." She had exposed herself as a user.

For several days I observed her movements. There was a secluded lane not two blocks from her place, where I would prepare her for the journey. To make her abduction easier, I purchased a vial of sodium Pentothal from a young man who worked at a hospital.

I entered the parking lot of her apartment building at nine PM on that Saturday night, and pulled into the slot next to her accustomed parking space. When she turned in, I was standing at the rear of my car with the trunk open. I called to her as she got out. "Excuse me, miss. My car won't start. Could you give me a jump?"

She was put out, as most people are by such inconvenience. For an instant, I wondered if she would recognize me, but she gave no sign.

She shook her lovely head. "I don't have any cables."

I flashed a friendly smile. "I have some here in the trunk."

She stepped forward a few paces, looking into the trunk until her eyes fell on the cables. Then she relaxed somewhat. She was not as close as I would have liked when she nodded and turned to her car. I surged forward and put my left hand across her mouth as I stuck the needle into her magnificent ass. She struggled and tried to scratch me, but I was well protected by clothing and gloves, as I lowered my face to the sweet scent of her hair.

The Pentothal did not take effect as quickly as when injected into a vein, and I threw my other arm around her and held her for the better part of a minute until she went under. I tossed her into the trunk and pulled out of the driveway ... just as a neighbor drove in. He nodded in passing, as if we had some common bond for being in the same place at the same time.

When we arrived at my house, she was still under. I undressed her and laid her on the bed. Then I locked the metal collar around her neck, covered her, and stood watching for some time. This was a very special occasion, the first guest in the secret room I had so lovingly prepared. I turned off all the lights except for one small

lamp, and her form was most appealing beneath the
sheet. Finally, I locked her in and went to bed.

At four AM, I awoke to her screaming. I twisted
around to the monitor in my bedroom closet. She was
kneeling on the bed in the dim light, pulling at the chain.
I reached for the control and zoomed the camera in to see
her face. She was sorely afraid. I threw on my trousers
and ran downstairs. When I came through the door, her
face turned white. She pushed away from me, jamming
herself against the headboard with the sheet pulled up
around her shoulders. She had stopped screaming and
now appeared to be in shock.

"Who are you?" she asked. "What am I doing here?"

"I am your teacher ... your spiritual guide. I will
cleanse the demons from your soul and make you into a
loving woman. Right now, I want you to get some rest. We
will talk in the morning."

With that, I returned to my bedroom to watch her on
the monitors. She was like a caged animal testing its new
milieu. She paced the space, stretching the chain to its
limits to determine her range of freedom. She searched
the bathroom and desk drawers looking for something
she could use as a tool or weapon. It was most interesting
because she was not yet aware of the cameras on her.
Eventually she gave up and returned to the bed. I fell
asleep making plans for the process of adjustment that
would begin in the morning.

"Adjustment?" Megan threw her head back and stared
out the window. The lights of a small town twinkled in the
darkness and she felt set apart from the world below. After
several minutes, she turned back and skimmed until something caught her attention—the same insipid phrase he had
forced Jane to say. She could hear the sneer in his voice.

After a few days, I decided it was time to move forward with our relationship. She had acclimated very
quickly and seemed to be somewhat comfortable with
me. She even told me about personal experiences like the

time she fell off a horse and broke her arm at age thirteen. Still she resisted my advances, unable to proclaim affection. I could wait no longer to satisfy my desire for her.

I understood the female need for modesty, and had given her some lingerie to make her more comfortable. She knelt on the bed in a lacy teddy and watched my preparations with great interest. I brought in a large metal tub containing a large block of ice, and centered it below a heavy noose that swung from a metal ring in the ceiling at the foot of the bed. I don't know if she understood my purpose, but she fought valiantly as I bound her wrists and ankles with rope. I put a pair of five inch heels on her feet—this an important embellishment, since it would both keep her feet from freezing and give her traction to avoid a mishap.

She struggled as I forced her to stand on the ice while I put the noose around her neck and tied it off. She had not yet learned. Alas, she actually believed me capable of hurting her. Perhaps she thought that I intended to kill her then and there.

We were nearly eye to eye now. "Darling, please make love to me."

She stared at me with unseeing eyes, some of her glossy blond hair caught in the loop around her throat. "What?"

"I want you to say that."

"Why?"

"I care too much for you to rape you. I must be invited into your bed."

Her face contorted. "You're mad."

"Perhaps, but it's the only way you'll come down from there alive. I estimate you have less than one hour before the ice melts enough to shut off your breathing. I'll give you some time to think it over."

It was the first moment she understood. In spite of her terror, I was buffeted by the wave of relief that surged from her body. I left her there and went to my room to watch her on the monitors, not knowing how well my scheme would work—or if it would work at all. At first she pulled at her bonds until she nearly slipped off

**the tenuous perch. Then she settled down as if waiting
for something to happen.**

**I moved one camera to observe her feet. It took far
longer for the ice to melt than I had anticipated, but she
was ultimately forced to stand on tiptoe, thereby accentuating the beautiful line of her calf. By now the rope had
tightened noticeably around her throat, and she called
out. My heart leapt for joy when she said the words. This
first mating was wonderful. She was now pliable and
loving—everything I had hoped for ... no, everything I
had dreamed of.**

"Enough!" Megan pitched the pages into her briefcase and closed it. She lifted the coffee to her lips and took a
thoughtful sip, glaring out at the inky nothingness below.
"No. Too much."

Chapter 11

Wind blew the rental car's door shut with a jarring thud as Megan shielded her head with her purse and dashed the short distance from the parking lot to the hospital's main entrance. Her mother held the door and waved her on.

"I wasn't sure you'd make it. Been raining like this for days. There's flooding down on Sutter Creek."

She kissed her mother on the cheek. "Now Mom, you knew I'd make it. Piece of cake compared to driving in New York on a good day."

Sarah Roarke shook her head. "Don't know if it was worth your while coming. Your grandma's not herself." She turned down the hallway of the one-floor hospital with Megan on her heels. "Morning, Hilda," she called to a passing nurse.

Megan edged through the door behind Sarah. The room was large, and it would have been quite airy if the big windows were open to the sun. Now the drizzling rain seemed to cast a damp pall over everything. She dumped her purse onto a chair and moved to the bedside.

Her grandmother reclined on the bed, staring at the ceiling. Never a tall woman, she seemed even smaller now. Her skin was ashen, her eyes glistening and vacant.

Megan took the withered hand. "Good morning, Gramma."

The old woman's eyes moved in her direction. "Wha? Earline!"

Sarah positioned herself on the other side. "No, Mother Roarke. It's your granddaughter, Megan."

The old woman gave a slight nod. "Earline."

Megan looked up. "I don't think she knows me. Who's Earline?"

"Her sister who died about forty years ago."

"I can't believe she's like this. What happened to her?"

"We don't know exactly. The paperboy found her keeled over in her garden. It looks like she fell pretty hard."

"Will she get better?"

Sarah reached out and stroked the withered brow. "Why don't we go sit in the cafeteria?"

"Where is Dad?"

"He'll be in tomorrow."

"How's he taking this?"

"I don't think it'll sink in until he sees her."

Megan stirred cream into a steaming cup of coffee and gazed at her mother. Sarah didn't age the way other women did. Her hair was still thick and dark. She had the same light in her eyes, and the skin of her face and throat was remarkably firm for a woman of sixty-two. But she seemed to be shrinking. The impressive rib cage of her youth had sunken, and her shoulders were getting narrow.

"So, what's Gramma's prognosis?"

"We don't know. They're still running tests."

"Well, what do they think it is? Alzheimer's?"

"No. It's more severe ... brain damage, like a stroke."

"Then she may never be herself again!"

Sarah leaned forward. "I think you should prepare yourself for the possibility that she may not survive this."

"Oh, God." Megan dropped her forehead into her palm. "I should have come sooner. I want her to know how much I love her."

"She knows that, Honey." Sarah drew herself erect. "There are things I need to say ... mother things."

Megan's head came up.

"You are still a young woman. This is the time to live your life, and you should not be preoccupied with death. But at my age, death is a neighbor who lives down the road. He walks among my family and friends. It changes your perspective.

"Your grandmother is ninety-two years old. She was loved by people from miles around, and she lived a rich and fulfilling life. For many of those years, you were her joy. Her delight. That gift, you have already given. She never needed spoken words to know how much you loved her."

"Oh, Mother." Megan broke down and sobbed.

"Let go of it, Honey. Death is inevitable, but people never really die as long as a part of them lives on in us." Fighting back her tears, Sarah pulled herself up and moved around to bury Megan's face in her shoulder. "And there is much of her in you."

Chapter 12

Filled with reservation, Megan lurched along the hallway. Harmon Jarvis only had three working modes—preparing for a meeting, in a meeting, or following up on one. And that, he did over the phone. She had never heard of someone being summoned to his office during working hours. Was she going to be called on the carpet? Or fired?

She hesitated outside the door to collect herself, then pressed forward into the office. "Morning, Chief."

Jarvis stood up to greet her. "Good morning, Meg. Have a seat."

She slipped into one of the guest chairs in front of the large wooden desk, feeling at a loss with nothing in her hands. "You wanted to see me?"

"Yes. I understand you've been receiving some sort of mysterious submissions."

"Oh, that." Megan nervously brushed her skirt. "Who told you?"

"Achal."

"It would be Achal." Megan smiled weakly. "He's concerned about me."

"So I've heard. Are you two getting serious?"

Megan shook her head. "We haven't made plans, if that's what you mean."

"But you are seeing each other."

"I think that's an accurate statement."

Jarvis weighed his words. "You may feel it's none of my business, but I have strong feelings about hanky-panky between my people. What happens if you break up? Do I lose one of you?"

"I don't believe that would happen."

"You don't believe you'll break up? Or you don't believe that you would leave because of it?"

"I give you my word. I won't leave because of it."

"I'll hold you to that." Jarvis fell heavily into his chair and extracted a thin cigar from a box on the desk. He took a tool from the drawer, dressed the end, and lit up. "Now, to the issue. What is it you're reading?"

Megan shifted in her seat. "Ostensibly, the opening chapters of a novel. A new one arrives in the mail every Friday."

"What's it about?"

"It reads like the memoirs of a serial killer. Each chapter is the story of one victim."

"How many chapters have you seen?"

"Five."

"And you don't know who the author is."

She shook her head. "He sent a letter with the first chapter saying he's been published in another genre and wants to try his hand at horror."

"Does this qualify as horror?"

"Well, there is no supernatural element. But it is horrible."

"Do you have a synopsis?"

"No."

"So you don't know the plot."

"I don't know if there is a plot. It's more like an autobiography."

"How many chapters do you anticipate to complete the book?"

"Based on the average length of the ones I've seen, he'll have to kill about thirty women."

"Do you believe this is a published author, or is it some hack trying to force his way through the back door?"

"Well, he's not a novice. He has some writing experience, and he knows his way around fiction."

Jarvis frowned. "If it's not in your genre, I don't understand why you're spending time on it."

"It's different."

"You're telling me that this appeals to your professional desire to field something unusual?"

Megan nodded. "I've never seen anything like it."

"Let's go with that. How is it different?"

She drew in a long breath, and blew it out. "Usually, violent sex is depicted by external observation. The police piece things together after the fact, or the writer describes the act as it's being committed. Sometimes you get into less tangible issues like the killer's psychosis and how the crime plays into that. You with me?"

"I think so."

"In this case, rape and murder are almost incidental. The central issue is the killer's thoughts, and the actual crime is a convenient vehicle to portray his dementia."

"How does he achieve that?"

"He tells what he's thinking from the time he identifies a victim until she's dead, and his thinking is, shall we say, distorted."

"Sounds very dark."

"Yes. Maybe too dark to print."

"Too dark?" Jarvis threw up his hands. "What's too dark to print today? I used to believe there was a limit, but now we have real killers storing body parts in refrigerators and performing fellatio with severed heads. And that's reported on the evening news, for God's sake. Can this manuscript be worse than that?"

Megan shrugged. "I guess you'd have to read it."

"I intend to." Jarvis snubbed out his cigar. "You're turning the corner here, Meg. I'm going to buy two or three of the projects you brought in recently. Future successes in purchasing will increase your production load, and GBF wants us to get everything into print within one year of signing the contract with the author." He sat back and forced a weak smile. "In other words, I need you one hundred percent. Can't have you wasting time on pie in the sky."

"Oh, Harmon. I only spend fifteen minutes a week on it."

"Which is one precious hour every month. At this rate, it will be seven or eight months before you have it all, and I don't think it's efficient to deal with a manuscript piecemeal."

He clasped his hands. "Here's what I want you to do. Copy me with what you have in hand. If I don't see the potential, we'll toss the rest as it comes in. If it looks good, Heather can collect the chapters until the package is complete and you can evaluate it as an entity. Agreed?"

"Yes, sir." She snapped a salute. "Are we done?"

Jarvis nodded.

Megan found her feet and moved haltingly toward the door. She pulled it open and turned back. "Will you do me a favor?"

"If I can."

"Read all of it."

"Why?"

"I hated the opening pages."

"I probably will, too. But I will read it, if you do me a favor."

"What?"

Jarvis grinned. "Get back to work. Now we're both wasting time on this thing."

Chapter 13

From the head of the table, Harmon Jarvis smiled at the group assembled in the large conference room—eighteen editors, Gladiator's Director of Marketing, and a stranger seated on Jarvis' right.

"As you know, our merger with GBF will be effective in two weeks. The deal is assured and our new owners want to get a running start. To that end, they've sent one of their people to help us develop a cohesive marketing philosophy."

He glanced at the visitor. "I'd like to introduce Franz Littman."

Jarvis moved his chair aside as Littman walked to the podium. A compact man of about fifty, his large nose and dark eyes were shadowed by a shock of brown hair in need of a trim—reminiscent of an English schoolboy. But he turned to face them with the adult intensity of a man who seldom laughed.

Megan suppressed a sigh. How many times had she sat in this bleak room while men and women proffered ideas of stellar importance? And how many of those ever bore fruit? None. Zilch. *Nada.* She crossed her arms and sat back to await the spate of charts and graphs.

"Good afternoon. Thanks for coming."

Though not very deep, Littman's voice reflected the confidence of his physical bearing.

"Within the next week, I hope to meet each of you individually to discuss the unique requirements of your genre specialties. For today, let us address some general issues."

He pulled a small note card from his coat pocket. "In preparation for this merger, we wanted to analyze the United States fiction market. To do this, we hired an American company that conducts research polls, and worked with them to develop a suitable questionnaire.

"The survey was limited to adults who purchase six or more novels per year. Since Gladiator does not publish romance, we focused on genres consistent with our imprints—mystery, suspense, horror, science fiction, and so on. The results are quite surprising."

Jarvis gazed at him dryly. "We like surprises."

"Good." Littman scanned the group. "I could ease into this with supporting data, but I want to cut to the chase. The American publishing industry is systematically destroying its own market."

He waited for the stir to die down. "I know it's hard to believe. It is, however, true. In this modern age of computers, publishers know how well a given release sells—down to the book. What our computers cannot tell us, is how many of those books are actually finished by the buyer.

"With the possible exception of romance, it appears that twenty to thirty percent of purchased novels are never finished. And that number would be higher, if not for the fact that many readers feel compelled to get their money's worth by reading the whole book.

"A young woman said she bought a book from one of our competitors that was so bad, she did not just write off the author—she wrote off the entire house!

"I spoke with an aspiring young writer who is a disciple of one of Gladiator's premier authors. When I asked if he finished this author's latest release, he said that he had for two reasons. First, it was his mentor. And secondly, he paid twenty bucks for the damn thing.

"You see? Every time this happens, we lose a little market share. When someone has a bad experience, he will be less likely to part with his money the next time he wanders into a bookstore. Or he may pass it up entirely.

"Another problem is formula writing. The word 'formula' has many connotations. Every house has a preferred formula for what it wants to publish—religion, suspense, romance, or science fiction. This is realistic because it relates to editing efficiency and efficacy of distribution channels.

"But what has evolved in American literature is a formulization by many major authors whereby each book is a copy of the preceding success with no change other than the names and places. Up to a point, this has proven successful, but there is a limit.

"One example where formulization worked extremely well was Ian Fleming's series on James Bond. Although we knew Bond would prevail, each book was sufficiently different in the location and players ... particularly charisma of the villain.

"Unfortunately, modern American writers are not so adept at coming up with this kind of variation. After a time, the most devoted of fans get tired of the same formula, also a reason for declining sales in today's novel market."

Megan sat a little straighter.

"Another type of formulization is length. The longer the better, this year. The shorter the better, five years from now. Some houses even have minimum or maximum limits on word count. *Shogun* was eleven hundred pages. *Jonathan Livingston Seagull* was barely over a hundred pages, with illustrations. By what distorted logic does length determine a book's quality or its potential financial success?"

Harmon Jarvis peered at him over the rim of his glasses. "You're saying that a book should be as long as it needs to be."

"Precisely. But what we see is the unwarranted padding of fiction. Too many authors are writing excessive and useless detail: seventeen-page flashbacks, three-page descriptions of fixing breakfast, irrelevant characters, and whatever else it takes to make a seven-hundred-page book out of a three-hundred-page story."

"And your research supports this?"

"Yes." Littman motioned to the west. "Twenty percent of readers out there want the words. They are disappointed when the book ends, no matter how long it is. But the vast majority are tired of skimming, even skipping entire pages, to get past the padding and pick up the thread of the story."

He shook his head. "If padding is undesirable to the reader, how can it possibly benefit us? Higher cost of production and shipping causes us to raise the price, thereby exacerbating buying resistance at the point of sale."

Megan leaned forward. "Are you suggesting that the industry is wholly responsible for its marketing problems?"

"Absolutely not. There are many detrimental trends at work in the United States—conversion to visual media, changes in educational emphasis, breakdown of the family unit, and an increase in the daily demands on the time and energy of adults—not to mention the Internet.

"What I do want to say is this. Faced with erosion of our market potential by these powerful forces, we must field the best possible product to retain our market share, let alone expand it."

Littman paused in thought. "And in order to become profitable in the near term, we must capture market share from our competitors. Here again, product quality is the key, and that is primarily determined by the decisions of our editors. You must accurately qualify and select novels that have great potential."

He glanced around. "This leads me to an important point.

Every editor in New York has a set of criteria on which selection of novels is based. It may be company policy, written or tacit. It may depend on the education or background or personal tastes of an individual editor. 'Spy thrillers are out and ecology is in.' 'A woman in jeopardy must save herself.' 'You can no longer sell a book based in Vietnam.' I even know of a case where an editor rejected a manuscript because it was 'Not his cup of tea.'"

Anger boiled up, and Littman seemed to loom larger. "We are not printing books for our own edification. It is not your job to select novels that appeal to your personal taste. Your job is to print novels that will make money.

"Business prospers by selling a product that people want to buy." He scanned them with steely eyes. "Tear up your list of selection criteria, whether it exists physically or mentally, and replace it with one simple question. Will people like to read this?"

Megan sat at attention. Much of what he said mirrored her quiet inner thoughts, things she might hesitate to say publicly.

Littman continued. "I do not want to leave you with the impression that we are asking more of you without offering something in return. You all hold the title of Acquisition Editor, but you are so bogged down with production of what you have purchased, that you don't have enough time to acquire. As it turns out, our British operation is short on work right now. I suggest that we farm out some of your copy editing and production duties to them so that all of your time can be used to find new material."

He waited for them to assimilate the significance. "Furthermore, I want you to believe that I am here to help. My office is on the northeast corner, down the hall from Harmon. If you can nail down any specific problem that I can help you with, my door is always open."

Megan asked, "I have a question. Is your door is open now?"

"Certainly."

"Do you have any fresh ideas on where to look for new material?"

"Actually, I do have a couple." He collected his thoughts. "First of all, I have been affiliated with several writer's groups in this country, and have served as judge on many of their novel contests. We should invite them to send copies of all novels submitted."

"Why not just the winners?" Bernie Yellanik blinked, as if surprised by his own voice.

"Because the winners are rarely the best ones submitted. It would be better to see them all."

"Would these societies go to all that trouble?"

"Why not? It's certainly to their advantage to advertise that all entries will be submitted to New York."

"Sounds logical. What else?"

"Well, this is premature, but we are trying to get a handle on how much fiction is being published by small presses, and if this might be a source for us. At least we know that these books have proven acceptable to a professional in the community, who has deemed them to be of sufficient merit to venture his or her own capital. Perhaps we could buy the rights to reprint their best works."

Jarvis asked, "Are there many independent fiction houses out there?"

"There are hundreds of small presses that print nonfiction—perhaps a source for our nonfiction lines. But with the difficulty fiction writers face in punching through the ramparts which New York has created, some of these presses may have ventured into fiction. And there are some small houses that deal only in fiction. At this moment, I don't know how prolific it is."

"How can we determine that?"

"I have people pouring over lists of small presses right now. Once we decide which to contact, it will only cost us a handful of stamps to qualify the idea."

Megan realized she was holding her breath. Was it possible that the merger would pay off? Did GBF have expertise that could make a material difference? If so, it would be one source of relief in a life of spiraling pressure.

Chapter 14

The offensive warbling penetrated his dream. Colunga rolled over and thrust his hand toward the phone. The receiver gyrated through the air and spun to a raucous collision with the floor. "Son of a bitch!" He flopped his shoulder over the bed's edge and felt around, finally bringing it to his ear.

"Yeah?" Oscar grimaced and held it two inches away as the excited voice of Hank Oliphant assaulted his tympanic membrane.

"Oscar, did I wake you?"

Colunga turned the clock around. "No, Hank. Six o'clock is kinda late for me. I've already played eighteen holes and fixed breakfast for the DAR."

"Sorry, but you wanted to be notified if anything turned up on these bodies."

Colunga pulled himself upright and swung his feet to the floor. "Talk to me."

"We found another buried skeleton."

"Where?"

"Off a service road on the Nepaug Reservoir. Do you know where it is?"

"Christ, Hank. I'm not a forest ranger."

"It's west and a little north of Hartford, between Canton and Bakersville."

"Are you on the scene?"

"Yes."

"I'm coming up."

"There's nothing to see but a couple of ribs sticking out of the ground."

"Are they exhuming the body now?"

"No. Captain Chalmers wants to call an archaeological team on this one."

"I'm coming up anyway."

"Suit yourself. After you turn west toward Bakersville, it's about two or three miles on your left—not much more than a driveway."

Oscar dropped the phone into the cradle and pulled on his shorts. In the bathroom he brushed his teeth, and ran a comb through his graying black hair with his other hand. He threw on his clothes and headed for the door, but pulled up to open the dresser drawer. There was the unused black comb Julia had given him because she said he always looked unkempt.

He had few reminders of her—most of her personal things given away, or thrown away, because they only sustained his grief. He had her teddy bear that he sometimes slept with, the cheap pocket watch she gave him the Christmas after her mother died, and this stupid comb.

Oscar gripped the wheel with one hand and fought the map with the other, both irritated and amazed at how cantankerous a sheet of paper could be. He had passed Canton, and now concentrated on maintaining the speed limit while finding the turnoff to Bakersville. A sign with an arrow drifted into sight. He threw the map on the passenger floor in disgust, knowing that the reservoir was only a few miles away.

Gauging distance had been a hard thing to adapt to in Connecticut police work. That distance on a New Mexico map would have been twenty miles. Here it was four. He took the left and relaxed slightly. How far could he miss? If he came across a sign saying "Welcome to Bakersville" it would only be a few miles out of his way.

He pulled the comb out of his pocket and held it up in front of his eyes. The sun bounced from the car's hood and produced strange patterns from the glossy black teeth. Why did he bring it along? It was a last minute impulse. Of all things to cherish, a dime-store comb that would have been ground to dust in his pocket, or lost years ago had he not put it away.

The road ahead blurred slightly. "Julia, my baby."

He remembered how he breathed a sigh of relief when she went off to Arizona State. She would have friends and campus security and dedicated city police to protect her, not to mention the instincts that a girl her age must have. How then, did this murderous maniac lure her away? What charming device, or instrument of fear, did he use to lure her into the seething pit of his own sickness?

Oscar pulled off the road and jammed the gearshift into PARK, his vision and concentration compromised by emotion. He remembered little of the flight to Phoenix, but the morgue stood out like yesterday. Those morbid corridors, so common to his experience, had seemed unearthly—as if he'd been transported into a nightmare of his own creation.

Like a disembodied spirit, he had watched as the steel drawer slid silently from the wall and clanged against the stops.

"May I be alone with her?"

Oscar had not seen Julia undressed since she was twelve. He pulled the sheet from her body and gazed upon the full breasts and hips of an adult woman. She had taken a terrible beating, and the bruises on her wrists and ankles confirmed that she was helpless. Oscar winced at the memory ... the pain as he had bent double and wept upon his crossed arms, inches from her pathetic lifeless face.

He opened his eyes with a shudder, to see the lush green trees of Connecticut stirring in the morning breeze. Something moved nearby, and he whirled around. Hank Oliphant stood beside the car rapping gently on the window.

Oscar found the switch. "Morning, Hank."

"Morning, Lieutenant. Whatcha doin'?"

"I was on my way ..." Oscar pulled a handkerchief from his back pocket and blew his nose. "Where is it?"

"A hundred yards down the road." He pointed. "On the left."

"Get in, Hank."

Seconds later they turned onto the short access road and nosed up to a steel cable which barred the entrance between Hank's unmarked car and a State Patrol cruiser.

Oliphant walked up to the tall trooper stationed there. "Sam, this is Lieutenant Oscar Colunga."

He snapped a salute. "Sam Layton, sir."

Oscar glanced around. "Seems awfully quiet."

"Yes, sir. The forensic boys are on their way, but nobody's showed up yet."

Oliphant glanced at Oscar. "Want to go up and take a look?"

"Yes."

They skirted around the cable on the left end and walked up the trail.

"Who found her?"

"A young couple from Hartford out on a flower walk. They moved off the path to have a bite, and there she was."

"I don't understand. Were they digging in the ground?"

Oliphant's head wagged back and forth slowly. "According to the ranger, it was a quirk of nature. They redirected some drainage channels a few months ago, and she was uncovered by the resulting erosion."

"Are you sure it's a female?"

"No, but it seems like a safe bet based on the pattern we've seen up here."

"What happens now?"

"Well, it takes awhile to assemble an archaeological team, so it'll probably be a day or two before the digging starts in earnest. In the meantime, our forensic people will do their thing with what's exposed. And I have to set up round-the-clock security to make sure nobody messes with the scene."

He turned off the trail and headed up the hill. "She's about two hundred yards in. Like I said, not much to see at this point."

Oscar followed him silently. Early morning sun was virtually shut out by the canopy of branches. He gazed at a patch of wildflowers in passing, and sucked in the scent of green plants and dark earth. What irony that this should be the resting place of such violence.

Oliphant stopped and stepped aside to reveal the grave. Only the ends of two ribs were actually exposed, but they were not protruding from a depression. The erosion had lowered the entire surface evenly, and the body's outline was readily apparent—especially the rib cage and pelvis.

"Considering the lay of the land, I would expect the skull to be visible." Oscar went down on one knee near the shoulder. "Where's the skull?"

Oliphant assessed it with a frown. "Maybe it's bent back at a sharp angle."

"Not likely, Hank. Shallow graves tend to be uniformly shallow."

Chapter 15

Achal Bedi sat at the bar at Wolfe's, watching the evening news. Four drug-related murders, three dead in fires, and two street people starved. "And a partridge in a pear tree." He looked around, but nobody noticed his quiet outburst.

Megan was late, but it was not unexpected. Most everyone was late according to some personal schedule. Once Achal had a friend who had to be led by forty-five minutes. It was something ingrained. One thing he had noticed about Americans—the one who lived closest was the last to arrive. It was some inverse sense of urgency.

He glanced over as a vision of loveliness slid onto the barstool at his left. The power and intelligence behind those green eyes always made him feel like a little boy. "Good evening, Meg."

"What's good about it? Littman tagged me at the elevators and chewed my ear for twenty minutes."

"Well, he's got his work cut out."

"I guess." Megan dropped her chin into her palms and sulked. "What do you think? Does he know what he's talking about?"

"I hope so. I agree with most of it."

She spun around in surprise. "You do?"

"Sure. I don't like padding as a reader or editor. And I've let a couple of authors go because I got sick of their formula."

"What if they're not your cup of tea?"

"My cup's pretty big, Meg. If it's science fiction, it usually falls in." He reflected. "Although I have printed a few things that started out like a dried tea bag on the saucer."

"Like what?"

"*Deluvian Formation*, for one."

"Wow. That's one of the best sci-fi novels ever published."

"True, but it took me a year to get there."

"You spent a year on one book?"

"Off and on."

"Why?"

"Because it was a powerful idea—guaranteed best-seller if he did nothing more than a credible job of writing. Unfortunately, his first manuscript was not credible. Worse, I didn't like the author when I met him."

"Dan Condon?"

Achal nodded. "Some writers go through a period of arrogance, usually about two or three years into their career. They've learned a little bit about the craft, and think they know everything. You ever notice that?"

"Oh, never."

"Well, I caught this guy during his arrogant period. He wasted ten pages of description to set up a restaurant scene. But after I kicked it back two or three times, he gained a little humility."

"And turned out to be one of your best authors."

"Probably my top earner."

"So, I assume you like him now."

"I hate his guts."

Megan covered her mouth and laughed—a deep, throaty, female sound that always stirred something in Achal.

The bartender wheeled around and rushed over. "Sorry, Miss Roarke. I didn't see you come in."

She recovered her composure and turned, eyes still smiling. "It's okay, Ralph. I'm in no hurry."

"You want your usual?"

"Ya know, I forgot to take my iron pill this morning. How about a rusty nail?"

"Coming right up."

Megan gazed at the television set over the bar. "If you dislike Dan Condon so much, how can you work with him?"

"No problem. He doesn't like me, either."

"Then why are you still together?"

"We make too much money for each other. We can't afford to break up."

She laughed again. "Sounds like a marriage."

"In a way, it is. But we're stuck with—"

He stopped and spun around as Megan waved her hand violently and leaned forward, straining to hear the young Asian woman on the screen.

"According to Lieutenant Oscar Colunga of the Connecticut State Police, the remains were discovered in a shallow grave near the Nepaug Reservoir in northern Connecticut. It will be several days before the team of forensic archaeologists can unearth the body, but based on a preliminary estimate of the grave's age, one source indicated that it may be Annette Chesson, a junior at Elander College who was last seen over eight years ago. She left the diner where she worked at nine p.m. on a Saturday night, and was not heard from again."

The pretty reporter turned a page. "In other news ..."

Achal studied her ashen face. "What is it, Meg?"

She gathered up her purse and clutched it against her chest. "I've got to go back to the office."

"Right now? We have dinner reservations in thirty minutes."

"Go on without me. I'll meet you there."

Megan opened the second drawer on the left and extracted the stack of black envelopes, peering into each until she found Chapter Four. She dumped it out onto the desk and skimmed it.

I finally found Sandra, quite by accident, working in a sandwich shop near a small college in Massachusetts. I knew her the moment I saw her. It was an act of God. I was not looking at the time, just hungry.

Megan's eyes inched forward, pausing on the opening words of each paragraph.

I entered the parking lot of her apartment building at nine PM on that Saturday night, and pulled into the slot next to her normal parking space.

The chapter was over twenty pages, and the printed sheets slid across the desk, some of them falling to the floor as Megan pushed them aside. She skimmed pages of detail on what he did to the unfortunate woman to make her proclaim her love for him. Near the end, she slowed and read with concentration.

... had been together now for over two months, and I was beginning to believe that she loved me as much as I loved her. It was a match made in Heaven. That night I brought her into my own bedroom. Even though she was earning my trust, I chained her hands to the headboard.
It was early summer and the windows were thrown open to drink in the cool air and aromas that made my rural exile such a pleasure. An ideal night for lovemaking, the moon was full and we were bathed in a soft glow as in a fairy tale. We made love thrice. It is a lovely word, don't you think? Thrice, like some ancient Roman writing. A poetic and historic use of the English language.
At dawn, I awakened her and kissed her tenderly. She proclaimed her love for me and suggested marriage. At

first my heart soared like an eagle. This was the pinnacle of all my dreams. I had spent a lifetime hoping that it was possible to cleanse the evil from a beautiful woman's soul and return her to the childlike receptiveness that society had so callously destroyed.

As I had suspected, the expense and trouble of setting up my secret nest was justified. I had always believed that any woman would come to appreciate my capacity for love and devotion if given enough time.

Unfortunately, I had to go into New York on business that day. I told her that I would perform the ceremony as soon as I returned. She protested that she wanted a big wedding with all her family and friends around. It had been her dream since childhood, she said. I locked her away and left for my appointment.

During the day, bad thoughts began to cloud my mind. Her desires were impossible. Her disappearance had made national news and triggered a massive hunt by police in seven states. How could she just emerge now, saying that she had chosen to go away with me? Impossible.

That night, I told her we must marry in secret—that it must be between us and she could never leave the house. Then her true colors emerged. She said she would rather die than be cooped up in one place for the rest of her life. If I really loved her, she said, I would want to show her off to others, to present her as my life's companion so we could do things that married couples did.

I tried to explain it to her, but she would not listen to reason. She became furious ... violent. She called me terrible names. She asked if I was stupid enough to believe that she could love an insane monster like me. She tried to bite me. She scratched my face. Now I realized that all her tenderness and lovemaking had been a sham—a scam to take advantage of my love for her. All along, her intent had been to con me into letting her go.

This was most disappointing. I had long believed that I understood the extent of the female's ability for deception, but this exceeded my wildest imagination. What evil could pervade so lovely a creature to permit such treachery?

I lashed out with inhuman strength, catching her alongside the jaw. She collapsed onto the bed and I left her there without another look. I went upstairs to my den and got very drunk. It was not until noon the next day that I found the fortitude to look upon that perfidious face. Only then did I realize that she was dead. My blow had broken her neck, and she lay in a wretched pile on the bed with her head at a grotesque angle.

I sat looking at her for some time. I touched the soft, porcelain skin, now cold and unyielding. I laid her out on the bed and held her. I kissed her cheek and wept. After an hour, I took a long drive. It may have been the worst day of my life.

I knew that I must dispose of her body soon, but I could not bring myself to be immediately cut off from her beauty. I decided to keep her head for a time. It was a dangerous and foolish decision, I know, but it was necessary for my peace of mind. I buried the body by placid waters, then drove to a chemical company in a nearby city and purchased two gallons of formaldehyde.

"Buried by placid waters?"

Megan spun around to the windows, replaying the news report in her mind. A college student, working in a diner, abducted on Saturday night, and buried at a reservoir. The book's victim was identical, except that she worked in a sandwich shop.

She rubbed her temples. There was something tugging at her memory, something out of place the first time she read that chapter.

"Of course! Who wears heels behind a deli counter?" She dropped her hand. "But in a diner ..."

Megan reached for the phone and dialed information.

"I need a number in Hartford, Connecticut."

Chapter 16

Oscar Colunga sat in his office trying to work up the energy to rise and go home. He looked through the big window to the outer office where his four staff members usually sat. It was six o'clock and the only one left was the dedicated Kathy Huntsinger. As he watched, she stood up and approached his door.

"I'm taking off. Anything you need before I go?"

"I don't think so, Kathy. You better get home to your daughter."

At that moment, his phone went off.

She smiled. "You going to answer that? It is after hours."

"What the hell." He lifted the receiver. "Colunga, OSI."

The woman's voice was shaky. "Are you the officer investigating the death of this woman they found by some reservoir?"

"Yes, the Nepaug Reservoir."

"Can you tell me if the body was ... complete?"

His feet dropped from the desk and he lunged forward to smash the RECORD button on his answering machine. "What do you mean by complete?"

He glanced up at Kathy and made a motion to trace the call. She scurried toward her desk.

The woman's reservations came across the wires. "I mean, was her head on her body?"

"I'm sorry. We won't know that until the body is exhumed." He knew she would bolt at the slightest pressure. "Are you a reporter?"

Her answer was long in coming. "Just curious."

"May I ask why?"

"Oh, it's probably nothing."

"Tell you what. Let me have your number and I'll get back to you when we have that information."

"No. That won't do."

"We should know more in a week or so." Colunga felt her slipping away. "I could mail you something then, or fax if you prefer."

"Thank you, Lieutenant. You've been very kind." She hung up.

He bashed the receiver into the cradle and wheeled around to Kathy. "Did you get it?"

She waved her hand and listened intently. "No. But they did trace it as far as New York—area two-one-two." She hung up and crossed the large outer room to his door. "Sorry. Was it important?"

"Well, this woman calls up and asks if the head is still attached to the body we just found."

"Why would anyone do that?"

"I can't imagine. She couldn't have gotten it from the press. And she didn't get it from us. We're not even sure the head is missing." He leaned across and stopped the recording. "Kathy, we need to find this woman!"

"But all you know is that the call originated in Manhattan. How do you intend to ID her? By her voice?"

"It's a start. I'd guess she's between twenty-five and forty, and a professional woman ... probably called from her office."

"Great. You've narrowed it down to about a million." She made a dour face. "You don't have a prayer."

"We might not have enough now, but I've got a feeling

we'll hear from her again." He shook his head in thought. "Do we have those gizmos on our lines that ID the caller?"

"I'll have to check with Susie at the front desk. I don't really know."

"If not, I want them installed tomorrow."

Chapter 17

The rented two-seater wheeled into the dirt parking lot in front of the real estate office sporting the sign DUGGAN'S PROPERTIES, coming to rest in a small cloud of dust between a Jeep Cherokee and a green Jaguar. The building was like a picture postcard for Connecticut, a low wide structure with gently sloping roof, set back into the trees along a winding two-lane road near Pleasant Valley. Tudor trim and mullions of the multi-paned windows were painted dark green in harsh contrast to the white stucco.

Megan hauled herself out of the small convertible and stretched her long legs in the midday sun, breathing in the sensuous aroma of verdant forest and living earth. She glanced at her watch. About ninety minutes on Saturday. What would the drive be like on a weekday? Certainly a lot more than the ten-minute subway ride to her apartment.

She brushed a crease from her shorts and approached the building, finding the large reception area deserted. A woman, somewhat plump, emerged from the office on the right. She wore a dark blue business suit and white blouse with integral bow at the neck. Her curly brown hair looked like a helmet.

"Miss Roarke?"

"Yes."

The woman moved closer and extended her hand. "Welcome. I'm Joan Kirtch. We spoke on the phone." She smiled up with gleaming dark eyes.

"It's a pleasure to meet you in person, Joan." Megan returned her smile. "I've never looked at houses before. How do you go about it?"

"Well, we could go over catalog listings here in the office." She lifted a set of keys from the reception desk. "But I think it would be best to look at a few places first ... give you an idea of the area and what to expect around here."

"Fine." Megan followed her out to the Cherokee and climbed aboard. She fell silent as the vehicle picked up speed, gazing at this alien world of natural things. Wildflowers and plants carpeted the land beyond the shoulders of the road, and sunlight filtered through tall trees that seemed to rotate in note of their passage.

"I hope I haven't misled you, Joan. I'm not actively looking to buy right now ... just get a feel for the area to plan for financial requirements."

"You made that very plain on the phone, and I don't mind at all."

Megan smiled. "How far is this place?"

"Just around the next bend."

Joan slowed and turned off onto a dirt driveway. Fifty feet in, the grade became quite steep. As the Jeep clawed its way upward through the embracing trees, the house rose into view like something being thrust up from the Earth. They topped the rise and came to rest in a clearing that served as front yard and parking lot.

It was a huge A-frame backed up against the wooded hill, a broad deck projecting forward from the main level with a three-car garage below. The front façade was native stone, framing glass that formed a two-story triangle encompassing the first and second floors. Dark shake shingles on the steep roof gave a massive appearance to the structure.

"It's a mansion!"

"Yes, it is quite impressive." The realtor pulled up in front and led her up the long staircase to the deck.

Megan turned and drew a breath. The valley stretched out below, a patchwork of green and yellow merging at the far side where the trees formed an impenetrable wall.

"Why would anyone leave this place?"

Joan opened the door and stood aside. "In this case, divorce."

Megan entered and stared in awe. Still furnished, the living room stretched ahead and to the far wall on her left, rising some thirty feet to the ceiling's apex. An open wooden staircase spiraled upward to the second floor balcony, which ran past two rooms at the rear. The first, and apparently larger, had a wide, shuttered opening set into the wall facing the front windows.

Through a door on her right was a library with a large picture window in front and books lining the interior walls.

She moved hypnotically through the doorway directly before her. A heavy walnut table and matching china cabinet gleamed dully in the dining room on the right, and down the stairs to her left was an informal dining area flanked by an enormous kitchen with red-tiled floor and copper pots over a large cooking island. The effect was like a cavern with sunlight streaming through latticed windows spanning the rear wall.

She turned back to the realtor. "I love it."

"Would you like to see the bedrooms?"

"I don't know if that's a good idea."

Joan smiled. "Afraid you'll like it too much ... won't want to leave?"

"I don't want to leave now."

Megan followed her up the staircase and gaped openly as they passed through the master bedroom. It was spacious, with large, openable windows looking out over virgin woods at the rear. She moved through the doorway to her right and passed through a large dressing room with twelve feet of closet, then into a spacious bathroom with oversized tub and dual shower heads.

Megan spun around to Joan. "How much does something like this cost?"

"He's asking four hundred."

She froze and blinked twice. "Four hundred thousand dollars?"

"Lots of places go for more in this area, but this is rather unusual. Because of the A-frame construction, there's less than two thousand square feet finished, and it only has two acres of land. Most people who move up here are looking for a little more in one of those categories."

"Even so." Megan felt herself trembling and sat down on the tub. "I could never afford that."

"Do you have anything to put down? Equity in another property?"

"Well, they tell me I'll receive something from my grandmother's estate. But I have no idea how much."

"She passed away recently?"

"Last week."

"I'm so sorry." Joan regarded her. "Perhaps this isn't a good time to talk business details."

"No, I'm all right." Megan brushed her hand across her eyes. "If I could bring the loan balance down to two hundred, what would the monthly payments be?"

"Right around two thousand. Could you handle that?"

"I'm paying almost as much for my apartment in Manhattan. But I'd have to buy a car." She thought for a few seconds. "Are there other people who live up here and work in New York?"

"Many of them."

"Are there car pools?"

"Of course."

"That might make it easier." Megan arose and circled to

the front wall, throwing open the great shutters to gaze across the valley. "It's beautiful beyond belief."

"Yes." Joan stood beside her, sharing the view. "Too bad you're not actively looking."

"Even if I were, I couldn't spend that kind of money."

"Well, you would be generating net worth instead of funneling your money into some landlord's pocket. You should also consider tax benefits to see how it affects actual cash outlay. And we may get the owner to come down on the price."

"You think he would?"

"We can always make an offer."

Megan gazed down on the living room. "I couldn't even afford to furnish this place."

"Maybe we can include some furniture in the deal."

"Seriously?"

"It was a nasty divorce, and he wants to rid himself of everything that reminds him of her."

"How do you know that?"

She winked. "We all know each other hereabouts."

"Oh, it's coming too fast. I need to get out of here."

Joan squeezed her elbow. "I know. Let's look at a couple more places ... give you a comparison on what kind of value this represents."

Megan nodded gratefully. "Good idea."

The tires spun loose of the gravel as Megan left the small lot in front of the realty and set out toward Highway 44. In spite of the distance covered, her time with Joan had been surprisingly short. It was 2:30 as she turned east. After all these years in the area, she was going to see Hartford.

Wind slipped over the windshield and whipped her hair, smelling sweet and clear. Overhead, a flock of starlings soared in fluttering spirals, forming the only pattern in an unbroken sky. Traffic was light, and she was nearly oblivious to the world around her.

Suddenly, she stiffened. Something had penetrated her euphoria. Megan glanced in the mirror and plowed to a stop. She backed up onto the shoulder to read the sign: NEPAUG RESERVOIR.

She slapped the lever into gear and surged onto the road with a screech of tires and spray of gravel. A local man in a weather-beaten pickup, rounding the gentle corner behind her, laid on the horn and swerved to miss her. She waved apologetically and stared at the scene opening up before her.

A dozen vehicles were packed into a short road on the right, and several more were parked along the shoulder—some sticking out a foot or more onto the pavement. Megan checked her mirrors and slowed, coming to rest behind a Connecticut state cruiser.

"This is stupid, Meg." She got out and walked haltingly toward the crowd milling around the police lines. The atmosphere was anticipation, like a race crowd waiting for the next crash. She passed by a van from a local television station and slipped sideways behind the crowd, coming to rest on the left flank with the police tape against her waist.

Megan gazed up the gentle slope to the point where the tree line obscured everything beyond. Three official-looking men in suits were conversing a hundred yards up the slope. One man was slight of build, one heavy, and the third was Native American or Hispanic.

"All right, folks. If you don't have official business here, let's break it up and go home."

She wheeled around as a tall state trooper wended his way through the vehicles and approached the crowd. Their eyes met and he veered directly toward her.

"May I help you, ma'am?"

"Oh, I just happened to be driving by." Megan gazed up

at the square jaw and wide brim of his hat. "Is this where they found that body?"

"Yes, ma'am. But I'm afraid there isn't much to see right now." He smiled amiably. "I'm sure you'll see news reports as things develop."

She turned to go, and then swung back. "Who's in charge here?"

"Lieutenant Oscar Colunga." He pointed up the slope. "That's him, with the black hair. Would you like me to call him over?"

Megan gazed at Colunga too long, and the trooper had his hand to his mouth before she could eject the word. "No!"

He turned back. "I'd be glad to get him down here for you."

"Really. There's no reason. Thank you so much." Megan pivoted and fled toward her car.

Up the slope, Hank Oliphant stopped in mid-sentence, realizing he was being ignored. "What is it, Oscar?"

Colunga peered down the hill. "*Que mujer!*"

"What's that mean?"

"What a woman!"

Oliphant turned. "Jesus, you got that right."

"I'll be back." Oscar set out down the hill at a fast pace as the small red car sped away. Even to his keen eyes, the license plate was well out of range.

"Afternoon, Sam."

"Afternoon, Lieutenant. How's it going up there?"

"Slow. I may call it a day, but I was wondering who that woman was."

"Oh, just a Lookie-Lou. I have to shoo them away from time to time."

"She appeared to be very attractive from a distance."

"God, you should have seen her up close. She had the most amazing green eyes." He grinned. "I was tempted to trump up a citation to get her name and address."

"I wish you had. Us single guys could use a lead like that."

"Actually, I tried to keep her around ... even suggested calling you over, but she was in a big hurry."

"*Que lastima.*" He smiled. "You know what that means, Sam?"

"No, sir."

"It means 'what a pity.' Too bad." Oscar turned his head eastward, watching the dust settle on the road. "*Que lastima. Que mujer!*"

Chapter 18

Elevator doors hissed open and Colunga stormed across the hall to the Manhattan offices of the FBI.

The petite, dark-haired receptionist looked up. "May I help you?"

"I'm here to see José Cruz."

"Do you have an appointment?"

"I wouldn't drive all the way down here without one."

Her lips curled up. "Your name?"

"Oscar Colunga."

"Ah yes. He said to send you right in." She pointed down the long corridor. "Third door on the right."

He trudged down the hall with trepidation—embarrassment. He and Cruz had once been like brothers. Now, separated by a mere two hours, they rarely saw each other, and this time he had to ask a favor.

"Aye, *Hijo*." Cruz sprang from his desk and embraced Colunga, then pulled back to arm's length. "I am so happy to see you!"

"Obviously." Colunga smiled into the shining eyes. José hadn't changed since college. His five-foot-seven frame was still trim and athletic. There was no sign of age in almost cherubic features, accented by thick eyebrows and a slightly oversize nose.

"Come in. Come in." Cruz offered a seat at a small table right of the desk and closed the door. "You want coffee?"

"No thanks. I poured in a gallon on the way down here." Colunga scanned the room. "This is the first time I've seen your office. It's twice the size of mine. You must be doing well with the Bureau."

"Not too bad. I keep getting kicked up the ladder. Only problem is, I seem to get farther from the action with each new rung." He moved over and sat down across the table. "How are you doing, *Hijo*?"

"Professionally?"

"No, personally."

"Better, I guess."

"I been worrying about you. It's more than six months since we've seen you."

"Sorry, Joe. I've become somewhat of a hermit since moving to Hartford."

"Have you made any friends up there?"

"I haven't had any interest in socializing."

"That's not good, *Hijo*. You need to be around people. It's your nature."

"I know, but it was a good move to get away from the southwest for a while."

"Because of Julia?"

Colunga blinked hard. "You remember when I gave her that Kachina doll for her fifth birthday? How she looked when she opened it?"

"Like you'd given her the moon."

"After she died, I saw that smile every time I passed a store with a Kachina in the window. I saw her face in the sunsets and her eyes in the stars on autumn nights. Everything reminded me of her."

"I understand." Cruz lowered his head in reverence. "Did they ever catch the man who did it?"

"He never came to trial."

"What a shame." He gazed at Oscar. "Sometimes I wish we never grew up, *Hijo*—still back there in the desert scaring jack rabbits with your padre's M1 carbine. Do you miss those days?"

"More than you could imagine."

"*Seguro.* That was a better time of life." Cruz eyed him. "Can you stay for lunch?"

"I'm clear until tomorrow morning."

"Good. I want you to come home to dinner ... stay overnight. My wife misses you, too."

"I would be delighted."

"Excellent." He grinned. "Now, what could be important enough to bring you into this town?"

"Business." Colunga sighed. "One of my data analysts came across some alarming statistics recently. It looked like we might have a serial killer operating in the state. Then we discovered another body at the Nepaug Reservoir. I assume you heard about it."

"Yes. I have been following closely."

"You have? Why?"

"Partly curiosity, and partly because it's the kind of thing we frequently get called in on—homework, you might say."

"You always had good instincts, Joe." Colunga shook his head slowly. "One thing we kept from the press was the fact that she was decapitated."

"*Madre de Dios!*"

"I've been saying that a lot lately. I tend to revert to Spanish when the shit gets deep."

"You asking our assistance?"

"Yes, but not in the way you probably expect. I won't know if we need you on forensics until our own people have done their thing, but there is a related issue that you are better equipped to deal with than we are."

"Which is?"

"Just after we discovered this girl, I received a phone call from a woman who seemed to know some particulars of her death. I'm pretty sure she knew we wouldn't find a head with the body."

Cruz leaned onto his elbows as if he suddenly felt heavy. "Did you ID her?"

"She wouldn't give me anything. And we didn't have enough time for a trace, except that she called from Manhattan."

"That covers a lot of people."

"I know. It's seems like an impossible task, even for the FBI."

A grin crept across Cruz's face. "Damn you, Oscar. You still know how to push my buttons, don't you? Just like the time you sent me on a wild goose chase so you could ask Helen Casteneda to the prom."

"Hey, I really needed those fishhooks."

Cruz chuckled. "All right. What have we got to go on?"

Colunga produced a small envelope from the breast pocket of his coat, and dumped the miniature cassette from his answering machine onto the table. "I didn't have any way to copy this, so I made a recording for my use on a standard cassette and brought you the original. Can you handle it?"

"Sure. But what do you expect us to do?"

"Whatever you can. Perhaps her accent will tell us about her origin or education. Was she calling from a building or home? A public phone? You guys have experts for that sort of thing, don't you?"

"We got experts for everything. I'll see what we can do."

"Thanks, Joe. I owe you one."

"You owe me several." Cruz picked up the small tape and fingered it. "But now you've piqued my curiosity."

"Why?"

"Something's rattling around in my brain. How many women are involved?"

"We have missing persons reports on fourteen women, and eight or nine dead bodies that fit the profile."

"Which is?"

"Ages from sixteen to mid-twenties. Slender and attractive, shaded toward beautiful. All killed by noninvasive methods and dumped in the northwest corner of Connecticut."

Cruz leaned back and stared out the window. "Have you ever been to the Statue of Liberty, *Hijo?*"

"No."

"The Empire State Building?"

"No."

"Okay. We're going to take the afternoon off. Then tomorrow, I'm going to put my data analyst in touch with your data analyst."

Chapter 19

Megan strolled into the bathroom, molting her soggy clothes en route to the shower. She never looked forward to winter, but a respite from this heat wave would be most appreciated. She worked shampoo into her hair as the cool water pummeled her face and shoulders, flowing down the taut stomach to erupt like a miniature waterfall from her vulva. She ran the soap over her body in practiced patterns, then rinsed and stepped out onto the mat to dry herself. She donned a terry cloth robe and wrapped a towel around her head.

Moving to the bedroom, she approached the small desk and stared at the black envelope centered in the pool of light from the reading lamp. It seemed darker than the surrounding shadows, as if absorbing ambient energy.

She shook her head. All the other chapters had arrived with the regularity of a scheduled flight. She extracted the pages and checked the incoming date stamp. It was initialed by Heather and had actually arrived on Thursday—six days late.

Megan estimated the pages. It was a long chapter, maybe too long to write in a week. Or had he written the first seven chapters previously, and paced their submission one week apart? If so, it could be catching up with him.

With a sigh, she settled in to read. All her resolve to ignore the book was for naught. Harmon's direct order wasn't enough to stop her. Megan recognized her own compulsion, and resented it. But she no longer fought it.

Delicious Pain — Chapter 8

Providence. An interesting word. My dictionary defines it as divine guidance. I thought about this as I turned west onto Interstate 295 to bypass the city of Providence. Being Sunday morning, there was plenty of time and it was my intent to take one of the back roads across northern Connecticut on my way home.

I had met some good women since moving to New York. One of them was from Boston. She was about my age, and her daughter was a freshman (or must we say freshwoman?) at a university out west. Now free to roam at will, Dora had invited me to spend the weekend with her to see the sights of Boston.

Being a history buff, I was taken with the Northeastern Seaboard. For the first time in my life, dozens of historical sites were within one or two hours from home and I spent a good deal of time tripping around to them. By this time I had ranged from Valley Forge to the Old North Church, but nothing got to me as much as walking the beach at Walden Pond. I didn't actually see his cabin. My friend told me it had stood around a slight bend to the right, but the pond was bigger than I had expected, surprisingly serene.

There are those who worship Thoreau as some sort of mystical guide, while others think he was simply a kook who disliked people. Whatever he was, there is no doubt that he left an indelible mark on American lore. Perhaps it was the writer in me, but walking the same beach as Thoreau was exhilarating and, for that brief moment, I sensed an association with history that has never been equaled in my experience.

From there we traveled east to Gloucester, a scenic coastal village north of Boston. We had an early supper, being desirous of spending a long evening together in the privacy of her boudoir. I remember sitting on a large restaurant patio, cantilevered out over the water, as the cool evening breeze began to blow. She had lobster. I opted for a seafood fettucini, since I have always found Maine lobster more trouble than it's worth.

Next day, she was unexpectedly called away on business. I lay in bed while she dressed, watching a race on television where a car lost a tire and flew backward into the infield, injuring several people. Much too soon, she was ready and I dropped her off at Logan Airport.

So, I found myself with a great deal of time on my hands as I turned westward toward Connecticut. I felt disconnected, snubbed, and morose. My wonderful weekend had been cut short and I was now moving randomly with no place to go—no path or purpose other than to amble in the general direction of home.

At least the choice of back roads was propitious. By now I had nearly memorized the long open stretches of Interstate 95, but up here the trees pressed upon the road, and underbrush fairly snagged in the wheel covers in places. On several occasions I pulled over and entered the woods to drink in the flora and fauna of Nature's song.

As a boy from the hills, I only feel at home in the woods. I have always had a strong affection for God's handiwork, ever since I can remember. There is an innocence about the natural setting that is lost in the concrete jungle of our cities. Unfortunately, I never had the skills to do anything close to the land, but I have always dreamed of being a rancher or farmer.

"Wunnerful." Megan got up and wandered into the kitchen for a glass of milk, shouting back at the darkened bedroom. "You don't know your character from a hole in the ground. One chapter he's maniacal and ruthlessly clever. The next, he's walking through the forest like a Boy Scout."

She returned and sank into the chair. "What's more, your imagery is forced and amateurish. The flora and fauna of Nature's song?"

And so, it was in this Xanadu that I came upon Melissa. I had already experienced the bitter disappointment of spontaneous reaction to opportunity, and vowed never to let it happen again. But there she was, standing in a brief top and briefer shorts, with her thumb stuck into the air at a rakish angle.

Actually, I did not chastise myself as I slowed to pick
her up. At that moment I had no idea what would come.
Based on her youth and its implication of innocence, I
would have been happy to convey her to the next town
and let her off to seek her fortune. In fact, I felt sorry for
her as she huddled against the door and fed her story to
me a bit at a time.

She was a runaway, a dropout from Vernon High she
said, and I knew that the world might be very cruel to
her before it was over. I even offered council, saying that
it would be better to return home and try to reconcile
her differences with her parents. But she was resolute.
Her father had molested her since she could remember,
and she felt it was time to say no.

She said it had started when she was five or six. Her
father would take naps with her, holding her tight and
kissing her on the cheek or neck. By the time she was nine
or ten, he was kissing her on the mouth, and forced
intercourse before puberty. It was hard to believe she
would open up to me like that. Perhaps I represented a
kindly father figure, or she may have been lying to engen-
der my sympathy. Now I believe the latter to be true.

Somewhere along the road, something changed in
her. She had asked me to take her to the bus depot in
Hartford. Now she moved a little closer and asked where I
lived. I told her it was not far, and she asked if she could
spend one night with me. She hadn't slept in two days,
she said. If the authorities were looking for her, it would
be smarter to wait one or two days before catching a bus,
she said.

I was against it. Had she been one of my choices, I
would not have given the law a second thought. But there
are all sorts of problems that can arise when an older
man gets involved with a juvenile. You see my dilemma?
It's much like having no cash. You could eat at the Ritz
and charge it, but you can't buy a hamburger at a fast
food restaurant. I declined.

Then she made a fatal mistake. She moved close to me
and ran her hand up and down my thigh. I looked over,
seeing her for the first time. She was pretty. That's the
best I can do. Older women can be beautiful or exquisite.
Young girls are pretty. I realized that her breasts were

fuller than I had thought. Her thighs and calves were much too thin for my liking, but her skin had a marvelous glow and she smelled wonderful.

I grasped her wrist firmly and laid it in her lap. "Don't do that. It's not proper for a young woman."

She giggled and kissed my cheek. "Maybe I'm not as young as you think. Can I stay at your house tonight?"

Those words shook me. Was it possible that this pretty child could share my bed for one night and go safely on her way? I bypassed Hartford and headed for home. I was going to try a serendipitous experiment—to entertain not in the hidden room, but in my own home.

I must admit that I greatly enjoyed this intrigue for a while. I took her home as I would a date, everything open and aboveboard. She said she needed to clean her clothes, so I offered her a gown and helped her load the washer. Then I fixed her a thick steak and some properly cooked vegetables, along with a bottle of excellent chardonnay. I lit a pair of candles and we sat and talked while the sun set.

Since her arrival, there had been no overt gesture, but she had made her intentions quite obvious in the car. Now in total darkness, I moved around the table and untied the sash on her robe.

She pushed away and retied it. "What are you doing?"

"I want to put you to bed, pretty child."

She stared up at me with phony ignorance. "But you said it was not proper for young girls."

My anger was rising. "And you said you were not so young."

"I'm sorry if I misled you, sir. I just needed a place to stay."

"You can stay here, if you fulfill your part of the bargain."

She caught me by surprise. Springing from the chair with the speed of a cat, she ran to the rear windows and began screaming for help. She had a very loud scream, the kind that many actresses never achieve. I stood my ground and calmly asked why she was screaming. Fortunately, she did stop immediately, probably because I had not advanced on her.

I said, "Please, I am sorry for this misunderstanding. I promise I won't touch you."

She brushed her tears aside and managed a smile. "I'm sorry, too. Tell you what. Let me stay the night, and maybe I'll feel comfortable with you tomorrow."

I agreed ... anything to keep her quiet, but my mind was gorged with thoughts. Were her actions the result of childish innocence? Or were these the deceits of a woman who had already learned how to manipulate men? And could I now allow her to stay the night unfettered, free to steal away if I slept for even one moment?

What if she went to the police and cried statutory rape? What if she ran to one of my neighbors and asked for help? My secret room would only stave off the most cursory of inspections. Any detailed examination would reveal the monitors and leads that now permeated the house.

Everything would be ruined and I would be undone. And for what? This scrawny whelp? This gangly child with the personality of a carp? The risk was not acceptable. I hit her on the jaw and she sagged to her knees. Now the haughty look of control faded as her eyes rolled back in her head. I gathered her up and carried her downstairs.

Megan felt her eyes cross. "We can't print this. Women would be camped out front." She got up and turned off the lights in the rest of the apartment, then trudged back into the bedroom. Now the stark white paper seemed like the only point of light centered in a universe of darkness.

Reading from a standing position, she skimmed several pages full of torture and indignities as her captor tried to induce cooperation from the terrified girl. For some reason, she did not give in.

Megan turned the last page and read carefully. She read the last paragraph again, then collapsed into the chair.

"Dear God!"

Mindless of the hour, her hand lashed out toward the phone.

Chapter 20

Colunga chewed the last bite of his dried ham and cheese and glanced up at the clock as Oliphant came through the door.

"Evening, Hank. When you said a little late, I thought you meant six or seven. It's nearly ten o'clock."

"Sorry, Oscar. Everything takes longer than it should."

"Always. What've you got?"

Oliphant eased his girth into a swivel chair by the desk and pulled a folded paper out of his breast pocket. "Preliminary report on the woman at Nepaug. I thought you'd want to see it."

Colunga reached across the desk and scanned it. "Still no ID yet."

"Nope. My guess is Annette Chesson. Without dental comparison we may never know for sure, although these forensic archaeologists are nothing short of miraculous." He paused. "They can tell a lot about health, lifestyle, and cause of death from a skeleton—when a society went from hunter-gatherer to agrarian, for example. The men usually went right on doing whatever they did before, but there were changes in the bones and joints of the women."

Oscar grinned at his exuberance. "I know."

"You do?"

"I dabble in the anthropology of the Southwest." Colunga turned his attention to the report. "Female. Blond. Five-seven. Body type ... well-proportioned? That doesn't sound like a technical term."

"I think it means stacked."

Oscar pulled a file from the pile on his desk. He set aside a photo and turned a few pages. "Seems to fit Chesson. Height's right." He spun the photograph around to Oliphant, a studio portrait of the young girl in a low-cut blue formal. "This qualify as well-proportioned?"

He leaned forward. "No question."

"What kind of fiend could destroy such beauty?" Colunga pitched his reading glasses onto the desk. "And why?"

"Damned if I—"

Oscar reached for the warbling phone. "Colunga."

"Mr. Colunga, we spoke once before."

"Yes, I remember." He pinned the phone to his ear with his shoulder and hit the RECORD button while motioning to Oliphant, who slipped out of his chair and went looking for help.

"How are you tonight?"

"I've been better." She hesitated. "Would you answer a question for me?"

"If I can."

"Do you know of any case where a runaway from Vernon High was picked up on the road?"

"I'm not sure what you mean by picked up."

"Please don't make this difficult. I mean abducted and murdered ... never heard from again."

"Hmm. Let me check the file." It was a play for time. By now he had virtually memorized the reports. He pulled the folder and rustled pages for several seconds. "Yes, there is one case like that, but she was not from Vernon."

"Close to there?"

"A couple of towns over." He listened to her heavy breathing and racked his brain for some approach to keep her on the line. "You said you were not a reporter, right?"

"Right."

"Do you have a personal interest in one or more of these women?"

She responded slowly. "I'm afraid so."

"Give me your name and address. I'll come right over."

She expelled a thin laugh. "As far as you know, 'right over' could be California."

"I don't care. You know things about these murders."

Her voice drifted from a far place. "Probably just coincidence."

Oscar swallowed hard and tried to ignore the sweat rolling down the back of his neck. "If you know anything that could point to this man, you could be in jeopardy yourself. Have you thought about that?"

"Every day."

"Then let me bring you in. You'll be safer if we know what you do."

"You may be right."

"Please meet with me."

"I just can't."

"Then, may I ask you a question?"

She replied with silence.

"How did you know Annette Chesson's head would not be found in her grave?" He heard his heart pounding in his ears, feeling light-headed from the tension. He had taken the plunge. Now he awaited her reaction.

Her voice came across weakly. "Then it's true." Megan fell silent for several seconds. "I'll send you something—"

"Son of a bitch!" Oscar dumped the handset into its cradle to shut off the annoying dial tone. "Did you get it, Hank?"

The portly detective cleared the door two seconds later. "Sorry, Oscar. Nobody on duty knew how to do a trace. Why don't you have one of those intercept boxes?"

His face screwed up in disgust. "Bureaucratic snafu."

"Was it important?"

"Well, this woman called me once before about the Chesson case. Wanted to know if the head was with the body—before we knew."

Oliphant's eyes bulged. "Why the hell didn't you tell me about her?"

"Tell you what? That some curiosity-seeker phoned? That's never happened before?"

"Well, we could have tried to identify her."

"I've got the FBI working on it, Hank."

"You do?"

"Hey, ain't that what us desk jockeys are for?"

Oliphant grinned. "I guess so. Sorry."

"No problem, *amigo*." Oscar produced a bottle of tequila and some paper cups from a desk drawer. "Want a shot?"

"Sure." Oliphant sat back and tested the bitter taste. "So what do you know about this woman?"

The ambient light softened as Oscar switched off the glaring desk lamp. The room seemed cool and comfortable, in contrast to the humid haze that hung on the other side of the windows. He gazed at Oliphant for a few seconds.

"She's well-educated. Articulate. Sounds very attractive, for what that's worth. And she probably lives or works in Manhattan."

"That's all you know about her?"

"Except for what I learned just now." Colunga downed the shot. "This woman knows a lot more about these murders than we do."

Chapter 21

Megan left the elevator on the fourth floor and scanned the doors. Room 422 was to the right, bearing the words JT Investigations in black letters on opaque glass. She hesitated for several seconds, then pushed through.

It was a large rectangular room with incandescent light fixtures suspended from the ceiling by painted metal tubes. A mammoth wooden desk faced her in front of windows looking out onto Times Square. The right wall was littered with diplomas and plaques above a faded pink sofa, and a solid row of filing cabinets lined the left wall.

"Come in. Close the door."

Teldon sat behind the desk, scribbling on a pad with a fountain pen—a middle-aged man with receding blond hair, pronounced jowls, and ruddy complexion. He wore a cheap tan suit and dark brown shirt, open at the collar.

"Mr Teldon?"

He capped his pen with a show of irritation, and looked up. "My God." Teldon sprang from his chair and skirted the desk to take her hand. "Are you Miss Roarke?"

"Yes."

"Forgive me. I've read about this in books, but it's the first time in over twenty years that it happened to me."

"What's that?"

"The door opens, and this stunning woman walks in."

"Why, Mr. Teldon," Megan slipped her hand free, "I bet you say that to all the girls."

"I do. But this time I mean it." He winked. "Let's have a seat on the sofa."

Megan moved over and sat, glued to the right arm rest.

The PI split the difference and gazed at her. "Would you care for coffee or soda?"

"No thanks."

"Something stronger?"

"No, really. I have a luncheon engagement in a few minutes. Could we get down to business?"

"Of course. What can I do for you?"

Megan fished a folded black envelope from her purse. "I must know who sent this to me."

Teldon ironed it across his leg, then turned it over several times. "Not much chance of that, Miss Roarke. The label was done on a standard printer—probably ink jet and not distinctive like the old typewriters were. As far as the stamps, they're current standard issue, and they are stamps. Absence of a postage meter implies the action of an individual."

"Fingerprints?"

Teldon lowered his head. "You want fingerprints, take it to the FBI."

"What about the postmark? Can you at least tell me where it was mailed?"

"That's a possibility." He held it close to his face. "Maybe with special light or chemical treatment. But that equipment is at home. I'll have to get back to you."

"Fine." She pulled a card from her coat pocket and handed it over. "My home phone is on the back."

"Will you be there tonight?"

"Eventually." Megan slid forward, poised to stand. "I guess we should go over your fees."

"Two hundred dollars an hour, plus expenses."

Her mouth fell slightly open. "Rockford was only two hundred a day!"

"That was twenty years ago, and he didn't live in Manhattan." He smiled. "Don't worry. If I don't clear the charges with you first, don't pay it."

"All right." She gained her feet and walked to the door, pausing with her hand on the knob. "Stunning, huh? I probably wouldn't let one of my authors get away with that word."

"How about elegant?"

Megan pursed her lips and nodded subtly. "Not bad."

"Hi there, Super Agent. What's new?" Megan slipped into her usual chair at Wolfe's.

"You might be surprised." Irv Miller nudged the silver bucket at his elbow. "How about some champagne?"

"Do we have something to celebrate?"

"Yes. Your book is practically sold."

"Practically sold? Is that like partially pregnant?"

"You can't be partially pregnant, Meg."

"Well, how can a book be practically sold?"

"I thought your rewrite was brilliant. So I laid it on Duston Todd over at Intrepid, and he loved it. He wants a few changes of course, but nothing unreasonable."

Megan managed a weak smile. "That's wonderful news, Irv."

"That's it? No whoop? No cartwheels?" He bent over and looked up into her eyes. "You're about to become a published author. I expected a little more joy ... possibly a hint of elation."

"I'm sorry. You've earned better. It's just that I have a lot on my mind right now."

He gave her a little-boy grin. "What's the problem? Work?"

"That's one of the few things that is going well. I'm

starting to find some decent manuscripts and the merger is working better than we can believe."

"Buyer's remorse on the house in Connecticut?"

"I haven't bought it yet."

"Achal?"

"It's not Achal."

Miller sat back and shook his head. "I've run out of guesses."

"It's that stupid book."

"What book?"

"The one I told you about before."

He pulled the champagne from the ice and filled both glasses. "You mean that unidentified submission?"

"Yes."

"Dammit, Meg, I thought we had an understanding on that. You said you would blow it off if it continued to upset you."

Tears welled up. "I know, but it's gotten out of control. I'm beginning to believe it's based on real murders."

Miller stiffened. "You're joking."

"I wish I were." She reached into her purse for a handkerchief and daubed her running mascara. "I wish it could be a joke ... or a bad dream that would go away. I hate it, but I can't help reading it."

He sat back and considered her. "What makes you think it's based on the real thing?"

"Oh, a few random newscasts I've seen." She threw her head back and sniffed. "And I've been in touch with a police officer in Hartford, a Lieutenant Colunga."

"In touch?"

"I've called him twice to compare notes between the book and actual facts. Last night, I think he confirmed it."

"And you really believe someone is sending you true confessions?"

"In a way." Megan toyed with the stem of her glass. "No doubt he's fictionalized it to disguise names and places, but I think a fair amount of reality is coming through."

"What do you intend to do?"

"I'm going give this lieutenant copies of the eight chapters I have. Maybe he'll be able to piece things together, since he has access to all the records." She paused and took a thoughtful sip. "You remember the first time I mentioned this, and you told me not to take it personal?"

He nodded.

"Now I'm terrified by that prospect. If he's a real killer, am I some sort of target?"

"Oh, Meg. I can't believe that."

"What if it's true?"

He contemplated. "All right. Tomorrow morning, I'll start calling editors to see if anyone else is receiving it. How's that sound?"

Her distorted features broke into a friendly smile. "Would you do that for me, Irv?"

"You bet."

The storm clouds built behind her eyes again. "And if it is just me?"

He reached across and squeezed her hand. "We'll handle that, too."

Megan twisted the dead bolts into place and dumped her purse on the couch. She switched on the lamp and glanced at her watch.

"Ten o'clock. What a day."

Shedding her earrings, she kicked off her shoes and ambled toward the bedroom where a flashing red light cried out for attention. Megan turned on the desk lamp and sagged into the chair as she pounded the answering machine switch.

"Miss Roarke? This is Jessop Teldon. I have something for you."

She wrote down the number and reached for the phone.

"JT Investigations."

"Mr. Teldon. This is Megan Roarke, returning your call."

"Ah, yes, Miss Roarke. I was able to lift the zip code from your envelope."

"Where was it?"

"The area around Grand Central Station."

"Terrific. That should narrow it down to a half million."

"Perhaps a little less. But I did think of another approach after you left my office."

"Oh?"

"It occurred to me that this type of envelope is rather unusual ... that we might be able to determine the location of purchase. So I called twenty stores in the area, and three of them sell it."

"So we can't uniquely pin down a location."

"I'm afraid not."

"Any other ideas?"

"Not at the moment."

"All right, Mr. Teldon. What do I owe you?"

"Let's call it an even hour."

"Two hundred dollars, if I recall correctly."

"Yes, but I might suggest an alternative that would represent considerable savings. Why don't you buy me lunch?"

"Seriously?"

"I rarely go out with women nowadays, and I'd like to be seen with an elegant woman one more time before I die."

"Are you in ill health, Mr. Teldon? Do you expect to die soon?"

"You never know in this crazy world, Miss Roarke."

Megan laughed. "I'll think about it. Expect a check or a call within two weeks. Okay?"

"Very well. I hope to see you again, either way."

She stood to open the drapes, and gazed down on the

dark void that was Central Park. Reaching up to brush a strand of hair from her cheek, she was startled by the motion of her reflection in the window. Her head came around and she locked onto her own eyes.

"I will not be your victim. We will not play by your rules."

She lifted the receiver and hit the redial button. "Mr. Teldon, this is Megan Roarke. I really need to identify this bastard. Is there any stone left unturned?"

"Well it's a long shot, but I could examine some of the original manuscript pages for latent prints. We would have to rule out yours and anyone in your company who handled the documents. And if we come up with a few probables, you'll have to take that up with the authorities."

"I'll send you some pages tomorrow."

Chapter 22

The padded mailer on his desk puzzled Oscar. Communications usually came by fax or in a standard business envelope, seldom more than a few pages. Some instinct raised the hair on the back of his neck.

He slid the pages out and examined the first. It was typed, double spaced, and carried a receiving stamp in bold blue in the upper right corner. Dated roughly two months prior, it was initialed HB and gave no indication of the receiving party other than the near certainty that it had been processed by a business. Donning his reading glasses, he read the opening lines.

Delicious Pain — Chapter 1
The first woman, I killed for practice—mainly to see if I could. We have been taught from birth that murder is wrong, and it is difficult to override social conditioning.

Colunga picked up the phone and punched in Kathy's extension. He watched her head come up.

"Yes, Oscar."

He smiled at her. "How'd you know it was me?"

"I could tell by your expression."

"Would you come in here please? I've got something that needs special processing."

"Sure." She sprang up and entered the office. "What is it?"
He indicated the stack of paper. "This is evidence. Will you make a copy for me?"

"If you wish, but why not let Documents do it?"

"I have my reasons ... white glove treatment. Don't get your prints on it, and minimize handling to retain any prints that might be there."

"When do you need it?"

He glanced up at the clock. "I thought I'd walk over to Gallivan's for supper. Could you have it done in an hour?"

"How many pages?"

"About a hundred."

"No sweat. I'll have it on your desk when you get back, even if I have to work a little late."

"Thanks, Kathy. And one more thing." He turned the Rolodex and jotted several lines on a note pad. "Send the original in its envelope to José Cruz at the FBI. Here's his address."

"Any specific method?"

"Overnight. Traceable."

Colunga sat alone in his office. The blinds were drawn and lights were off in the outer room. Except for dim green hues from the exit sign and the neon spectrum from his desk lamp, the world was black and he was isolated from it.

He turned a page on the manuscript copy, realizing he was nearly at the end.

I really tried to make her understand. I gave her every chance. But she was too young, I believe. She had not yet developed the techniques for survival that I had observed in older women. Or perhaps it was her intrinsic defiance of authority that had caused her to be a runaway in the first place. I never did buy her story about her father's incest. And as I came to know her, I realized that she was

a social loss. The fact that she sought out junkies and losers was nobody's fault but her own.

She had created her environment and was now a victim of it. What's worse, I was her victim. She had deceived me into bringing her to my own home. I had underestimated her ability for manipulation, and the reality of that naiveté hit me hard. This mere child had fooled me and attempted to use me, and I chastised myself for playing her pawn—even for a few hours.

Consequently, I was not kind and gentle with her as I had been with my beloved Sandra, and at times it seemed almost a desecration of my little love nest to have this creature in it. My attempts to calm her and gain her affection had been a complete waste of time. Because of her defiance and foul mouth, I kept her bound and gagged most of the time. I used her for a coffee table while I watched television, setting my cold beer on her firm rump.

After several days, I realized she was hopeless. Unless she could switch her mind completely and instantly, she must be eliminated. I conceived of a new method to induce her to invite me into her bed. That very evening, I forced her into the bathtub in the hidden room. I laid her on her stomach with her head away from the faucets and put a leather gag on her. I tied her feet with a long rope and looped it through the D ring on the gag. Then I cinched it up so that her body was gracefully arched, her weight resting entirely on her pelvis—her nose perhaps ten or twelve inches from the bottom.

Her scream penetrated the gag as I turned on the cold water and my scheme became apparent to her. Had I any affection for her, I would have used tepid water, but I saw no reason to comfort her. She had done nothing to merit such consideration.

I sat on the edge and watched the terror in her eyes with relish. For a brief time, I thought the device might work. The only negative of this idea (which I never employed again) was that she could not say the words. I advised her to blink once for yes and twice for no.

As the water rose, she struggled violently but was unable to alter her position in the confining space,

**except to slide down until her knees pressed against the
tub and the cold water splashed on her legs. I adjusted
the flow to keep the level rising at the rate of one inch
per minute, and every minute I asked her to signal her
response to my invitation of lovemaking. On each occasion, she swore and called me names in muffled anger.
The words came all too clearly through the ineffective
gag, and I vowed to develop a better one.**

**Finally, the water was over her mouth. It apparently
leaked in around the leather strap, because she began to
sputter and cough. Again I asked her to acquiesce, but
she stubbornly shook her head with what little movement
she had. I watched in fascination as the water reached
her nostrils. She tried to arch her body more or thrust
her head out by whatever mobility she could muster, but
it was near the end.**

**I stood up to watch her drown, undone by her own
inability to adjust. In those last moments, the invisible
snakes crawled from her vagina and frolicked in the
bubbles around her face.**

Colunga expelled the breath he'd been holding. "You sick
motherfucker." From the mottled page, the eyes of the writer
stared back, leering with satisfaction—reveling in the horror
and disgust he had created.

Oscar pushed back, and opened the drawer over his knees.
In the dim light he could see the glow of cellophane on the
long forgotten pack. He drew it out, removing one of the
stale cigarettes while he fumbled in his coat pocket for a
match. He came to his feet as he lit up and walked to the
outer office. It was dark and comforting, the gray smoke
curling about him as he paced.

When his fingers registered heat, he dumped it into an
empty Coke can and nodded with satisfaction at the sizzle.
He returned to his office, the mysterious caller on his mind.

"Lady, you had every reason to be upset. The question
now ... fiction or fact?"

He read the last page again. Invisible snakes crawling from her vagina? What childhood abuse or social accident could lead to this kind of deviation in the human mind? Was his own daughter a victim of such distortion in her final hours? He sagged into his chair as the room went out of focus.

"We have a lead on your daughter's murder, Oscar."

"Who?"

"We don't have a name yet, but we think he's been operating here for about nine months. There have been four victims and one attempt in that time, all of them coeds."

"You got a line on him?"

"Maybe. The girl who got away says he was Caucasian, in his late thirties, driving a four-wheel-drive with Oregon plates." Captain Longstreet gazed at him with reservation. "I'm telling you this because we're friends, but you stay as far from this investigation as you can without leaving the state. We get a bereaved father involved, and the DA will throw it out. Understand?"

Oscar nodded slowly. "Oh, yes. I understand."

Chapter 23

The pillow felt cool as Megan rolled over onto her back and took in a long shaky breath. She threw her forearm over her face to block the candle's dim glow, which now seemed to pierce her eyes with unreasonable intensity. She sensed heat from the plethora of blood in her pelvis and euphoria from the lack of it in her brain.

Minutes later, her body approached normal tolerances. She turned her head to Achal. "Thank you."

"No reason to thank me."

"Yes there is. Where did you learn to use your tongue like that?"

"The first part or the last?"

"All of it."

"Hmm. I hope it's not indelicate to point out that I knew one or two women before you."

"Well, I'm grateful to each and every one of them." She turned to put her arms around him and pressed her body against his. "Can I expect more surprises in the future?"

"As long as you continue to surprise me." He kissed her hard and long.

She released him and sank into the pillow. "Do you think we'll be together for a long time, Achal?"

He stroked her taut stomach. "As long as you love me."

"I do." She pulled him down and held him close, staring past his dark hair. "But I don't want to end up like Irv and Lisa, together for years without commitment."

"It wouldn't be that way with us. I blew it the first time around, but I've matured. Next time it will be for life."

"You make it sound like a sentence."

"Being single is a sentence—worse than a bad marriage." He pulled away to look into her eyes. "Do you want to talk about marriage?"

"Not yet. I need to get my life in order first."

"Get your life in order?" Achal sighed and laid back, staring at the ceiling. "You've bought four good novels in the past month. Your job is assured. You've sold your manuscript. What's the problem? That damned book again?"

"Yes."

"What now?"

"I've decided to find the author."

"How?"

"I hired a private detective."

"You can't be serious."

"What's wrong with that?"

"Jesus, Meg. I thought it was silly enough when you called that cop in Connecticut. Now you're squandering your own money on a private eye?"

"I wouldn't say that."

"Really? What's he turned up, so far?"

"Nothing."

"What did you expect him to do?"

"I was hoping he could trace the envelopes or paper."

"How much did he charge you?"

"Two hundred."

"And you don't consider that squandered?"

Megan sat up with the sheet drawn tightly across her chest. "I'm not going to be a victim anymore."

"If a professional investigator couldn't run the guy down, what can you possibly do?"

"You have no faith in my creativity?"

Megan pushed her coffee aside and carefully wrote down the names and phone numbers. "Thanks, Mr. Teldon. I'm glad you keep such accurate records."

It was a bad connection, his voice sounding tinny over the phone. "By the way, Miss Roarke. There is one thing I neglected to mention during our last conversation."

"Oh?"

"When you sent me those original manuscript pages to analyze?"

"Yes?"

"I expected photocopies."

"You mean they weren't?"

"They were literally original sheets, produced by a printer. Could that be significant?"

"Probably not. Say you want twenty copies of ten pages. Might as well beat up your printer as hassle with getting it copied. The cost is about the same."

"Too bad."

"Yes, but I do appreciate the information on these stores." She paused. "By the by, I will call you for lunch next week."

Megan pressed the cradle switch and dialed.

"Shelley's Office Supply. Edith speaking."

"Yes, Edith. My name is Megan Roarke. I'm an editor with Gladiator Press, and I wonder if you could spare a minute to help me with some research."

"Gladiator Press? The publisher?"

"Yes."

"Certainly. What can I do for you?"

"I'm interested in colored envelopes, something similar to the standard nine-by-twelve manila with flap and metal clasp—in black. Do you carry anything like that?"

"We usually have a few."

"Do you get much call for them?"

"Very little."

"How little?"

"I think we buy two dozen around Halloween, and let them sell out during the year."

"Do you have any in stock now?"

"From here, it looks like two or three. Want me to check the rack?"

"That won't be necessary." Megan frowned. "So if I wanted a dozen of these today, it would require a special order."

"Well, I can't speak for other stores, but it would for us."

Megan's throat went dry. "Suppose another store did carry more than you do. Would the sale of a dozen trigger a reorder?"

"It might."

"How many people manufacture this type of envelope?"

"Only US Documents, to my knowledge. But there may be others."

"And US Documents would know who these others are?"

"Of course."

"Thanks, Edith. I can't tell you how helpful you've been."

"My pleasure." She hesitated. "Do you know any of the science fiction editors who work for your company?"

"I know Achal Bedi fairly well."

"Really? Please give him my regards. I read everything you print."

"I'll pass that along."

Again she flashed the switch and dialed Heather. "Get me the phone number for US Documents' New York distribution center."

Chapter 24

His desk was a mess. Oscar polished off the morning's first cup of coffee and stared at it, trying to decide where to start. The ringing phone was a welcome diversion.

"OSI. Colunga."

"Aye, *Hijo*. I just got the results on that tape you brought in."

"Good."

"The call was placed from an office environment. Switching noise indicates a commercial phone system, the kind used by large companies."

Oscar frowned. "Anything else?"

"She is well educated—originally from the middle states, with a dose of New York accent and a hint of Boston. Their guess is that she lives in the city now."

"Middle states. Like Illinois?"

"A little farther west. Somewhere in the region between North Dakota and Kansas."

"Any idea how long she's been in New York?"

"No way to tell that. Assimilation of accent is a very individual thing."

"Thanks, Joe, and I'm glad you called. I sent you another package that should arrive today."

"Oh? What is it?"

"The first eight chapters of a novel."

"What? You trying to broaden my exposure to literature?"

"Not exactly, although you may want to read it. I did last night." Oscar drew a long breath. "Each chapter tells about the abduction and murder of a female victim, and some of the details do fit cases we're working on."

"Where did it come from?"

"I believe it was sent by the woman on that tape, and I'm hoping you can ID her from fingerprints or something else your lab might come up with."

"I don't understand. Why would she send it to you?"

"A few days ago she called again to ask me about a second victim. I really leaned on her, but she refused to cooperate. Then this book shows up in the mail, and it's clear that her information came from the author. What is their relationship? Did she write it? Does she know who did? In any event, I want to find her."

"You think this book may be the confessions of a mass murderer?"

"I don't know. People can glean a lot of information from police reports and news items. That's my problem. Until I get a handle on this, I won't know whether to pull out the stops."

"Maybe you should."

"Why?"

"Oscar, Connecticut is not the only state involved. Since our last conversation, I've talked with some of our agents. We're looking into similar cases along the entire eastern seaboard. You may have stumbled across the first solid lead."

Colunga sat in stunned silence.

"Tell you what, *Hijo*. I'm going to personally push this manuscript through channels. I'll get back to you."

Chapter 25

Doctor Tibor Johansson introduced himself as Director of Forensic Anthropology from a museum in California. Below the thinning blond hair, his bushy eyebrows seemed to erupt over a hawkish nose. The teeth, set into an oversize jaw, were uneven and yellow. Johansson was certainly European, although his English was impeccable. He had been working day and night for nearly a week. But as Oscar eyed him across his desk, his policeman's instinct said the good doctor would sport the same loosened tie and rumpled coat leaving his house in the morning.

"I appreciate your coming over here, Dr. Johansson."

"It is my pleasure, Lieutenant. But please, call me Tibor. I find communication so much more efficient when informal."

"All right, Tibor. What do you have for me?"

"I have brought you a copy of our report." He drew two tomes from the wide leather case on the floor at his side, and dropped one on the desk.

Oscar felt the building tremble. "*Madre*. It will take me days to read that."

The older man nodded knowingly. "Indeed it would, and most of it is irrelevant to your needs. Consequently, I have inserted markers at key passages in your copy. I will direct your attention to the most critical information now. The rest you can peruse later."

"Good."

"Please turn to page four. Here we will deal with macroscopic features. It was a Caucasian female, approximately five and a half feet in height."

"How do you determine height when the head is missing?"

"From the length of long bones, spine, and other indications. A skull is not required, I assure you."

"Of course."

"Age, however, is a more difficult problem. We can estimate this in children based on size and bone development. Indications are more subtle in the adult. Absence of osteoporosis or arthritis suggest that she was a young woman, but I can't be more specific." The anthropologist scanned his notes. "However, we do know that she had not borne children."

The cigarette nearly tumbled from Oscar's mouth. "How can you tell that?"

Johansson smiled. "We paid a certain price for the benefit of walking upright. One such problem is difficulty in giving birth. The pubic symphysis, where the two pelvic bones come together in front, is often damaged during the trauma of labor, creating cavities on the inner surface known colloquially as postpartum pits."

He opened the report to an enlarged photograph and laid it on the desk, pointing at the region in question. "You see? Smooth as the day it was formed."

"If you say so." Oscar stared at the photo and shook his head. "What about the cause of death?"

"You must understand that when a body has been in the ground this long, deterioration complicates the evidence. Even cartilage is decayed. But I detect subtle indications of a broken neck."

"Are you sure?"

"We are certain that there is no skeletal damage to the body. This contraindicates, but does not rule out, an intrusive instrument such as a gun or knife. Nor can we rule out the possibility of trauma to the head. But hairline fractures in the remaining vertebra imply that the neck was severed just below the break. Would you care to see photographic evidence?"

"Wouldn't mean anything to me." Oscar spread his hands. "Could you venture a guess as to how the neck was broken?"

"Actually, I might. Because the indications are so subtle, I doubt that it was caused by a blow to the back of the neck. The proverbial blunt instrument usually causes more damage to adjoining vertebrae."

"Hmm. Under what circumstances could this kind of break occur?"

"Possibly compression, but I think the most likely cause would be a twisting motion."

"Like a heavy blow to the jaw?"

"Quite possibly."

Oscar gazed at him. "Anything else that might help us?"

"Well, she did ride a horse in her formative years."

"You're certain of that?"

"Yes. Changes occur in the knees and pelvic girdle when a human rides during adolescence—quite distinctive I assure you. What's more, she must have suffered an accident in her early years. The X-rays were most explicit. She broke her right wrist, probably during puberty."

Oscar felt the blood drain from his head. "Anything else?"

"One thing so minor, I'm not sure it would show up on a police report. She had a congenital defect. Her middle toe was subordinated to its larger neighbor on both feet."

"Translation?"

"It was tucked under and misshapen like a clove of garlic." Tibor pondered for a few seconds. "If there is more of salient value, I do not know what it might be. I suggest you read the report to compare it with your knowledge of the facts."

Oscar found his feet and extended his hand across the desk. "Thank you, Tibor. I may be calling you to follow up."

"As I would expect." He stood up and shook hands heartily, then turned to take his leave.

After two paces, Oscar called out. "One more thing."

He turned back. "Yes?"

"Do you have personal experience with these new techniques for locating bodies in open country? Elevations of gravesites and the like?"

"I have touched on it a few times. Very sophisticated techniques using special radar and selective applications of light, augmented by computer image enhancement."

Oscar skirted the desk and closed the distance. "How big an area is it practical to scan?"

"There are many variables that affect complexity and cost—open fields versus woods, age of the grave, native ground cover, and so forth. In theory, given enough money you could scan the Earth, but in practical terms it is desirable to define a specific search area."

Oscar shook his head. "Let's say I could narrow it down to ten acres. How long?"

"Perhaps a few days in open country. Considerably more in a forest, with much reduced chances of success."

"Damn."

Tibor smiled. "You are not in an optimum area here."

Oscar clapped him on the shoulder. "Thank you for your time and advice. I will read your report."

The tall man nodded and walked away. Oscar watched the outer door close and scrambled to his desk, clawing through the missing persons reports until he found Annette Chesson's. He turned several pages and stopped.

"'Radial fracture of the right ulna at age thirteen.'"

Next he took the manuscript from the drawer and turned to Chapter Four, scanning until his eyes fell on the passage: "'She even told me about personal experiences like the time she fell off a horse and broke her arm in junior high.'"

Oscar opened Johansson's report and skimmed the marked pages. *Radial fracture of the right ulna during adolescence.*

His eyes flitted like a moth from one document to the next. Was it concrete proof that the author was a killer? Tibor's report and the police report should match, and anyone writing about unsolved murders might pick up such information from a report, investigator, relative or friend— even a news item.

Oscar moved to the windows, staring down at the sparse crowd on the street. After several minutes, he drifted over to the seldom-used coat rack and lifted his old cowboy hat, blowing the dust off and resetting the curls in the brim with his strong hands. He held it across his chest to mute the pounding of his heart, reliving that crisp winter day in Arizona.

A thin strip of dirt road stretched ahead through dense stands of pine that climbed the slopes to hills and mountains beyond. The sky was unbroken and the intense sun scintillated thin ice crystals fluttering on the gentle north wind.

Oscar stepped from his pickup to reset the pump, the fresh blanket of snow crunching under his boots with each subtle move. He stuffed the nozzle into the filler and sniffed the sharp scent of gasoline, leaning over to check the hitch on the horse trailer as the owner strolled out of the shabby old garage, wearing greasy cap and coveralls and a three-day growth.

"Mornin', Oscar. What brings you up this way?"

"Just a little hunting, Zeke."

"Hunting? This time a year?" The aging man wiped his hand on a red rag and thrust it out. "Well, it's always good to see you, son. Care for a cup?"

"Yes."

Oscar sat on the wobbly chair, gazing at the decay and disorder around him. Walls originally white, now encrusted with patches of grime and oil, rising from cracked black floorboards. Windows pitted by years of weather and neglect. Ragged papers and rusting parts jammed into every available niche. Pinup girls and old posters of automobiles with bulbous exposed fenders, the V-8 printed in bold type to extol that wondrous advance of Mankind. Things old. Outdated. Obsolete.

"How've you been, Zeke?"

"Ah, I'm gettin' by. 'Course, it ain't like the old days. Ain't many people left in these hills. But I get a little work, and I got simple tastes."

Oscar nodded. "Anybody ever come through from the outside?"

"Not much since they moved the highway." The old man took a thoughtful sip, blowing first to raise a small cloud of steam in the chill interior. "One fella come by this mornin', though. Threw a fan belt on his Blazer. Too bad. I think she overheated ... maybe done some damage."

"What color was it?"

"Blue and white."

"Did you notice the plates?"

"Not really. Outa state, though. I'm pretty sure of that." Zeke set down his cup. "Seemed ta be looking over his shoulder. You on his trail, son?"

He eyed the old man. "Which way did he go?"

Oscar's body convulsed. He covered the six feet to his desk in less than a second and raised the receiver to his ear. "Colunga."

He listened several seconds, hand over the mouthpiece to mute his heavy breathing. "Yeah, Hank, I just talked to Tibor Johansson. Your body with no head is probably Annette Chesson."

"Are you sure?"

Oscar rubbed sweat from his eyes with his sleeve. "Drop by and I'll show you what he brought in."

"All right, but it'll have to be after work. I'm tied up on another case."

"I'll be here."

Chapter 26

"And your choice of salad dressing?"

"Bleu cheese, on the side."

The waiter pivoted and marched off toward the kitchen.

Megan glanced around the hotel restaurant. Several people openly stared while other eyes flitted in their direction. She leaned across the table to Lisa Thistle.

"The perfect exemplar for lack of privacy—a New York editor at a writer's conference."

The attractive brunette smiled. "I know just how you feel."

Megan took a sip of wine. "I'm so glad we could arrange to have lunch. I haven't seen you in months."

"I know. Strange that we must travel clear out to Colorado to spend time together, when we live in the same town—even stranger since you are my, ah, boyfriend's client." The dark eyes flashed. "God, I hate that word."

"Client?"

"You know damn well what I mean. It seems like we could have come up with a decent alternative by now, but I hate them all. Cohabitant? Significant other? Hi, this is my significant other!" Lisa made a face. "How significant, and other what?"

Megan nodded. "But that isn't the worst. The title clearly goes to POSSLQ."

"I guess I missed that one."

"Lucky you. Persons of opposite sex sharing living quarters—a cumbersome phrase to start with, and the mnemonic is audibly offensive." Megan brushed her hair from her face. "It's a continual thorn in the side for editors. My instinct is to stick with the old tried and true, like lover or fiancé."

"But fiancé implies that you intend to get married."

"Not anymore. It just gives you the right to fool around without guilt." Megan took a sip of water. "Speaking of that, there's something I've been wondering about. Would you answer a question for me?"

"Sure."

"How does it work for an editor and agent to share the same bed? Don't you get into problems with conflict of interest?"

"No problem. We don't do business together anymore, which has cost us both money on occasion. We are literally paying a price for this relationship."

"Are you thinking about marriage?"

"He thinks he'd make a lousy father." She sighed. "Sadly, I'm beginning to agree with him."

"That doesn't sound good."

"I guess it's my way of telling you we may be nearing the end of our run." Lisa sat back to receive the salad and paused for the waiter to depart. "My daughter is almost nine, and I'm starting to realize that I'll have to go elsewhere if I want a real home for her."

"I am sorry to hear that, Lisa. You and Irv seem like the perfect couple."

"Oh, we are. But it will never be any more than a couple." Lisa toyed with her fork. "What about you and Achal?"

"We're practically living together."

"Now, Meg, I'd hate to see my best friend turn into a POSSLQ."

"It won't come to that. We both need our private space at times."

"I don't see the problem. I'd move in with Achal in a New York minute, if he was available."

"Well he's not!"

Lisa laughed, wiping salad dressing from her lips. "Don't worry. I won't try to steal him from you."

"You better not. It's one thing to steal my authors, but something else to go after my man."

"You know me better than that."

"That's just the problem." Megan forked in a chunk of lettuce. "Remember Dougie Cranston?"

"Wellesley was a long time ago, Meg." Lisa drifted off for a few seconds. "Besides, all Dougie Cranston wanted was to get into a girl's pants. One week after I stole him from you, he dumped me for a high school cheerleader."

Megan grinned. "Justice."

Lisa eyed her. "So other than men, how are things going? Did the merger work out well?"

"Incredibly."

Her eyebrows raised. "Really?"

"Yes. We're trying some of their marketing suggestions, and it's starting to pay off."

"Like what?"

"I don't know if I should give our trade secrets to a competitor."

"Not even to an old school chum?"

Megan nodded. "Especially if that old school chum is you."

"Come on, Meg. If you are successful at something new, we'll all know about it before long. What's the big secret?"

She shook her head. "Nothing, really. We've started a new line for suspense. New authors, European distribution ... that sort of thing."

"Well, there's a news flash. I think I better jump up and phone my boss."

Megan smiled. "Go ahead. I'm sure he'll take serious and immediate action."

"Yeah, like the last twenty ideas I laid on him."

They exchanged a knowing look.

Lisa sat back and regarded her. "I was a little surprised to see you here, with the merger and all."

"It's part of my plan. I decided to beat the bushes for new talent."

"Is it working?"

"Well, I've attended several conferences in the past few months, and two or three interesting projects have turned up every time."

"Good." Lisa paused as the twenty-year-old waiter refilled the water glasses. She watched him walk away. "Nice looking young man."

"You're too old for him."

"He's not too young for me."

Megan made a wry face. "I like Irv's looks better. More maturity ... distinction."

Lisa played with her fork. "Yeah. I like his looks, too."

"Speaking of Irv and friendly competition, were you one of the other editors who was receiving that awful book?"

"What awful book?"

"The manuscript that arrived in black envelopes, one chapter at a time."

Lisa's lips pursed. "I don't know what you're talking about. I haven't seen anything like that."

"The story of a serial killer written in first person?"

Lisa shook her head.

"Didn't Irv ask you about it?"

"Not a word. Why?"

"Why?" Megan swallowed hard. "He said he'd talked to several horror editors who were reading the same thing. Why wouldn't he ask you? All he had to do was roll over in bed."

Chapter 27

The large black envelope had arrived in the morning mail. Oscar donned a pair of gloves and slid the contents out, rotating the pages to read the title.

Delicious Pain — Chapter 23
Downtown Boston was hot on that late summer evening. I left the hotel and strolled several blocks to a piano bar recommended by the desk clerk. It was friendly and cool there, and the first two beers went down like I'd just pulled a stump.
   I had fallen into one of the chairs at a small table by the piano. It was unintentional, but as the crowd began to flow in I realized that I had staked out prime real estate, at the pianist's elbow where it was easy to talk and joke with him—exactly where a groupie would sit.
   And so it was, apparently, that God smiled on me by causing two young ladies to steer toward my table. At first, I could not see the one behind. The one leading was a slim brunette, probably in her early thirties, and attractive enough.
   "May we sit with you?" She moved aside to reveal her friend.
   For a moment I sat there mesmerized, a strange mixture of brain activity paralyzing my reactions. During my youth, the women of the silver screen were big busted with hourglass figures. They stalked flowered rooms trailing ribbons and sashes from satin gowns, firm flesh

bulging twixt crossed ties, spawning desires that boys do not breathe even to best friends in secret.

Perhaps it was the angle, but I was that little boy again, sitting cross legged with popcorn spilling from my open mouth. Her waist was cinched up in an expensive black belt at least four inches wide. From there, lines flowed upward and downward in living arcs that celebrated woman. Her thighs were sweeping roundness, edging ever straighter to meet flawless knees below the short white skirt. And the purple leather top forced her large breasts together, forging an awesome line of cleavage. Her wide eyes and slender nose were engulfed by massive strands of honey-colored hair emitting erratic bursts of light.

Men dream of a romantic encounter with a woman like this. When I was a lad, I used to sneak my father's magazines out of his drawer after he passed out. Most were crime stories of women humiliated and murdered. But one was about a man meeting a magnificent woman on a train, who fell lovingly into his bed for the price of a few drinks. Adult reality had long since taught me that this was a pipe dream within the limitations of American society.

I stumbled to my feet, my half second of hesitation now dragging on me like an anchor. As in a dream, I panicked, fearing I would not arise in time—that the illusion would fade away like an image written on fickle fog.

"My name is Pamela, and this is my friend, Wysper."

Whisper. A perfect name, I thought, even before knowing how it was spelled.

The blond goddess jerked her head. "No. I want to sit at the bar." She spun away, haughtily, and stepped up onto a stool.

I exchanged a perplexed look with the smaller woman and sank back into my chair, feeling a twinge of embarrassment, knowing others would feed their egos on my misfortune. I was angry with God for teasing me thus. If he didn't want me to partake, why bring the carrot so close? I decided to get very drunk.

Soon I noticed that Wysper was in my field of view.

Except for my peripheral vision, she was the entire field of view if I sat comfortably in my chair. I had only two choices—change my location, or watch her. It cost no energy to stay put, except pulling out money for fresh rounds.

Falling nearly to her waist without a hint of curl, her hair was thick and massive like strands of fine spaghetti. When she whipped it around, the ends attained great speed. Each time, I expected the sound barrier to be broken.

She never bought a drink. They were always stacked up at least two deep in front of her. And as I watched her work the room, a pattern began to emerge. After each suitor was rebuked, she would toss her head with a virulent jerk, as if airing out her hair ... cleansing it of the male taint.

All men were equal in her eyes, maggots clamoring for the looks God had mistakenly bestowed upon her. And I hated her. Now I knew why I had chanced upon this place. Even God could not stomach such arrogance. He had sent me as an instrument to correct His error.

When I looked up, she was gone. For a moment, I was terrified. Then I noticed the large leather bag sitting like a sentry on her seat. She was down at the end of the bar working over a couple of men who hadn't paid her proper homage. The pressure was rising. My chest was starting to sweat. At any moment she might leave, and I couldn't let her do so without knowing how to find her again.

I had racked my brain for an approach that might work, but it was hopeless. We were on her turf—her theater of operations. She would spurn me as she had all others with clever repartee designed to make me feel the fool. Suddenly, I noted a thin case projecting from her purse.

I stood up and folded my raincoat over my arm. Moving to the bar, I laid the coat across her purse, leaning over to the dark-haired girl. "Thank you for almost talking with me."

She glanced briefly in my direction. "Maybe next time, huh?" Her attention was back on the man next to her. In fact, it had never strayed.

I darted into a men's room stall to see what I had taken. It was her checkbook with name, address, and phone number. I tore out the last check and dropped the folder through the legs of her barstool on my way out. It made a muted ping as it bounced off the crossbar, followed by a subtle splat when it hit the carpet.

I worked very hard over the next several days to find out what I needed without being detected. They were roommates, living in a town north of Boston. It was a strange unhistoric area, consisting of one-story homes and businesses constructed after World War Two. They lived on the second floor of a newer apartment complex.

They went out every night after work. The brunette went directly from work, but Wysper always came home to change because her prowling threads were inappropriate for day wear. I only hoped the routine would not change because it was a Friday night.

I watched her climb the stairs and enter the apartment. People were coming home from work and there was a fair amount of bustle in the area. I waited fifteen minutes and drove into the lot, parking on her driver's side with four feet of operating room. Twenty minutes later, she came out and locked her door. She was wearing a white top and short pleated skirt made of a heavy blue knit material. Her cheerleader legs tapered into a pair of high white boots, and her hair shimmered in the oblique sunlight. She was as breathtaking as the first night I saw her.

As she cleared the stairs, I got out and moved around to meet her at her car door. "Miss Eglund?"

She pulled up in a defensive posture. "Yes?"

I produced a badge I had bought in a pawn shop. "Bank examiner Forbes. I need to talk with you about your account at Yankee Federal."

The demon was actually taken aback. "What about it?"

"Intent to defraud." I was ready to run if she objected or seemed to recognize me. But I was confident that she would not remember me, counting on the fact that she dismissed all that was not of her own creation or under her control.

She gazed up at me. "What do you mean?"

I pulled her check out of my pocket. "Is this yours?"

She found her checkbook and rifled through it until she discovered the last one missing. She looked up in surprise. "Where did you get it?"

It was the closest I'd been to her, the first opportunity to really look upon her beauty ... perfect teeth slightly parted, clear robin's egg eyes accentuated by full cheekbones, and a square jaw that flowed upward to disappear under her thick mane. For an instant, I rued the task that had befallen me. It was not possible for me to make love to her since I detested her. This was an erudite sacrifice for my fellow men. Even so, I might have relented at that point, had she not shown her true colors.

Wysper stamped her foot and shrieked, "I asked you a question, asshole. Where did you get my check?"

I looked around with legitimate concern. "Please, Miss Eglund. This is a delicate matter. We should not air it in front of your neighbors." I gripped her elbow and opened the passenger door of my car. "Have a seat and I'll explain."

To this day I am surprised she complied. She was such a bitch! She made a face and her body shuddered in resentment, but she did get into the car.

An aside, if I may. This is something I will never understand. Why are women so trusting with strange men? Perhaps it speaks well of our society, but there was usually one critical moment when a woman could have saved herself by screaming, or fighting back, or breaking away ... or listening to that quiet voice of warning in her mind.

It was still daylight and people had been coming and going while I waited for her. But at that moment, no one was in sight. I looked over to see her sitting with arms crossed over her purse, her lip stuck out like a pouting child. That's when I hit her. The blow, delivered without great force to the side of her jaw, put her out like a light. She moaned and crumpled over the center armrest.

I fled the scene and drove around blindly until my brain convinced my nerves that we had gotten away clean. Then I pulled into a lot behind a darkened commercial building, chained her hands and feet, and tightly fastened the seat belt to hold her in place. This activity brought her around and she tried to scream. I covered her mouth and applied a gag that guarantees absolute silence and serves as a control device—the ability to inflict pain at will.

She tried to scream several times, but doubled over in severe agony on each occasion. Then she fought her bonds until satisfied that she could not reach the seat belt release. I unbuttoned her blouse and slid my hand in. She looked at me with revulsion and tried to pull away. I administered pain. She sat still. I told her to spread her legs. She refused until the pain. After a few exchanges, she did anything I wanted without hesitation.

Now she knew that I could control her. I fastened the chains on her ankles to the seat supports and undid the belt, pulling her over against me like a couple on a date. Then we set out for Walnut Mountain, a very secluded place where I had buried a former love many years ago.

It was unfortunate that our encounter was to be so brief, that she would not have more time to regret her mistreatment of men. But the trip was to take several hours ... long enough for her to contemplate the fate she had brought upon herself.

"Son of a bitch!" Colunga stuffed the pages into the black enclosure and stormed into the main room. "Kathy, make three copies of this, and send it to the lab for fingerprints. Also see if they can raise the postmark."

She looked up in surprise. "Right away."

He thought for several seconds. "What was the name of that shrink we sent the first eight chapters to?"

"Dr. Rita Takamura."

"Do we have the report yet?"

"No."

"I'll need her number."

Chapter 28

Oscar perched on the edge of an antique chair in the den of a pleasant bungalow near Bristol. Through the large picture window at the rear, tall trees cast stark shadows in the late afternoon sun. He turned as he heard pages fall to the desk.

"What do you think, Dr. Takamura?"

"Please, it's Rita."

"All right."

The petite woman collected her thoughts and spoke in a voice more commanding than her stature. "When you sent the original eight chapters, you requested an analysis from the perspective of fiction or fact."

"That's correct."

"May I ask where they came from?"

"They were sent to me by a woman in New York."

"What woman in New York?"

"She refused to identify herself, but she's probably an agent or editor."

"Why would she send a novel to a police officer?"

"She thought she saw similarities with actual murders up here."

"Was she right?"

"Dead on."

"And this chapter. Did she send it?"

"I don't think so."

"Why not?"

"It's different from the others ... mailed in a black envelope with no receiving stamp like the original chapters had." He paused. "Also, it describes a murder that took place in Boston less than three weeks ago."

Rita stared at him in amazement. "Accurately?"

"I don't have the report yet, but preliminary information seems to match. He used the actual victim's name."

"I see." She took a long breath. "Even before this chapter, certain factors indicated that this might be based on fact."

"For example?"

"His psychosis was very cohesive. I wondered if a sane novelist could write a fictitious character with that degree of consistency."

She stood up and moved to the windows, drawing the shears to look out. "If this chapter was written by the same man, I believe you have the chronicles of a serial killer in your hands."

"Can you be certain?"

"I am certain of less and less as years roll by, but this chapter confirms a transition I had predicted."

"A transition?"

"Yes." She paused in thought. "Have you had much experience with serial killers, Lieutenant?"

"Not a great deal."

"Well, theirs is a life of deepening psychosis. Frequently they start out with sexual aberrations in their early years— fondling and molestation of other children or killing animals. Eventually they move up to rape, or a series of rapes. At some point they start to murder their victims.

"This is similar to building up a tolerance for drugs or alcohol. Over a period of time the thrill wears off for things they have done, and they must become more adventurous. New challenges. Greater violence. Greater brutality."

Oscar nodded. "Sounds like our man."

"Exactly. On the first page he questions whether he has the ability to kill—some desire he's harbored for a long time. Later he has childish expectations for the dungeon he constructs. Sex and murder have been integral from the start. But by the eighth chapter, the pattern begins to change."

She ran her fingers through thick black hair. "He kills without any form of sexual gratification. Now, in this latest chapter, he murders a woman without the prospect of it—deliberately denies himself the option before he takes her."

"How do you interpret that?"

"I think he's becoming disillusioned. Experience has proven that his dreams cannot be fulfilled. He's disappointed and, I would guess, sexually dysfunctional."

"Impotent?"

"Yes. Otherwise, why would he pass up the opportunity to rape a woman who, by his own description, is one of the most beautiful women he's ever encountered? He could just as easily take her home as to some burial site. Especially with the hatred he professes, why not torture and humiliate her for several days rather than a few hours?"

Oscar gazed at her delicate profile—eyelashes protruding past a slender straight nose, and the subtle curve that flowed downward from her lower lip and turned along a strong jaw to meet her throat at right angles.

"Any ideas?"

"Several, but one is more disturbing than the rest." Rita turned and rested against the window sill with arms folded. "Humans rarely recognize fallacies in their beliefs. Some things may work against them for a lifetime, but they somehow manage to rationalize or blame their failures on someone else. Psychotics are masters at this. Am I making myself clear?"

"Crystal."

"Let me make one more point about this particular psychotic. Do you remember that several times he talked about good women—those raising children against great odds for example?"

Oscar nodded.

"He may decide that his failure is based on the kind of woman he's been abducting ... rationalize that they were too young or inexperienced. He may start to go after more mature women who can better understand or appreciate his efforts, those who were previously immune. And I suspect this latest chapter is a signal to that effect. I wish we had the intervening chapters, so we could better track his development."

"I'm not sure there are intervening chapters." He recognized his own surprise in what he was saying. "He may have written the first chapters earlier, and then decided to jump ahead for some reason."

"If so, that could be significant." Rita pushed away and walked to her desk, gazing down at the manuscript pages. "The more immediate question is why he sent this one directly to you."

"What's your guess?"

"To prove he murdered her?"

"Possibly. But there are many details that could not be known by investigating officers. It could be a complete fabrication."

"Any other ideas why he would send it to you?"

"My guess is that he wants to play with me ... make me a victim too."

"Would a fiction writer do that?"

"I doubt it."

She sat down and leaned onto her elbows, looking drained. "Either way, doesn't it bother you to be in direct contact with this man?"

"Very much. He knows the woman sent his stuff to me.

He knows who she is. He knows who I am. And I can't touch him."

"So, what are you going to do?"

"I'll check out the Boston murder to see if he could have killed Wysper. If so, we'll go through the rest of it looking for details that might tie him to earlier victims."

"And if you do?"

"We look for factual background in his writing that could be used to identify him."

"Who is this 'we' you refer to?"

"My staff and I." He glanced at the ring finger of her left hand. "Do you want to help?"

"Yes. I think we should go over his writing together—combine our expertise."

"That's a great idea." Oscar stood up and moved to the desk. "But my brain is going to shut down if I don't pump in some fuel pretty soon. Do you like Mexican food?"

She smiled up at him. "As long as the sushi is fresh."

Chapter 29

After reading the manuscript a fourth time, Oscar scanned the notes on his legal pad. He turned the manuscript over, paging backward until he located the passage near the front of Chapter Eight, then glanced at the clock—nine PM in Arizona. He pulled a worn phone book from the desk drawer and dialed.

With a distinct click, the ringing stopped. "Cyril Baines, here."

"Cyril, this is Oscar Colunga."

"My, my. A voice from the past. Where are you, old boy?"

"Connecticut."

"Well, we haven't heard a peep since you left Arizona. How are you getting along?"

"Just fine. You?"

"No worries. What are you doing with yourself?"

"I'm working for the State Police."

"How'd you end up way out there?"

"It's a long story." Oscar hesitated. "How's Ann?"

"Quite chipper. Would you care to speak with her?"

"Yes I would, but I'm up to my ass in alligators right now. How about I call you this weekend?"

"We'll look forward to it." He paused. "Am I to assume you want help with these alligators?"

"Yes. I need some information."

"Give it me best shot."

"You know more about racing than anyone. About eight years ago, a car threw a tire and went into the infield backward. Several people were hurt ... maybe killed. Could you run down the exact date?"

"Hmm. Any idea where?"

"Probably the continental US."

"That does jangle an alarm, but it's not coming to me. May I get back with you?"

"When?"

"Ten minutes, I should say."

"Of course." Oscar gave Cyril his number and said goodbye.

Oscar found his feet and moved to the window, gazing out at the yellow and blue points of light twinkling in the hot night air—sights and sounds of this small eastern city so far from his origins, but not far enough to escape the memories.

The four-wheel-drive with Oregon plates rested askew beside the road twenty-five miles northwest of Flagstaff, key in the ignition and tank empty. Once proud in its ability to eat up rough terrain, it now stood as a hollow shell that had failed its master in his hour of need.

Human tracks led northward through the snow—dark blotches, widened and exaggerated by the sun, that marked his trail like stepping stones.

The trailer ramp banged into the dirt and rang with a metallic peel as the quarterhorse backed out snorting and pitching nervously, trying to see over his shoulder.

Upward. Up the gentle slope to the tree line. Strange combinations of conifer and yucca pierced the four-inch icy mantle that was melting fast in the afternoon heat, becoming sodden. The tracks turned west and then north again—erratic, confused, now being obliterated by the horse's large hooves.

A cut between the rocks at the crest. There in the valley below, the thing scrambled through birches, clawing its way with hands and feet, driven by the terror of Hell.

Oscar dived for the phone and slid into his chair. "Cyril?"

"Found it straightaway. The exact date was the twenty-seventh of June."

"Thanks, Cyril. I'll call you in a few days." He cradled the phone and jerked the report on Melinda Grant into the light.

Last seen on June twenty-seven ...

Oscar dropped his head into his hands and rubbed his eyes. "*Hijo de puta!* You killed every one of them."

Chapter 30

At the top of the long staircase, Megan turned the corner and strode to the front table where Irv Miller was waiting. She dropped into the chair and blew a lock of hair from her face.

Miller smiled whimsically. "Bad day?"

"Yes. And it's only noon. I don't know how much will be left of me when it's over."

"Maybe this will help." He reached into his breast pocket and tossed an envelope onto the table.

"What's that?"

"An offer. Duston Todd wants your book."

"Thank God!" Megan extracted the page and scanned it. "I wish the advance was bigger."

"Every writer wishes that. Question is, can you live with it?"

"I guess so."

"We could shop around for a better deal."

"No! It's becoming imperative to eliminate uncertainty. I need a book contract in my hot little hand."

"All right. I'll tell Duston to proceed, and we'll go over the contract together when it comes in." Irv smiled. "I always feel let down when the deal is done. Maybe we should shout from the rooftops or fly to Cancún."

"Cancún? Do you have the time?"

"If you have the money."

"I don't. Even if it's a blockbuster, it will be two years before royalties start to flow in, and this advance won't make the down-payment on the house I'm looking at."

"You're going to buy a house?"

"Good question, Irv." She leaned onto her elbow and tapped her teeth with her fingernails. "I found one in Connecticut that I love, but it seems like a long way to travel every day."

"Depends where it is."

"Near Pleasant Valley."

"I know the area. I used to live up there."

"You did?"

"A few hills over, but not far."

"Why'd you leave?"

"I couldn't stand the drive any longer."

Megan nodded. "Exactly what I'm afraid of."

"Frankly, I wouldn't worry about that. I commuted for years before it got to me. But don't write off the idea too quickly. Even if you decide to sell in a few years, real estate is a good investment."

"You sound like my agent."

"I am your agent."

"My realtor, then."

"Who's that?"

"Joan Kirtch."

"I know her!"

"You do?"

"She's practically an institution up there."

"May I take your order?"

Megan turned and looked up at the crisp young waiter with short hair, slightly blacker than his uniform. "Curry shrimp ... hot."

"Soup or salad?"

"What's the soup?"

"Clam chowder."

"Is it red or white?"

"Red."

"I'll have the salad with house dressing."

"Would you care for a cocktail?"

"Water on the rocks."

"And you, sir?"

"The same, plus a gin and tonic."

"Very good." He slapped his order book closed and pivoted away.

Megan gazed at Irv. "Now that the business is put to bed, may I ask you a personal question?"

"Sure."

"How are you and Lisa getting along?"

Irv lit a cigarette and tilted his head back, expelling a thin trail of smoke into the air. "The handwriting is on the wall."

"I believe she said your 'days were numbered.'"

His head snapped forward. "She did? When was this?"

"A week or two ago. We had lunch at a conference, and she said you were having problems."

"Problems ... a simple word for complicated issues. Did she tell you what the problem is?"

"Something about you taking responsibility for her daughter."

"Oh, I could have lived with that. She's getting old enough to take care of herself." He leaned forward. "You don't know the worst of it."

"Which is?"

"Lisa wanted more."

"More children?"

"Um-hmm." He sat back and regarded her. "You know the definition of freedom?"

"What?"

"When the last kid graduates from college and the cat dies."

Megan smiled. "I didn't know you had children."

"Three by my former wife. The last one graduated this year, and the cat keeled over long ago. I'm not about to sacrifice my freedom now."

"But you're still young."

"I'll be forty-seven in December." He nodded with satisfaction at her reaction. "If I had a kid now, I'd be retired by the time he entered college. I want the freedom to travel and pursue other interests before I have to use a walker."

"So, you're at an impasse."

"Like you said once, you can't be partially pregnant. You have more kids or you don't. There's no middle ground."

"Maybe you should find a woman too old to bear children."

"The thought has crossed my mind."

Megan's brow knitted. "Speaking of Lisa, I have a bone to pick with you."

He stiffened. "Oh?"

"You told me you had found other editors who were receiving that serial killer book, but you didn't even ask Lisa about it. What's the story?"

Irv ducked his head like a boy caught with his hand in the cookie jar. "Sorry, Meg. I did ask a few people, but they looked at me like I was crazy. So I gave it up. I never specifically said I talked to Lisa, and I truly believed your fears were unfounded. Also, I realized that a random sampling of editors probably wouldn't turn it up, even if he was sending it out by the gross. Besides, you had so much on your mind at the time, it seemed like the constructive thing to do." He dipped his head and looked up at her. "Can you forgive me?"

"Maybe." Megan pouted. "But this increases my resolve to identify this jerk."

"You're trying to find him?"

"I hired a private detective."

His eyes widened. "Did he come up with anything?"

"Indirectly." She paused. "Did I mention that the chapters come in black envelopes?"

"I don't recall."

"Well, they do. So I tracked down a list of stores that ordered large black envelopes over the past few months—covering all the New York boroughs and northern New Jersey."

She blew out a gust of air. "But I don't know how much good it will do. Given a suspect, I could determine if he works or lives near one of the stores. Otherwise, what can I do?"

Irv shook his head. "Sounds impossible."

"Don't worry. I'll think of something."

Chapter 31

Oscar turned northward onto the exit from Interstate 95 toward the New London submarine base, noting that the foliage seemed a bit thinner at the Connecticut coast. As he accelerated to speed, bushes with great white flowers flitted by alongside, and the scent of juniper wafted through the open windows on the still summer air.

It was so different from the vistas of the west—mountain ridges falling into a valley floor filled to a smooth finish by millions of years of sediment, each range taking on its own hue of green or gray depending on distance and the subtle mist released by trees and desert plants. New Mexico was barren by comparison, yet spectacular in scope.

Here, one could seldom see beyond the trees. But at home, things a hundred miles away were clearly visible. If the spirit directed the eyes to look up, there was always something to behold—higher, farther, and grander.

He sensed a sadness in himself. "Homesick. Son of a bitch! You're homesick. Take a vacation when this is over. See old friends ... return to the center."

The exit sign to New London flashed through his reverie. He left the highway and followed signs along surface streets, finally entering the short road onto the base. He turned into the lot of the small building just right of the main gate.

Twenty minutes later a woman entered. Her graying hair

matched the color of her eyes, which were partly obscured by half-height glasses. In her fifties, she wore civilian clothes over a trim figure—a light blue blouse and black skirt.

She flashed a friendly smile. "Lieutenant Colunga?"

"Yes." He produced his ID card.

"My name's McKensie. Sorry it took so long, but I had to scare up a car."

"We could have used mine."

"I'm afraid we could not. Are you armed?"

"No, ma'am." He spread the lapels of his coat.

"Very well."

He followed her out to the small white sedan and they whisked by the sentry at the gate. Headed north, they crested a short hill past manicured lawns and buildings, then dropped down to a street that ran parallel to the Thames River. Oscar sat forward and gaped at the row of submarines moored on his left. The black hulks ranged in size and type, but the line seemed to reach the horizon.

"My God."

His escort nodded. "Impressive, isn't it?"

"Almost makes me feel better about taxes. Do many people get to see this?"

"Not many. We open the base to the public once a year. Otherwise you need a pretty good reason to come on. Security is tight, especially in the area where we're going."

She turned left to a gate in the twelve-foot chain-link fence that separated the sub pens from the rest of the base, and pulled up as the guard challenged.

Oscar started to reach for his ID, but the young man snapped a salute and motioned them on without a word.

He shook his head. "You call that tight security?"

"Don't worry. We checked you out long before you got here. Besides, he saw my name." She pointed to a gold bar pinned to her blouse. "My husband was a lieutenant commander before he passed away. My son works for base security. And I work for the Admiral."

"So it really didn't matter who I was."

She turned and lowered her head to peer over the rim of her glasses. "Not very much."

Oscar grinned. "What does Harold Gilley do here?"

"He's a supply officer. Buys the literally tons of stuff it takes to keep this place going."

She parked in front of a long two-story building, a combination of red and white masonry with a loading dock running its length. They went through a small door and Oscar examined the exposed red-and-gray pipes as he followed her up the stairs to the second floor. At the top, the room opened up into a large area with chest-high reception desk and offices along the perimeter.

Several people called out to her as Mrs. McKensie approached the desk. "Visitor for Mr. Gilley."

A uniformed woman pointed to an office on the west wall. "He's expecting you, sir. Go right in."

Oscar nodded and edged into the room. "Harold Gilley?"

The man rounded his desk and thrust out his hand. "Call me Bud. Everybody does."

Oscar pumped his hand vigorously. "Okay, Bud."

Gilley combed his thick black hair with his fingers. "Would you care for coffee?"

"No thanks."

"Then have a seat. I'll be right with you."

Oscar surveyed the office as Gilley refilled his cup from a machine in the corner. The desk was littered with papers, and every surface and pigeonhole in the government-drab office was stuffed.

"They told me to look for a landmark, some enormous tower. I didn't see one coming in."

"We tore it down. It was used to teach escape from submarines with older diving technology. But we have these little umbrella things now, so the tower was no longer needed. Took years to get it done though. The engineers were afraid it would collapse if they let the water out."

"If you wanted it down, what's the problem with that?"

"It was six hundred feet high. We had to control where it fell." Gilley banged a spoon on his cup and settled in behind his desk. "Now, how can the US Navy support our local police?"

Oscar crossed his legs. "We understand you were serving aboard fuel tankers in the Med roughly eighteen years ago."

"True. What about it?"

"We're trying to identify an Air Force officer who was assigned to the fuel distribution system for our bases in Morocco."

"Air Force? Why come to me?"

"We ran across an old friend of yours who says you knew more about that operation than anyone."

Gilley's brown eyes flashed and the square jaw yielded to a broad grin. "Who told you that?"

Oscar extracted the notebook from his coat pocket. "A man named B.G. Crabbe."

"Buster? I didn't think the old fart was still alive."

Oscar grimaced. "Buster?"

"When one is in the United States Navy, one does not call a buddy Bernard."

"One wouldn't be so gauche." Oscar eyed him. "Did you know some of the Air Force men who worked the pipelines?"

"Lots of them. Could you be more specific?"

"Let's say that he and a partner ran a thriving black-market operation. Does that help?"

Gilley leaned back in thought. "Amazingly, it does. There was an almost legendary pair in the black market at that time."

"Did you know them?"

"We may have crossed paths once or twice."

"Any chance you could remember a name?"

"I might, but there's no chance it will come to me right now. You have a number where I can reach you?"

Oscar fumbled a card from his coat pocket. "I want to thank you ..."

"No need. Glad to be of help." Bud stood up and came around to take the card. "But I don't understand why you drove all the way down here. This could have been done over the phone."

Oscar got to his feet. "I've wanted to see this base for years. It could be a once-in-a-lifetime event."

Gilley smiled and offered his hand. "Mention that to McKensie and you'll probably get the best tour any civilian ever had—assuming she doesn't consider you a threat to national security."

Chapter 32

Aware that she was the center of attention in the sea of men at the hotel bar, Megan stirred her rusty nail idly. She had already repelled three advances and was preparing to deal with those responsible for the two fresh drinks lined up behind her own.

She tensed as a handsome man glided onto the stool next to her and nodded amiably.

"Evening."

"Evening, yourself." She tossed her head and turned away.

"You with the writer's convention"—he leaned forward to peer at her breast—"Megan?"

She ripped her name tag off and stowed it in her purse. "How'd you know?"

"Lucky guess. Do your friends call you Meg?"

"I don't have any friends."

"Me either." He waved the bartender off. "Where you from, Megan?"

"New Yawk."

"Me too!" He ogled her with a toothy grin. "I hear all women from New Yawk are easy. That true?"

Megan met his eyes with a level gaze. "I hear all men from New York are gay. That true?"

"Must be." His head dipped sharply. "I'm a lesbian, myself."

The hint of a smile formed. "You're a lesbian?"

"Sure. I like to do it with women."

She broke into a short, throaty laugh. "Well, I'm a woman. Would you like to do it with me?"

His eyes rolled and his head tilted coyly. "Oh, what the hell."

Men stared aghast as he stood up to help her off the barstool. One started to his feet, but a companion gripped his arm.

The trip to the door was one of the longest she ever made, knowing that every eye was on her. She followed his broad back to the elevators, and hit him on the shoulder with her purse as the doors came together.

"That was the dumbest idea you ever had."

Achal grinned like a mischievous boy. "Didn't you enjoy it?"

"Maybe in some perverse way. But there was too much tension."

"I rather liked it. Did you see the looks on their faces?"

"Hurt and anger. And those poor men who wasted money on drinks."

"Those are the breaks of the game, my love."

"I guess. At least you didn't talk me into playing a hooker."

Achal considered it. "There's always tomorrow night."

She laid her head against his shoulder and giggled. "I would like to hear their conversation right now. We'll be the hot topic all night." She kissed him hard on the mouth. "Did you get your kicks? Is your ego gratified?"

He looked down at her with intense softness. "More than any time in my life. You are the perfect woman. Brains, beauty, and that insouciant playfulness that lights a room."

She conformed to his body, head back. "And you are the perfect man."

The silly bim-bom broke the moment, and the elevator doors parted to a group of surprised onlookers. She followed him down the hall to their room, where he threw off his coat and turned to embrace her at the foot of the bed. He kissed her tenderly. "I think it's time to consider something more permanent."

She buried her face in his chest. "I'm so afraid."

He lifted her chin. "Of what?"

"I don't know. Commitment. Growing up. I've done a pretty good job of avoiding it so far."

He held her more tightly. "Haven't we all."

Megan broke away and sprawled on the bed, face down with her head on crossed arms. "I just don't think I'm ready."

Achal eased down next to her, stroking her back. "Who's ever ready? Nobody feels adult until adult responsibilities are thrust upon them."

Megan shifted to her side, the whites of her eyes accentuating the deep green. "I love you, Achal."

"I know." He kissed her sweetly.

She pulled back. "How did you know?"

"Some things do not need to be spoken."

"Hindu philosophy again?"

"Yes."

She sat up and tossed her head back, the dark red hair forming rivulets down her white blouse. "I'm not ready for commitment. I don't know what's happening to me, personally or professionally. Will I make it as a writer? Do I want to live in New York in any event?"

Achal regarded her. "If we have each other, what does it matter?"

"Right. The prince and princess riding off into the sunset." She turned to meet his eyes. "Even as a dumb farm girl, I knew that people are not so simple. You want me now for what you perceive me to be. What if my dreams bomb? What if I get disheartened and sullen? Will you want me then?"

"Yes."

Megan twisted away. "No you won't. It isn't even your choice. If I don't believe in myself, it doesn't matter what you believe."

"I will always believe in you."

"Oh Achal, I don't belong here. In my family, generations of men and women based their self-esteem on the land. How much they had. How much they could coax out of it. Try as I will, I can't override those values." She brushed the tears from her cheek. "That's why I'm drawn to that house in Connecticut. It would give me a sense of personal worth, even though I know it's stupid."

"It's not stupid."

"Oh, no? Do you want to live up there?"

"I don't know." Achal ducked his head. "I've never tried to sleep without sirens and street noise."

"You see?" Megan choked slightly. "You see? Whatever I want is wrong for me."

He reached out to stroke her cheek. "If it's good for you, it will be good for me. We'll go up and see it together. All right?"

"No. It's not all right. One thing I have learned. If something becomes too difficult, it's probably not a good idea." She reached out for his hand. "I'll go take one last look in the next few days. If it doesn't feel right, you're off the hook."

Chapter 33

Kathy Huntsinger sat across the desk in the early morning light. Oscar stared dumbfounded at the stack of paper on her lap. She had obviously been working her fingers to the bone, and this at a time when her daughter was ill.

"How is Leah?"

"Oh, she'll be all right. It's just a case of measles."

"Listen, if she needs you, feel free to take off."

"It's no problem, Oscar, really. She's staying with my mother." Her pretty dark eyes glistened as she smiled at him. "Mom nursed me through the measles when I was little, so I think she can do the same for Leah. Besides, I couldn't think of taking off during an investigation as important as this."

He dipped his chin to look over his reading glasses. "It is not as important as your daughter."

"She'll be all right." Kathy scanned the top document on her lap and looked up. "Ready?"

Oscar lit a smoke. "Fire away."

"This first item relates to the girl he said he killed in Florida. He claimed that Jane's father was a lawyer from Long Island. No match on that, but there was a young woman from Long Island who disappeared on a vacation to Galveston about the right time. Her name was Laurie Sanders, and her father was a lawyer."

"Which implies that we may have a mixture of truth and fantasy."

"Exactly. He lied about things that seemed important, like where he lived at a given time. Other things he considered too insignificant to lie about. And if you're going to tell your life's story, it would be infinitely easier to write actual events than to make up entirely new stories, or invent alternatives for each minute detail. My problem is to determine which is which."

"How do you propose to do that?"

"By looking for things that lend themselves to a computer search, with a little help from gut instinct."

He glanced at the pile in her lap. "And you've done all this in the last few days?"

She nodded. "It's easy, once you get the rhythm. But understand, most of these are not results ... merely the questions."

"Right." Oscar smiled dourly. "So where are you going to get the answers?"

"From the FBI, NCIC, VICAP, and our own files. Eventually we'll have to do some legwork."

"Like?"

"Inquiries to other state and local agencies. We can only go so far with canned data banks."

Oscar shifted in his chair. "I'm almost amazed by the implications of this one example. If she was his victim, and if she was killed in Galveston, we know where he lived at the time. And if he was a charter boat captain, we can probably narrow it down to a few hundred names."

"True, but running a charter business seems like one of those items important enough to lie about."

"If so, he was consistent. He mentions later that he made a fair profit when he sold the boat." Oscar thought for a moment. "This seems good enough to dig into. Do you have the homicide report on this woman yet?"

"They're going to fax it."

"All right. When you get it, I want to talk to the detectives who handled the case. They may have information in their heads that never hit the sheet. And we should talk to her father."

"I agree, but we'll have to be judicious with our time. There are about forty possible hits here. He claims he was a sergeant in the Air Force. He says he was raised in Kentucky and learned to swim in Tennessee rivers. He says all sorts of things that may or may not be true, and each one could represent a lot of effort."

"You set the priority based on bang for the buck, and we'll work our way through them." Oscar shook his head. "Of course, this could be a wild goose chase."

"I wouldn't worry about that. As a broken-down mathematician, I'd say that the correlation between the book and actual crimes is outside the region of random probability."

Oscar's eyebrows raised. "You're a mathematician?"

"It was my major in school. The computer stuff was just a fallout from that." Her lips pressed tightly together and she rolled a new page onto the desk. "He says his first novel was accepted for publication roughly ten years ago, if his timing is to be believed."

"Do you believe his timing?"

"It's consistent. Bodies have been falling around here for about that long."

Oscar snuffed out his cigarette. "I don't know, Kathy. If it was me, that's one truth I would shade."

"It still might be worth a look. There are roughly forty thousand books published each year. However, only a fraction of those are novels, and a fraction of those are by new writers. And if we assume he doesn't write romance, we can cut that list by fifty percent. We may be able to distill it down to a reasonable number, even spanning two or three years."

"If he really is a writer."

"Yes, I thought about that. So I asked a local writer's group to evaluate samples." Kathy laid a typed sheet on the desk. "They can't tell if he's published, of course, but they think he's writing at a professional level."

"Based on what?"

"Imagery, flow, and mechanics."

Oscar gazed at her dryly. "Didn't get a word."

"Well, imagery has to do with the way a writer uses words. When he describes a scene, can you see it? Do you know what a character looks like, and who he or she is? There's really more to it than that, but they thought his imagery showed experience."

"There's really more to it? Sounds like you know what you're talking about, Kathy."

"Oh, I've done a little writing. Mainly short stories."

"I see." He squinted. "What about the next thing?"

"Flow. Have you ever been reading a book and gotten lost—where you had to back up a paragraph, or page, to figure out what's going on?"

"Certainly."

"Did you ever have to do it with this guy's writing?"

"I backed up several times, but it was because I couldn't believe what he was saying, not because I got lost."

"Right. And the third thing is mechanics, how he handles dialogue, punctuation, and proper manuscript format for submission." She dropped her eyes to the page. "They say his mechanics are virtually flawless."

Oscar nodded. "Okay. Let's say he had a book published. What if he used a pen name?"

"I don't know if it matters." She smiled at Oscar's bewilderment. "If we can cross-correlate new authors who moved to New York a year or two before publication, we may end up with a list in the dozens ... maybe less. Then all we have to do is look up their real names."

Oscar's head shook slowly. "But the work required to track all this down could be phenomenal, especially when we're not sure it's true."

"That's my job ... to narrow the range enough to make the search practical."

She picked up the next document. "For example, he says he bought a home in New England that had been formerly owned by a rich classic car buff. If true, and if we can find the former owner, we'd have our man cold. There are magazines that cater to car buffs. We can compare their lists with state records of people who sold houses in this area at that time. Or we may just get lucky and come across some other buff who knows the man we're looking for."

"And if he lied about that?"

"Then we will spin our wheels a bit, but the computers will do most of the work."

"Reasonable ..." Oscar stopped in mid-sentence and spun around to the phone. "I'm sorry, Kathy. I told them we weren't to be disturbed. It must be urgent."

She nodded as he lifted the receiver.

"Colunga."

"Oliphant here."

"Yes, Hank. What can I do for you?"

"You can explain how you knew to look for a dead girl up on Walnut Mountain."

"Did you find her?"

"Not exactly. We found two. One grave is several years old, and the other is brand new. Now, how did you know?"

"The murderer told me."

"You know who he is?"

"Of course not."

"Then, how?"

"He sent me a letter about the girl who was killed in Boston a few weeks ago, Wysper Eglund."

A Bronx cheer reverberated over the lines. "Christ! I'm busting my ass out here, and you're sitting around your cushy office playing some sort of game?"

"Listen, Hank. I wasn't certain she was up there. I had to treat it like a tip."

"Tip, my ass! I'll be at your office in thirty minutes, and you better lay out everything you have, or I'm going to kick your Mexican butt halfway to the Rio Grande."

Oscar nodded solemnly to himself. "Any time you want to try, *ese.*"

Chapter 34

The morning was brooding and overcast and his armpits felt like a soggy sponge as Oscar entered the OSI office at ten AM. Nodding to the officers already at work in the big room, he walked over to the coffee pot and drew off a cup in the mug Kathy cleaned for him each night. He stirred in two sugars and a large splash of creamer, and headed for his office.

Kathy called out, "Your mail, Oscar."

He diverted and took the stack from her, noting the large black envelope before it hit his hand. "Another one?"

She gazed at it absently. "Looks like."

"Did you read it?"

Kathy was irritable. "I didn't even open it."

"But there might be some new information."

"I have enough to work on already. I can wait until you've seen it."

He sipped the hot bitter fluid. "Any word from José Cruz on the manuscript?"

Kathy's head shook slowly. "Want me to call him?"

"No. I'll do it in a few minutes."

Oscar paced into his office, closing the door behind him. He set down the mail and coffee mug and removed his coat, tossing it onto a chair as he sagged into his own. For some time he stared at the large envelope lying placidly among the smaller ones scattered on the desk, then rifled his drawer for gloves and a letter opener.

The pages spilled out, to his surprise only a few. "What the hell is this?" He squared them away and began to read.

Delicious Pain — Chapter 24

I have already stated too often that many of my loves came to me without proper planning, a matter of providence and opportunity. I also had come to realize that it was a waste of effort to take young women. Aside from lacking the experience and maturity to adjust to their new lives, we had nothing in common once the channels of communication were established. Having become a master of my trade, I vowed to pick a woman of great depth and beauty—a kindred spirit who could appreciate my capacity for compassion and adoration.

While this decision came to me in a flash, seeds of the idea had been germinating in my subconscious for some time—like the itch that is not assuaged by scratching. As I went about my daily routine, my perception was extended like a nervous deer sensing subtle movement in the trees.

For a while, I thought it would be my insurance agent. She was a comely woman with flashing eyes, a ready smile, and voluptuous body. One time we had lunch together and she complained about the size of her thighs. Having just watched her bend down to pick up her napkin from the floor, I found no fault with the unbroken curve and told her so. To my surprise, she was not offended ... possibly even flattered.

Then I came across a wondrous female working as a teller at my new bank. I had seen her walking to lunch on several occasions as I sat at the drive-up window. Although she usually wore long skirts, the fluid line of her lower body was striking, ending in relatively thick ankles that radiated sexuality over her high heels. Her hair was long and dark, falling into sweeping curls. The taper from her shoulders to her waist was pronounced, and while her face was somewhat widened in proportion to her weight, her tanned skin had the sheen of porcelain.

For several months I altered my schedule, going
inside to get a better look and to establish a rapport with
her that could later be used to my advantage. Alas, this
device failed me, for I discovered that she was married
and a mother of three children.

Now I faced a dilemma. Having spurned the insurance
agent in my own mind, I found it impossible to rekindle
my interest in her. If she was second best to the bank
teller, she must be third best to others. For nearly a year,
I searched for the perfect candidate. I was looking for
something that scarcely exists in normal society—a
woman with the looks of a movie star and the bearing of
a Nobel prizewinner. At times I was dejected.

This had always been a thorn in my side, and the
reason I never married again. Certain ideals had been
formed in the innocence of my youth, as I watched those
busty women take command of the silver screen. They
did not walk or talk like ordinary mortals. They drifted
through men's perceptions like a dream.

Actresses were not real women, but fabrications of an
insipid lie ... pawns of an industry wherein powerful
men exerted their male dominance while beating the
American public into a farcical frenzy and amassing
untold wealth. Phantasms of what the female could or
should be—regal and dominant in public, but lusty
whores in bed.

What sadness I felt. What disappointment as I matured and realized that these fantasies were dispelled by
the harsh realism of the adult mind, rendering the female
incapable of guiltless lust. What devastation as that reality
crept over me, that this wild animalistic verve was absent
in real women.

This may be my greatest failing and (if there is any
justification for what I have done) my greatest defense.
Try as I will, I cannot shuck off the expectations of those
innocent days of youth. They gave me the will to hope that
something better would someday replace my painful and
pathetic existence. I believed in the power of love and
sexual delight. I expected, when I matured to manhood,

to find that *joie de vivre* in the women I met. It did not happen. It does not exist. It was a bad joke played by a hollow society on an unsuspecting child.

Then I met a living, breathing personification of all those traits I had spent a lifetime longing for. The embodiment of everything female and fine. There was no guile in her Heartland upbringing, no deceit in her dealings with others. Oh, she was harried and over-worked—at times hostile or short. But never malicious. Even at her worst, the intrinsic decency and concern for others came through like a beacon to the weary mariner.

The light in her green eyes warmed my soul. The reflections from her rosewood hair formed the aura of a saint. And when she smiled at me, my red world of pain and despair dissolved into a placid blue.

So I decided to make her my next, and final love. It will be the pinnacle of my life. Perhaps I will at last find peace.

In any event, Mr. Colunga, by the time you read this my mission may be accomplished. If not, it will happen soon. I wish you the best, and hope we meet in another life.

"You blue-balled bastard!" Oscar took a deep breath and stared out the window. "Are you deliberately trying to get caught?"

In a cold sweat, he reached up to rub his pulsating temples. Then his head snapped up. "Or do you want me to prevent this one?"

Chapter 35

Oscar lunged for the phone and hit the auto-dial button for José Cruz's office in New York. As it rang, he pounded the desk, only vaguely aware of the tension in his shoulders that threatened to rip muscle from bone.

"Federal Bureau of Investigation. May I help you?"

The perky voice of the dark-haired receptionist did nothing for his mood. "This is Oscar Colunga. Gimme Cruz."

"One moment, sir."

Oscar rotated his head and tried to calm down. "Come on, Cruz. Pick it up!"

The jovial voice shattered his hysteria. "Aye, *Hijo*, what's shaking?"

"Listen, Joe, I need your help."

"Shoot."

"That manuscript I sent you for analysis?"

"What about it?"

"Do you have the results yet?"

"No. You want me to call the lab?"

"Please. And get back to me right away if they have anything."

"What's going down, Oscar?"

"I think the woman who sent it to me is going to be the killer's next victim. We've got to find her, Joe!"

"*Madre* ... I'll get right on it. You in your office?"

"Sure. You have the number?"

"Ahh ... yes. Give me a few minutes."

Oscar snarled at the dial tone and dropped the receiver in place, moving to the doorway at a near-run. Kathy seemed to sense his urgency as he called her over with a toss of his head. She sprang from her desk and followed him back into his office, closing the door behind her.

"What's wrong? You look like you've seen a ghost."

"Read this." He picked up the latest chapter and stuffed it into her hands, striding to the windows to stare out at the placid city.

An eon later Kathy looked up. "What does it mean?"

"It means he intends to kill her."

"Who?"

He wheeled around. "The woman who's been sending me this shit."

"How do you ..?"

"I just know. I saw her once, but didn't realize who it was. She has green eyes and red hair. Rosewood, he said. That means red doesn't it?"

She nodded numbly. "And he sent you this announcement?"

"Why not? I have no way of getting to him. He has all the time in the world."

Kathy's wide eyes were fixed on him. "What are you going to do?"

Oscar slumped into his chair and stared at his large hands. "I don't know, Kathy. Can you suggest anything?"

"Well, there are books in the library that list publishers and agents. We could call around in New York to see if anyone recognizes her description."

"Get them."

"They're reference books. I'll have to make copies."

"Screw the copies. Bring the damn books!"

Kathy dashed out, leaving Oscar staring at the phone in a sweat. "Come on, Cruz!" He ripped off his tie and loosened his shirt several buttons as he surged into the outer office. "Where's Bart?"

Stan Zelinski looked up in surprise. "He went over to records."

"Get him back up here. And call Operations. They have a trooper named Sam Layton. I want him on the phone within five minutes. If he's writing a ticket, I'll pay for it."

Oscar spun around and dived for the phone. "Yeah?"

"It's José, *Hijo*. I just spoke with the lab. No joy on a positive ID, but they did make up a list of New York publishers and agents most likely to handle this kind of novel."

"Fax me a copy."

"All right, but do you have enough manpower?"

"I'll let you know when I've seen the list. You'll be in your office?"

"I won't budge."

He dropped the phone and bellowed. "Stan? Have you found Layton?"

"Holding on line two."

He brought the receiver up and punched the button. "Sam?"

"Yes, Lieutenant."

"You remember the woman with red hair and green eyes up at Nepaug?"

"I'll never forget her."

"I need to find her. Can you think of anything that might help?"

"Well, the car was rather unusual—a Miata, I believe. And it was licensed in New York."

"Good. That might cut the field a little."

"Maybe more than you think."

"What do you mean?"

"It was a rental, and you know the exact date."

Oscar's fingernails dug into his palm as he waited for the next connection. He glanced up at the clock. He had been at it for an hour and this was only the twelfth call. He leafed through his portion of the FBI list, estimating how long it would take to get through it. For a moment he scanned the outer office, now a flurry of activity like a telephone sales office as his people worked their lists.

"Editorial."

He swung back around. "Yes. This is Lieutenant Oscar Colunga of the Connecticut State Police. I'm trying to locate an editor who may work for you. I don't know her name, but she has green eyes and red hair."

The soft female voice responded, "I'm sorry, sir. We don't have an editor like that."

"How long have you been with the company?"

"Nearly two years."

"Do you know of anyone who fits that description?"

"I'm sorry, no. Would you like me to ask around?"

"I would be eternally grateful. Please call me at the following number. It's extremely urgent."

He repeated the number for her and moved his ruler down to the next line as Kathy burst into the room.

"We may have gotten lucky, Oscar. I just talked to an editor who thinks she knows our woman ... says she works for Gladiator Press." She glanced at the note in her hand. "Her name is Megan Roarke."

His eyes flitted to the rental car list. "It's a match!" He took the paper from her hand, and dialed frantically. "Please connect me with editorial."

He looked up at Kathy, afraid to let hope show on his face. "This is Lieutenant Oscar Colunga with the Connecticut State Police. I'm trying to locate your editor, Megan Roarke. It's most urgent."

His heart stopped until she spoke. "I don't think Megan's in today, but I could connect you with her assistant ..."

"If you would." Again he waited, feeling his life was ebbing away with each second.

"Heather Bounton. May I help you?"

"I hope so, Heather. I need to speak with Megan Roarke immediately. Is she there?"

"I'm sorry. Who is calling, please?"

"I'm a police officer from Connecticut."

"Your name?"

"Colunga. Lieutenant Oscar Colunga."

She took her time writing it down, asking for the spelling of his last name. "Well, Meg isn't here. She went to look at a house she is thinking of buying."

"Young lady, I must reach her!"

"I'm sorry. You can't reach her right now. She's on her way up to Connecticut."

Oscar jerked, as if hit in the mouth. "On her way to Connecticut?"

"That's right."

"Tell me how to find her."

Heather expelled a gust of air, plying her trade as interference runner. "You can't find her. She's on the road."

Oscar covered the receiver. "She's on her way to look at a house ... in Connecticut. How can we find her?"

Kathy's eyes widened. "Through her realtor?"

He dropped his hand. "Do you know who her realtor is?"

"Why, yes." Heather's surprise showed through her decorum. "It's in my log. Would you like the number?"

"Certainly!" He waited, straining every fiber of his being to avoid the shout that wanted to erupt from his gut.

She told him the number, and then said, "It's in a place called Pleasant Valley."

"Thanks." Oscar smashed the cradle button and dialed

the number, suddenly aware that his blood pressure was too high to measure with standard equipment. "Dammit, pick up the phone!"

"Michael Duggan speaking."

"Mr. Duggan, this is Lieutenant Oscar Colunga of the Connecticut State Police. I need some information, and I need it now!"

The friendly voice faltered. "Of course. What can I do for you?"

"You have a client from New York. Megan Roarke."

"Ah, yes. A lovely lass."

"I understand she's on her way to look at a house you're selling."

"Quite right. In fact, one of my agents just left to meet her at the property."

"Thank God."

"I beg your pardon."

"Is there a phone at the house?"

"It's out of service. Is something wrong?"

"Maybe. Is there any way you can reach your agent?"

"She has a cell phone. Do you want me to call her?"

"Yes! Tell her to get Megan Roarke back to your office."

"Hang on." An aeon passed before Duggan came back on the line. "I can't seem to raise her." The tension was contagious and Duggan began to react. "Do you want me to go up there?"

"No! I need you to lead me in when we get there. Give me directions to your office." He scribbled the map onto a yellow sheet, and nodded to Kathy. "Get me a chopper, and get Cruz on the line."

"What?"

"Sorry, Mr. Duggan. I was talking to someone else. Notify your local police to get someone to that house immediately, and stay put until I arrive. Understand?"

"Yes, sir. I'll be waiting for you."

Oscar slammed the phone down and stared at it. Ten seconds later, it went off. "Yeah?"

Kathy nodded across the room. "It's me, Chief. The helicopter is on its way, and José Cruz is holding on line four."

He hit the button. "Joe?"

"Yes, Oscar."

"I've found her. She's looking at a house in Connecticut. You want in on this?"

"*Seguro!*"

"Meet me at Duggan's Realty in Pleasant Valley, Connecticut. Three miles east of Winsted on Highway 44, follow 318 north. It's about a mile in."

"I'm on my way."

Oscar dropped the phone and charged into the outer office. "Kathy, when will that chopper be here?"

"Five or ten minutes."

"Damn!"

Chapter 36

The road ahead twisted pleasantly through the overhanging branches that nearly touched at places to form a darkened tunnel. Megan exerted gentle pressure on the accelerator, taking in the placid beauty of the world passing into oblivion at the edges of her vision. The drive seemed longer now, a strange effect since it was only the second time she had made it.

Even so, the country in her reacted to the display of light and shadow, the insurgence of Nature's irresistible pull. She winced at the error in judgement that had planted her in New York City, and wished she had the guts to quit and leave it all behind—to write, to dream of that ethereal goal that would free her soul. Her inheritance was far greater than she could have imagined. How irrational could she afford to be in the pursuit of peace?

Megan recognized the fear of making another bad decision. Was it wise to saddle herself with this expensive obligation? Even if money proved to be no object, she would be tying herself down to a fixed facility, inhibiting her mobility ... reducing her options personally and professionally. When she first saw the house it seemed like a living dream, but she had strong reservations now. No wonder Joan Kirtch had to plead with her to take a second look.

A blaring horn snapped the scene into focus. Drifting

around a gentle curve, she was a foot across the center line. The oncoming car swerved onto the narrow shoulder, dust and gravel spurting from its undercarriage. She jerked the steering wheel to the right amid a cacophony of screeching rubber and high-pitched oaths from the passing driver.

She squared the car away and sat up straighter, grasping the wheel with both hands as she passed a sedan parked on the right side of the narrow pike, a scant six inches off the road.

Rounding the next curve, Megan recognized the mailbox and steep driveway. "Okay. Let's see if a two-wheel-drive can make it." She made the turn at fifteen MPH and sped up the slope. Surging over the crest, she locked the brakes and came to rest like a cat clinging to a screen door.

"Well, that was exciting." She shut off the engine and walked toward the long stairway, noting the realtor's 4X4 sitting in the shadow of the great deck. At the top, she placed her hands on the rail and leaned heavily, drinking in the view—knowing it was the last time she would see it.

Finally, she turned and walked across the deck to the front door, dreading the job before her. She hardly knew Joan Kirtch and certainly didn't owe her anything, but it was always distasteful to say no to another's wishes, especially when they had so much at stake.

Megan opened the door and walked into the mammoth room. "Hello! Joan? Are you here?"

She was met with stony silence. "Joan?" She ambled through the rear door and scanned the kitchen and dining room. They sat empty and silent, as if permanently abandoned, shrouded in a gloomy mist created by the sun's rays filtering through a light scattering of dust.

Megan turned and headed up the stairs to the second level. "Joan? Where are you?"

She gripped the handrail tightly, unsteady on her feet. The silence was oppressive and she did not sense the presence of another. No cough or creak of floorboards, no hint of human breath. Even the sound of her own gentle breathing seemed to echo from the walls and glass.

Megan crept to the doorway of the large master bedroom and peered inside, feeling like a trespasser venturing into someone's private and personal domain, expecting a loud challenge at any moment. The drapes were drawn, the room dark in spite of sunlight that forced its way in around the edges.

"Joan?" She took two paces toward the dressing room on her right and then stopped with a shudder. Slowly her head came around, and she was gripped with apprehension at the sight of a woman's boot projecting from the far side of the bed.

She steeled herself and moved haltingly around the bed, kneeling on it to stare down at the crumpled body. "Joan! What's wrong?"

There was no hint of movement ... no sign of life. Megan reached out to shake her shoulder and then pulled away, covering her mouth with her hand as she stared at the dark red gash around her throat.

"My God!" The next few seconds were lost to her numbed mind as her automatic responses took over. She backed off the bed and toward the door, realization and panic beginning to set in.

Then she sensed it ... another presence in the room. Instinct spun her around to face the man standing in the dressing-room doorway. He smiled. "Good afternoon, Meg."

For an eternity her eyes stared blindly, her mouth too dry to speak. At last, the words rasped through her constricted throat. "What are you doing here?"

"Oh, I heard you were coming up and thought I'd like to see the place."

"How did you find it?"

"Simple. I asked your realtor to show it to me a few days ago."

"My realtor ..." Megan's eyes strayed to the lifeless form on the floor. "Is she dead?"

"Quite."

"What happened to her?"

"Sorry to say, I murdered her."

She turned back to him. "You can't be serious."

He nodded.

"Why?"

He took a step forward. "She was in the way. I had to eliminate her so we could finally have our time together."

"Our time together? What are you talking about?"

"Oh, Meg. You disappoint me."

Megan's body shook and her vision clouded. She knew she was about to pass out. With a shriek, she spun around and ran for the door. He caught her well inside and threw her down on the bed. She rolled over and scrambled to the head, jerking one of the bed lamps from its resting place. With the added strength of adrenaline, she found her feet and brandished the lamp like a club.

"Get out of here and leave me alone."

He nodded and stood his ground. "Most impressive, Meg, but I can't let you go. I went to so much trouble to set up this event."

"What do you mean?"

"All that writing I did to keep you upset for so long ... to set the stage with fear."

She stared at him, comprehension slowly creeping across her face. "It was you ..."

"Yes. And I must say I was delighted by the effect my work had on you. Instead of one brief encounter, I was able to feed off it for months." He smiled, greatly pleased with himself. "I think it may be the most clever idea I ever came up with."

"You're crazy."

"Many have said that."

"You won't do to me what you did with the others."

Megan surged forward and took a mighty swing with the lamp. He sidestepped and diverted the blow, catching her in the chest with a hard right. She sagged to her knees in debilitating pain, clutching at her heart. Moments later she sank to the floor unconscious.

Megan awoke to the pain in her sternum, taking several seconds to remember where she was. She tried to bring her hand to her head, but was unable to move. Panic seized her again as she realized that she was naked and tied spread-eagle to the bed. She opened her eyes to see him straddling a backward chair on the edge of the bed to her left, running his eyes over her body. She pulled at the ropes with all her strength, but the unyielding bonds cut into her wrists and ankles.

He looked into her eyes with a reassuring smile. "Now, now. Don't fight it. I've tied you so that the ropes will tighten and cut off your circulation if you struggle." He arose and moved around the bed to loosen the bonds. "I'll help you this one time since you didn't know. But if you do it again, too bad."

Megan closed her eyes and lay still, thoughts of torture, pain, and humiliation jumbled together in her brain—a curtain of fear that shut off her normal rationality. She fought to clear her mind.

"What are you going to do to me?"

"Same as the others. You are going to invite me to make love to you."

She glared at him in defiance. "Never!"

"How can you be so sure?"

"Because I wouldn't give you the satisfaction ... and I know it won't save me."

"True, but the method of your demise is at my discretion.

It can be quick and painless, or quite horrible. And you may have the option of living. I'll take you home with me—if you're a good girl."

He lifted a metal attaché case to the bed and opened it. "You see? I have brought some interesting devices for us to play with."

Megan lifted her head and tried to see into it, aware for the first time that her panties were still in place. "Are you going to threaten me with hanging or electrocution?"

"Oh, no. You've seen all of that before. I've thought up a much more creative method for you." He produced a stick of explosive with a long coil of green fuse attached.

"What are you going to do? Blow my head off?" A wave of sick fear washed over her as she watched him squeeze a heavy fluid from a tube and spread it over the stick.

"Nothing so mundane." He pulled a knife from the case and moved around to kneel between her legs.

She watched in horror as he poked a small hole in her underpants and threaded the fuse through it. Then she convulsed at the pain as the explosive was forced inside her and her panties pulled up to hold it in place.

"You insane, pathetic bastard! How can you do these things?"

He returned to his chair, holding the fuse's end before her eyes. "You misjudge me. I don't want to see you blown apart. Hell, Meg, I love you. All you have to do is return that love, and I'll not harm a hair on your head." He lit the fuse and dropped it on the floor. "Fifteen minutes, exactly. That's all you have."

"You don't have that long. They'll be looking for me."

"Not even a good try, Meg. Realtors are usually out with clients for hours. We have lots of time." He took out a long silk scarf and tied it around her eyes. "But I think the effect will be better if you don't know how much time is left on the fuse."

Megan fell silent, knowing she could not reason with the madman. She heard his footsteps to her left, and the sound of the drapes being violently thrust open.

"It's a beautiful day. Too bad we can't cuddle together and look out at it like lovers. Maybe a stroll through the woods ... a far better prospect than yours."

Megan's mind was ablaze. She was experiencing deja vu. Her naked fear was being replaced by cold logic. Never had she been faced with a situation too extreme to control, but rape and murder had never been an issue. There had to be a key to survival—something he had written—something she knew about him.

Suddenly the air was shattered with the raucous sound of chopper blades. For a moment, her heart leapt at the possibility of someone coming to her rescue, but hope faded with the receding sound. He was right. Only Heather knew where she was, and Joan's people would not be concerned for at least another hour.

"We could be a couple, Meg. As free as that helicopter that just passed overhead. Anywhere you wanted to live. Anything you wanted to do with your life. It could all be yours."

The stench of burning fuse and carpet assailed her nostrils. She tested her bonds in spite of herself.

Chapter 37

Oscar hit the ground an instant before the skids did, and ran toward the low white building. A man appeared at the door, wiping his hands on a towel like a European shopkeeper. Oscar slowed and came to rest a few feet away.

"You Duggan?"

"Yes. You the policeman who called?"

"Right. Where is the place?"

"Just over the ridge. I tried to call my agent again, but there was no response. You want me to drive you there?"

"No. We'll take the chopper, but I'm supposed to meet an FBI agent here."

"Suit yourself. Want a cup of coffee while you wait?"

Oscar stared at the corpulent middle-aged man, a panoply of emotion washing over him. Didn't he understand the danger here? Wouldn't it be great to do a day's work without fear of losing a human life?

"There isn't time!" Oscar wanted to grab him by the neck and shake him. "There isn't time. We have to go."

Duggan recoiled. "Take it easy, young fella. I'll get you there."

Oscar started to herd Duggan to his bird, but spun around. The blue and white FBI helicopter appeared behind its sound, skimming over the trees like a soaring hawk. He waved it to earth and ran forward before it touched down, dragging

Duggan along by the sleeve.

José Cruz threw open the door and pulled them inside. "Where to?"

Duggan, gasping from the brief exertion, nodded toward the north and shouted over the blades. "That way. Follow the road about two miles."

José turned around. "How you doing?"

Oscar rocked back and forth in the rear seat. "I couldn't save Julia, and now ..."

"Take it easy, *Hijo*. We're only two minutes away." He turned to the handsome black pilot. "Don't spare the fuel, Paul."

With a sickening jar the chopper lifted and the blades rotated forward at maximum angle. Oscar closed his eyes, remembering the last time he had looked on the face of evil– that winter day in Arizona.

Down the hill from the rocky crest, the horse's ears framing this humanoid thing like a gun sight–Oscar's quarry scrambling on hands and knees, crawling on its belly, turning like a swimmer in a pool to watch the avenging specter bound to exact the toll for violation of Nature's law.

Murder. Not for food or survival. Nor for revenge or protection of family or land, but for the sake of one man's sociopathic distortion, his defective brain putting him above the law of civilized humans ... outside its protection, to be shot on sight like a venomous snake or rabid dog.

The horse snorted and bucked as the apparition scrambled up a steep gravel bed toward the cool dark bosom of the trees, then lost footing and plummeted downward, struggling to extract the weapon inside his coat.

The sharp crack of a 30-30 rifle echoed from impartial mountains. In the spring, a rotting heap was found by hunters–another innocent victim of a senseless accident.

***

Oscar ripped the 9MM automatic from his shoulder holster and worked the slide.

Cruz eyed him. "You sure about this?"

"I know he's there. I can feel him."

"Don't get trigger-happy on me, *Hijo*." Cruz pulled his 357 and checked the cylinders. "We need him alive. There is much to answer for."

"He's as safe as a babe in its mother's arms."

"Listen to me, Oscar. This is not the man who killed your daughter. No matter what he has done, he's entitled to a fair trial. Agreed?"

"May he live to be a hundred."

Chapter 38

Now he sat next to her, groping her breasts, fingernails running along the subtle mark of her rib cage ... kissing her sensitive stomach and the inside of her thighs.

Megan lay on the bed trembling, not from passion as a man's caress should bring, but fear and loathing. How had she ever found excitement in the touch of the male animal, and how could she ever allow it again? She quivered and cried out. How slight the difference between human sexuality and bestiality?

For a moment, a smile flitted across her face—some absurd irony clutching at what was left of her sanity, realizing that she would never need to face that question. She was dead, and if by some cruel twist of fate she should physically survive, her soul had died already. Now she wished he had left the blindfold on. At least she would not have to look upon his arrogant self-delusion.

"You know the words, don't you Meg?" His voice was calm and dry, like a doctor conducting an exam. "Say them."

"No."

"You want to lie here until it goes off? You won't do anything to save yourself?"

Her panic had faded into resignation. "You've already ruined me. I don't care to live."

"Now Meg, everyone wants to live. Besides, how bad could it be? I'm a reasonable man."

Megan sneered at him, "Reasonable man? You're insane."
She forced herself to meet his eyes. "How can you do this to
another human being? Have you no sense of ..." She broke
down and cried.

He brushed the tears from her cheeks and tried to kiss
her, but she jerked her head sharply to the side. "No! Don't
touch me, you fucking animal."

He tried to turn her head ... pull her lips to his, but
suddenly stiffened, surprise showing in his face as if he had
been stabbed. He sprang erect and sat on the edge of the bed
in thought.

She studied his profile, doubting her ability to assess his
emotion. He seemed to be afraid. "What?" She shuddered at
her instinctive response to be concerned for him.

He turned slowly to meet her gaze. "I just realized. That
was an FBI helicopter that went over a few minutes ago." He
launched himself to his feet and closed the metal case. "Sorry,
Meg. And you will never know how sorry I am. But I can't take
the chance that they are up here looking for you ... or me."

Megan heard the words form in her throat, unable to
suppress the absurdity that spilled out. "They couldn't know
you are here."

"I can't risk it." He looked at the fuse, now creeping onto
the bedspread. "You only have a few minutes. See you in
another life."

"No!" she cried out in shock. "You can't leave me like
this."

He was gone. Now she understood her irrational reaction. As insane as he was, he was her only hope. She lifted her
head and stared. The flame was now clearly visible, and a
wisp of smoke curled up from the burning bedclothes between her legs. She pushed with the instinct of a woman in
labor, eyes wide at the vision of destruction should it explode
inside her. She grasped the ropes on her wrists and pulled
furiously. Her right leg broke free.

***

"There!" Duggan leaned forward and pointed over the pilot's shoulder. "That's the house." His voice was shrill and trembling. He had been infected by the tension around him, now sensing the danger to his employee and friend. "Can you set it down in the clearing in front?"

"It'll be tight. Hang on." Paul Jones pulled the stick back to kill their velocity and came to a hover over the small parking area.

Oscar was scanning the house for signs of life when the front windows blew out. He stared in horror as the entire plane of glass erupted and spilled out like a chilling waterfall, crashing to the deck in slow motion under the relentless influence of gravity.

An instant later the shock wave struck, and the helicopter pitched dangerously to the side. Paul pushed the stick over hard as the skids swung back underneath, clipping treetops with a frightening fusillade of snapping branches.

For a moment Oscar knew they would crash. Then all went quiet and the helicopter stabilized. The four men gaped at the house, now lying straight ahead, as the last few slivers bounced on the deck like tiny prisms.

Seconds dragged by until José found his speech. "Set her down, Paul. Let's go see if there's anything left."

Chapter 39

Diplomas and plaques littered the wall behind Dr. Andrew Mather, head of psychiatry for the Fairlawn Medical Center outside New Britain. The good doctor had taken a phone call, and now Oscar fought to avoid impatience as he observed the intelligent features and athletic body of the man who would recover Megan Roarke's mind.

With a slight shrug he allowed his gaze to drift through the large windows to the manicured grounds. The view was somewhat obscured by snowball bushes that had grown to enormous size just outside the window. Above and beyond, sunlight danced from the fluttering leaves of large poplars lining the driveway. And beyond that was the real world, where most people went about their lives filled with love and hope, while a few managed to defile the dignity of Man by allowing perverted thoughts to spill into reality.

Oscar pawed his bleary eyes. He had not slept in two days, driven by the haunting realization that he had come within minutes of saving Megan, only to lose her to the dark side. Could he have done better? Perhaps worked a little harder or been a little smarter? Would it have made the difference? Possibly. But there was no point in castigating himself. It would only interfere with his course, confuse his mind, and detract from his resolve. The bastard who did this had to be tracked down—removed from the society of rational human beings forever, by whatever means required. He snapped around at the distinctive sound of the receiver settling into its cradle. The psychiatrist gave an amiable nod. "Sorry for the interruption. It was an important call ... a large endowment that could mean a lot to our work here."

Oscar grunted. "No problem, but I am most anxious to know how Megan is."

Mather contemplated the stocky policeman who sat clutching a battered cowboy hat. "Are you conversant with the field of psychology, Lieutenant Colunga?"

"Not very ... a few seminars here and there, mainly in conjunction with my work."

"All right." Mather locked his hands behind his head and leaned back. "Megan's mind seems to have found a way to protect itself from the trauma she suffered—like a switch that shut it down, probably at the moment she thought she was going to die. The closest I can come to a description of her condition is catatonia." He paused in thought. "I don't know how extensive the damage is yet, if she's processing sensory input for example. We're trying to determine that now."

"How badly was she injured by the blast?"

"Oh, physically she's fine. Eardrums are intact, eyes clear. As far as we can tell there is no permanent damage. But mentally, she's in a comatose state."

Oscar frowned. "How long do you think it will be before I can talk to her?"

"I don't know, and I think you need to prepare yourself for the possibility that it may be some time." Mather slumped forward onto the desk, meeting Oscar's distressed gaze. "As I said, her condition is not one we have dealt with before, and we are moving slowly to define the proper treatment."

Oscar shifted in his chair. "In other words, you don't know how to bring her out of it."

Mather stared at the desk. "I'm afraid you are correct."

"Listen, Doc, I need her. She can identify a man who's killed dozens of women. This bastard selected her and stalked her for months, finally catching her in a vulnerable place, and murdering another woman in the process. I know what this asshole does to women, and I want him off the streets."

"I appreciate your objective and your commitment, but I cannot rush her treatment. We may lose her entirely. Do you want to risk that?"

"Of course not." Oscar choked off his anger. "Is there anything I can do?"

Mather seemed to brighten. "Yes, I believe there is. What can you tell me about the events leading up to her trauma?"

"More than you want to know." Oscar's head shook ponderously. "I have a report for you in my case, but I can give you the highlights."

"Please do."

Oscar twisted his wedding ring and collected his thoughts. "Megan works for Gladiator Press in Manhattan. Awhile ago, she began to receive chapters of a novel about a serial killer, told through the eyes of the murderer. She could see common threads between his writing and some of the cases we're currently working on, and she called me twice to ask questions about our investigation."

"She spoke to you, personally?"

"Yes. Then she sent me a copy of what she had, the first eight chapters, telling about murders in the range of eight to fifteen years ago—maybe more."

"And this novel matched actual cases?"

"Yes. The writer had intimate knowledge of certain details. So we started a search for Megan, assuming she knew who the author was. Then I got a new chapter in the mail about a murder only a few weeks old, and a subsequent one where he told me about his intent to abduct Megan."

"Addressed to you?"

"Yes."

Mather whistled. "How did he know about you?"

"I don't know, but he did. In the last chapter he called me by name."

Dr. Mather stared in wonder. "That is an incredible story. Do you think Megan realized she was in communication with a murderer?"

"I'm almost certain she did at some point."

"So we can assume she was suffering considerable anxiety for a period of time."

Oscar glanced at the ceiling. "Depending when she caught on, it could be as much as three months."

"And was this writing graphic? Violent?"

"Very. Specific details on how he forced his will upon his victims, and how he murdered them—even cut the head off one and kept it because he 'loved her so much.' The most disturbing thing was his obvious insanity while he was doing it."

"No wonder her mind shut down. It's bad enough to be attacked by someone off the street ... when you have a chance of survival. But if she knew this man's psychosis ..." He paused. "Can you imagine the trauma when she realized she had become his victim?"

"No, I can't."

"You're right. Nobody could." Mather gazed at him. "That explains a lot, but specifically what did he do to her?"

"It's not a pretty picture."

Mather gave him a reproving nod. "I've been in this business for twenty years, and I've heard or seen things beyond belief."

"Well, he claims he has too much respect for women to rape them. They have to invite him. One girl, he stood on a block of ice with a noose around her neck. He always arranges something that will give them time to come around."

"And in Megan's case?"

"He inserted a stick of dynamite into her ..."

"Into her vagina?"

"Yes, with a slow-burning fuse."

"Hmm. Fits his psychosis. Phallic. A sexual insult."

Oscar stared at the psychiatrist. "That's it? 'Fits his psychosis'?"

"I'm sorry. We tend to become emotionally anesthetized after a while, just as you might get used to seeing dead bodies." Mather looked away toward the fresh world outside the windows. "Tell me why she wasn't killed. Did he relent at the last minute?"

"No. He fled before we arrived on the scene, leaving her there to die ... to be blown apart." Oscar stopped, considering his options. "If I tell you the rest, it must be in strictest confidence. Should this information leak out, it may compromise our case when we come to trial."

"It will not leave this room."

Oscar took a deep breath and expelled it slowly. "He had her tied down on the bed, undressed except for her underpants. He poked a hole in them for the fuse and pulled them up to hold the stick in place. When the fuse reached the flimsy material, it vaporized, allowing her to eject the explosive. She had pulled her right leg free, and managed to kick it off the bed an instant before it blew. It didn't even reach the floor. But it was beyond the lip of the mattress, and that was enough."

"Good God!" Mather arose and edged toward the window. He stood there gazing out for some time. "Weeks or months of intellectual fear, then a fraction of a second from a terrible death. No wonder her mind shut down." He turned back. "Thank you for leveling with me. It may help in her treatment, but knowing what trauma she suffered is most disconcerting."

"Yeah. Disconcerting." Oscar stood up, his mass seeming infinite. "May I see her now?"

Mather moved forward and clapped him on the shoulder. "Of course." He nudged Oscar in the direction of the door. "You realize that she probably won't react to you, but I'm glad to have you in her corner."

Oscar fell in alongside him and they trudged silently down the long corridor to the ward. He nodded to the state trooper sitting outside the door, and followed the doctor into the room. There he saw the inert form of the woman he had come to care about, looking more like a corpse lying in state than the beauty he had seen on that warm Connecticut afternoon. Her hair had been cut short, and was snarled and matted with sweat. The striking green eyes stared, half open, at the ceiling.

"*Madre de Dios.* Is she suffering?"

"We don't know." The doctor drew Oscar to the bedside and leaned over her. "Megan, I've brought a friend. Lieutenant Colunga of the State Police. He's going to find the man who did this to you."

Oscar watched in awed anticipation. For an instant, he thought he saw her lips quiver, but the moment passed with no further sign of movement.

Mather lifted an eyedropper from a bottle on the nightstand and carefully administered droplets to moisten her eyes. He watched her for some time and finally turned to the policeman. "Sorry. I had hoped that your presence might solicit some response, but as you see ..."

"May I sit with her for a while?"

"Certainly. Talk to her, Lieutenant." Mather turned on his heel and left.

Oscar drew up a chair and took her hand in his. "I'm sorry, Megan. We tried to get there, but we were too late." He stared at her face, feeling inept and foolish. "I don't know if you can hear me, but I promise I'll get the man who did this to you."

Chapter 40

Dr. Andrew Mather traced the steps down the long hallway as he had thousands of times before. He glanced over at the pleasant man next to him. "It's very kind of you to come all the way up here. I wish I could tell you that Megan will be glad to see you, but I doubt she will be aware of your presence."

"I understand, and thank you for explaining her condition. I just want to see her and know there's hope. So many of her friends have asked about her over the past few days."

Mather smiled. "I know. Several have visited her already, but I'm afraid they've been distressed by her condition. I hope our discussion will make it easier for you."

"I appreciate your kindness, Doctor." He glanced down the hall. "Is that the room? The one with the police officer outside?"

"Yes. There's another policeman in with her, I believe. He comes to visit once a day."

"Really? Who?"

"A lieutenant with the state police."

"Lieutenant? Why so much interest by the police?"

Mather pulled up a few feet from the door. "Don't you know the circumstances?"

"All of a sudden, I'm not sure. I heard it was an attempted rape."

"It was, but they're afraid the man who attacked her will try to finish the job."

"Good Lord! I had no idea."

"No matter. It needn't concern you."

"You know, it might be inconsiderate to break in on this officer. Perhaps I should wait in your office until he's gone." Mather paused at the door. "Fine with me. I'll let you know when she's alone."

The man spun away down the hall as Dr. Mather pushed the door open and stole into the room.

Colunga was sitting in a steel chair next to the bed, head bent forward over the hand he gripped tenderly in his own. He glanced up, the strain showing in his sallow cheeks and bloodshot eyes.

Mather moved to him, evaluating him with a doctor's concern. "Are you all right, Lieutenant?"

"Yeah." Oscar pulled himself erect and brushed past him, calling over his shoulder. "Thanks for everything, Doc. I'll be back to see her later."

The door swung shut on silent hinges and the man approached the bed. He stood transfixed for some time. "Megan, how are you?" After a long silence, he looked up in dismay. "She doesn't seem to know me."

Mather nodded. "As I said, she has tuned out the world around her."

"I know, but I thought she might react to me."

Mather smiled reassuringly. "In all honesty, I hoped so, too. Every time someone visits, I hope it will jar her back to reality. But I'm beginning to doubt it will be that easy. It may take us weeks or months to bring her out of it. And I'm sorry to say that we may never be able to. We would like to believe that we can always ferret out complexities of the human mind, but sometimes ..."

A nurse burst into the room. "Dr. Mather. That call you've been waiting for has come through. Do you want to take it now?"

The doctor glanced over. "It is rather important. Do you mind?"

"Not at all. I'll stay with her until you return."

As the latch clicked, the man took her hand and bent down, his face only inches from hers. "Megan, it's me."

Her eyes widened and her breathing became even more erratic. Her back arched slightly and the muscles tensed in her arms, but she was unable to move. Almost imperceptibly, her lips parted and a hint of sound hissed forth.

"What did you say?" He bent his ear to her lips.

"Oh, Darling. Please make love to me."

Chapter 41

Oscar lit a smoke and leaned back, taking in the view from the low restaurant perched beside the small bay at Stonington, Connecticut. The water reflected subtle golden ribbons from gentle surface swells in the setting sun, and the air smelled fresh and damp. A squadron of sea gulls raged overhead while a pelican foraged in gentle swirling arcs over the boat channel. His eyes darted briefly to the entrancing woman on his right.

"Sitting here, looking at this beauty, I wonder what we've done to ourselves with this so-called civilization. Would we suffer as much if we were still swinging from trees?"

Rita Takamura stared at the scintillating patch of ocean. "Maybe not. But then, we probably wouldn't have many of the noble aspects of Mankind, either."

"Noble aspects? Like war? Insanity? Murder?"

"No. Like art and music ... love." She turned to stare into his eyes. "One thing I've learned from psychology. Human beings are complex. Even those with the darkest emotions and most heinous distortions have some merit—some glint of personal worth. Some spark of joy at times."

"What about our man? Does he have glints and sparks?"

"You've read his work—at times depressed, sometimes euphoric. I know it's hard to conceive of a man like this experiencing the same positive emotions we do. But in his own way, I'll bet he does."

"It is hard to conceive." Oscar snuffed out his smoke and waved at the waitress for another round of coffee. "What makes a man go crazy like this, Rita? How can he be so far removed from reality?"

She was clinical and serious. "How removed do you think he is?"

"He's insane. Mad."

"Why? Because he reacts to the pain he has suffered? Because he acts out fantasies of revenge that normal men don't?"

"Normal men don't have such fantasies."

"Oh, really? Think back to your youth. Didn't anyone ever humiliate you? The gang in the vacant lot, or some pubescent girl who made you feel like dirt?"

Oscar winced at the memories that flooded back. "Sure."

"Didn't you want to make them understand that you were an important and intelligent being, instead of the fool they made you out to be?"

"Well, yes ..."

"Did you ever think of ways to get even? Even once?"

Oscar's face went rigid. "It sounds like you're defending him."

"I'm a doctor. It's my job to defend the mentally ill. These people weren't born defective. They're a product of environment—broken homes, alcoholic parents, divorce, child abuse, poverty, incest. Given a different path, most of them would be as normal as you or I."

He stared into his coffee for some time. "But this guy isn't normal, and I have a feeling we'll have to wallow in his insanity to find him."

Rita sat back and dropped her hands into her lap. "We? Have I been enlisted by the police?"

"You said you wanted to help that first day I came to your house."

"But we weren't certain we were faced with a genuine

murderer then. I will help, if you can guarantee to keep me out of the action."

"You have my word." Oscar beamed as the waitress refilled their cups. "How do we go about it?"

Rita took a fleeting glance at the darkening ocean and sighed. "I'll need everything you have in your files. Past victims, possible victims, what you've uncovered so far ..." She took a sip of coffee and reached for the sugar. "But even if I profile him dead on, it won't tell you who he is or where he is."

"Rita, we're batting zero right now. I've got to get a lot of balls in the air, hoping one will come down in fair territory."

Her exquisite features hardened. "And you want me to be one of your balls."

"Yes."

"Very well." She pushed the coffee cup back. "But enough of this wretched brew. Let's walk through town."

Oscar smiled for the first time in days. "With all that's going down, you expect me to stroll idly through a picturesque place with a beautiful woman?"

"Um-hmm."

"Good idea." He drew his wallet and plunked down several bills. "Ready?"

"Yes." She arose and led the way toward the door. Outside, she took his arm and leaned against him with the slight pressure her weight would allow. "It is a lovely night, isn't it?"

Oscar rolled his head up to gaze at the emerging stars. "A lovely night ... and a lovely woman. How can I be so lucky?"

"Clean living?"

"Does that mean no fun?"

"Umm," she purred. "I'm afraid it does. And I'm afraid I'm guilty of the same thing."

They climbed the stairs that led up to the quaint main street where they had left the car. Rita's hand suddenly tightened around his wrist.

"Tell me about her, Oscar."

"Who?"

"Megan Roarke."

His throat went dry. "Megan? I don't know much about her."

"I'll bet you know more than you think. She was an editor?"

"She is an editor."

"Sorry. I didn't mean to speak in the past tense." Rita fell silent for a few paces. "Is she pretty?"

"Very."

"And you care for her?"

"Yes."

"Why?"

"Why not? She's a human being."

"Yes, but is there more to it? Are you taking this personally?"

Oscar stopped and gazed down the street. "I failed her."

"It's not your fault."

"Yes, it is. When the chips were down, we found her in a matter of hours. If only I'd tried a week earlier ... a few minutes earlier."

"You didn't have a description before that. What were you supposed to do? Call up everybody in the publishing industry and ask if they had a female editor?"

Oscar shook his head. "There must have been some key ... something I could have used to reach her."

Rita disengaged her arm and turned to look up into his dark eyes. "And so you blame yourself."

Oscar stood awkwardly with no place for his hands. "Who else?"

"Listen, you did nothing to contribute to this man's psychosis. You did not set him upon her. It was a miracle that you came as close as you did."

"Still ..."

Rita turned away, walking hurriedly toward the car. "Please take me home."

Oscar glanced around and quickened his pace. He knew very little about women, but anger had to be met head on. "Are you upset with me?"

She spun around and looked at him through her tears. "Yes."

"Why?"

"Because you are so sad." The diminutive woman raised up on her toes and kissed him lightly on the mouth. "Let's go home. Whatever your specters are, nothing will happen to make them worse before the dawn. Tonight you will sleep on a clean, soft pillow."

Chapter 42

Oscar sat in Dr. Mather's office, talking to himself. Every wasted minute tore a piece of his soul away. He had developed a constant muscle spasm in his back, compounded and sustained by the fact that he wasn't sleeping well. When he closed his eyes, past tragedy played across his mind and he lay awake in dread of tragedies to come.

He gazed out the large windows at the pristine grounds, momentarily fascinated by great rooster tails of water that spurted from the many sprinkler heads. There should have been some pleasure in that, like he used to feel when he found running water in the desert. But there was no pleasure in his life now. He was a man without family ... a dull man at best, driven by some dark obsession that no one seemed to understand.

Even the night he'd shared Rita Takamura's bed was filled with tension and apprehension. Sensing his pain, she had taken it in stride, but Oscar was embarrassed. He was not himself, and it wasn't fair to anyone around him, especially to the woman who had offered consolation.

He wheeled around as the door burst open and Dr. Mather blew into the room. "Afternoon, Doc."

"Good afternoon, Lieutenant." He hurried to his desk and plunked down a pile of legal papers, sitting down amidst an aura of confusion. "The paperwork required for a simple grant can be staggering."

Oscar smiled weakly. "I hope you get it."

Mather folded his hands on the desk. "Sorry to be so caught up with our problems. I assume you're here to see Megan."

"Yes and no."

The doctor's eyebrows lifted. "Yes and no?"

"I'm very concerned about Megan's safety."

"Oh? Why so?"

"Because I become more certain every day that her assailant knows her—may even be a close friend or associate. If so, he probably knows where she is."

"Sounds highly probable. But you have her guarded twenty-four hours a day."

"True, but there are ways around that."

"Like what?"

"A diversion that gets the guard off the door. Stealing in through the windows. Poisoning her medication during a visit. I assure you, if he wants to get to her, he will."

"Why would he still need to kill her?"

"I'm certain she knows who our killer is. If so, she'll finger him the moment she comes out of it. He can't afford to risk that."

Mather nodded. "So, what do you propose?"

"I want to move her to another facility—quietly, with no fanfare and no record."

"Lieutenant Colunga, that would be the worst thing you could do."

"Why?"

"Because we have one of the finest staffs in America. Her prospects for recovery are far better here than they would be elsewhere."

Oscar looked at him dryly, too tired for emotion. "Her prospects for recovery are zero, if she's dead."

"I believe you are exaggerating the risk."

"Listen, Dr. Mather, I'd rather leave her under your care. But ..."

"No buts about it. I am her physician, and I forbid it!"

Oscar arose, pulling a sealed envelope out of his breast pocket. "Sorry, Doc. It's done." He tossed the envelope across the desk. "I have authorization from her parents. I have an ambulance waiting out front with qualified personnel on board. And I have a court order. Please see to her immediate release."

Chapter 43

Dr. Clarence Hubble pulled the tray out and hesitated, his left hand on the sheet that covered the body, his wizened blue eyes playing across Oscar's face. "Are you ready, Lieutenant?"

Oscar nodded, weak in the knees, the scene identical to that day long ago when it was his own daughter on the slab in Phoenix. The sheet fell away and he took a deep breath, forcing himself to scan the form outlined by the shiny metal surface beneath.

Wysper's skin was pallid and gray with random blotches of brown and black induced by contact with the soil she was buried in. Her skin had dried and folded into itself in deep crevices as the once supple tissue was consumed by maggots and burrowing things and bacteria from her own body. Her state of decay was far more appalling than the dried bones and leather of other corpses he had viewed during this hateful case.

Made up for a horror movie, he expected her to rise up and reach out to him at any moment. Oscar spun away and walked around the end of the table, shoving his hands into his pockets against the cold air that clutched at his mind.

"Will you be able to learn anything useful from an autopsy?"

The aging medical examiner brushed a shock of white hair from his broad forehead and returned Oscar's gaze. "You might be surprised. Look here."

Oscar stole a quick glance. "Strangled?"

Hubble nodded.

"Anything else?"

"Well, her bonds were apparently metal." He pointed to her ankles. "You see these thin bruises?"

Oscar moved down for a closer look. "Looks like ordinary prison manacles."

"Yes, I'd say."

"And her wrists?"

"They were chained together." Hubble lifted the hand nearest Oscar. "You can see the bruises where some of the links cut in."

Oscar bent down to inspect them. "Yes. A small chain. Have you measured the links?"

"Three-eighths to one-half inch ... fairly small but still very sturdy."

"And how was it secured?"

Hubble rotated the arm. "Probably by a small lock. See this mark?"

"Um-hmm. Is there any evidence of a gag?"

"No obvious indication." Hubble lowered the arm and gazed at her head. "But I could check more closely for evidence of occlusion or taping of the mouth."

Oscar shook his head slowly. "He said that he used some sort of gag which guaranteed absolute silence, and allowed him to administer intense pain."

"Who said? The killer? Have you caught him?"

"We haven't caught him. Let's call it qualified information."

"I see." Hubble hesitated, chewing over some thought. "Actually, you may have explained something that puzzled me."

"What's that?"

He reached over and turned the head away from Oscar, pointing at a small red V on her neck. "You see this?"

The image seemed to swim. Oscar produced his reading glasses and moved in close.

Hubble pulled a sharp pencil from his coat pocket and pointed. "The reason it looks blurry is that it's made up of many such marks slightly offset. Then it shifts about a half inch to here and the pattern is repeated. There are similar marks at other locations."

Oscar straightened. "What is it?"

"We may be able to tell when we get it under the microscope." The ME gazed at him. "You want my best guess?"

"Absolutely."

"I think it's a burn."

"A burn? From a cigarette or a ..." Oscar shook his head, not liking his own idea. "What could cause a burn like that?"

"It would be pure speculation."

"Go ahead."

"Electrical—a high voltage discharge."

Chapter 44

Boston's weather was overcast and cool, summer finally yielding to the onset of autumn. Oscar left the car and climbed to the second floor of the apartment building, wishing he could spare her this interview. But he could not. Wysper's roommate was the most direct link to his quarry. Pamela Drummond had seen the killer.

He took a deep breath and rapped on the door. After some time it banged against the chain, and an inquiring eye peered through the crack.

"Miss Drummond?"

"Who wants to know?"

"Lieutenant Oscar Colunga of the Connecticut State Police." He produced his ID wallet and held it close. "My office set up an interview for this afternoon."

She scrutinized the identification, seeming to be in a daze. "Is it two o'clock already?"

"Pretty close."

"I wanna check with your office."

"All right." He pulled a card from his coat pocket and passed it through the slit. "Ask for Kathy Huntsinger."

The door closed and Oscar turned to scan the dingy patch of lawn stretching toward the parking lot. A little girl with long brown curls sat on the dried grass cooing to her dolly, unaware of evil lurking around her—not in some distant place or future time, but right here one month ago.

He shook his head, struck by the realization that this featureless landscape was the last thing Wysper ever saw as a free woman. He sensed how terrified she must have been during her brief ordeal. How did those other women cope with it for days?

Hearing the chain latch released, Oscar spun around to see a woman with long dark hair motioning him to enter. By the time he closed the door, she had already slumped onto the couch. No lamp glowed, and the drapes shut out most of the muted daylight. She wore the darkness like a mantle of despair.

He stepped across the worn green carpet, taking a seat in an armchair opposite the aging coffee table. Memories flitted across his mind—college days when he lived in furnished apartments and could move everything he owned in a station wagon.

Oscar stared at Pamela Drummond. She was thirty-two according to the file, but she looked like a thirteen-year-old girl wearing mummie's housecoat. The collar bones and tendons of her throat stood out against shadowed hollows of surrounding flesh, and her hair hadn't been tended for days. Eyes averted and shoulders hunched, she sat with clasped hands cradled between her knees and rocked back and forth. Clearly she'd been crying for some time, and the glaze in her eyes told him she was on something.

Oscar leaned forward like a concerned parent. "Are you all right, Miss Drummond?"

Her eyes seemed to float upward to meet his. "Juss fine."

"Can I get you something? A glass of water?"

"How about a glass of bourbon?"

"I think you've had enough."

"Not nearly enough." She fought to keep him in focus. "But I ran out this morning."

Oscar shifted uncomfortably. Even under the best of cir-

cumstances, it was risky for a policeman to interview a woman
one-on-one. He should have requested a policewoman from a
local agency to back him up.

"Perhaps this isn't a good time for you."

"Not a good time?" She fell back against the cushion.
"Yes, this is not a good time for me."

"May I ask what's wrong?"

"Sure." She made a grandiose gesture with her right hand.
"Isn't that what cops are supposed to do? Ask questions?"

"Then?"

"Then what?"

"What's wrong?"

"I thought you knew. My roommate was murdered."

"That's why I'm here, but you seem very troubled."

"Troubled?" She looked around with resignation. "You
could say that."

"You and Wysper were close?"

"Close?" She lunged forward. "You want to know the
truth?"

Oscar nodded.

"I hated the bitch." She brought both hands up over her
mouth. "Oops. Guess I shouldn't say that to a cop ... 'specially
now."

"You're not a suspect."

Her hands fell away and she looked painfully morose. "I
guess you shouldn't speak ill o' the dead, but she used her
friends. Wysper didn't give a damn about anyone else."

"So, why did you go out with her?"

"It's not easy for a divorcée to meet men. She introduced
me to everyone around town. Sometimes, we even had fun."
Pamela keeled over, lying in a fetal position on her right side.
"I always hoped to find a good man among her rejects."

"Did you?"

"Yes. But she took him, too. She wouldn't let another

woman win, even if she didn't want the guy. Even if she didn't like him. It was a big ego thing. Sometimes she put moves on men to get them in trouble with their dates ... or wives." She struggled up onto her elbow. "You got anything to drink?"

"Sorry."

Pamela managed to pull herself erect. "I've been on the wagon for hours. The hangover is setting in."

"How long have you been drinking?"

"Since Tuesday." She gazed at him in a fog. "How long is that?"

"Too long." Oscar frowned. "Perhaps we should reschedule this."

"No good. My bags are packed," she jabbed her index finger into the air, "and the flight blasts off at six."

"You're leaving town?"

"You got it."

"Why?"

"Don't you see? If he preferred skinny brunettes to statuesque blonds, it would be me on that slab instead of Wysper. The man knows who I am. He knows where I live!"

"You're afraid he'll come after you?"

"Bingo!"

"I've seen the police report. You didn't ID him. In fact, you have no idea who he is."

"You know that. And I know that. Does he know that?"

"So you're going into hiding."

"Where nobody can find me."

"I see." Oscar grimaced. "In that case, I would be very grateful if you could answer a few questions."

"I'll try, but would you do me one teeny-weeny favor first?"

"Name it."

"Could you fix me some toast with butter on it?" She waved to the alcove at the rear of the living room.

He hauled himself up and moved toward the kitchen. "Where's the bread?"

"I think it's out on the counter."

She had to be right. Everything was out on the counter—opened cans and cooking utensils, all with something drying in or on them. Oscar shook his head. It looked like the aftermath of a tornado, but the things he needed were in plain sight among the rubble.

"You want two, while I'm at it?"

The drunken voice floated over his shoulder. "Yes! And aspirins, over the sink."

Oscar loaded the toaster and turned. "Did you and Wysper ever go to a piano bar downtown?"

"You mean Eddy's?"

"Did you frequent more than one piano bar downtown?"

"No. Just Eddy's." She paused. "You know anything about Boston?"

"Not much."

"Funny place. The guy on your left is on welfare, and the one on your right is worth millions. Old money. New money." She was slurring heavily. "Problem is, they're all married."

"Do you know most of the men who hang out at Eddy's?"

"Wysper knew them all. She was real tight with the bartender, and she was after the piano player."

"Why?"

"I dunno. He wasn't much, but any entertainer was a big deal in her eyes. She wanted to be a movie star."

They fell silent while Oscar located the aspirin and searched for food. He found a carton of milk in the refrigerator and poured the dregs into a spotted glass from the strainer by the sink, then buttered the toast and moved over to set it in front of her.

"Thank you, Mister—what was your name?"

"Colunga."

"Thank you, Mr. Colunga." She downed the tablets with a slug of milk and shoved in a piece of toast. "You may have saved my life."

"Could be." He smiled reassuringly and sat down. "You look better already."

"I feel better." She reached for the second piece. "Now, where were we?"

Oscar pulled a small recorder from his coat pocket. "Mind if I tape this?"

"Okay by me."

He set it down and switched it on. "Did you notice a stranger at Eddy's, a few nights before Wysper disappeared? Someone who was not a regular?"

"Nobody special, but it's by the big hotels. Lots of people fall in." Pamela eyed him. "I don't understand why you're asking me about this. I already told the police everything I know."

"We're investigating similar cases in Connecticut, and I'm looking for things that wouldn't show up on a report."

She gave a satisfied nod. "Like what?"

"How about a man, sitting near the piano, who offered to share his table with you?"

"Hell, that happened all the time when they got a load of Wysper."

"This time you started to sit with him, but Wysper veered off to the bar."

"Oh, yeah." She drifted off for a moment. "I do remember something like that."

"Good. I want you to think back—remember everything you can about that particular night."

Pamela brought her hand up to her eyes. "I'm sorry. They're all a blur."

"Wysper may have been wearing a white skirt and purple top."

"No help." Her hand fell away. "That was her favorite outfit."

"Was there a night when she misplaced her checkbook?"

"Yes." A light came on in her eyes. "We found it under her stool when the lights came up."

"Can you remember what happened earlier? Around the time you came in?"

"I think we met for happy hour down the street. Then we walked up to Eddy's. It must have been eight or nine, because the piano player had already started. And there was this guy sitting at our favorite table. A loner."

"What happened?"

"Our eyes met as I approached the table, and there was this unspoken invitation to join him. It was all right by me, but Wysper was pissed because 'her' table was taken, so she decided to sit at the bar and talk to Burt."

"What did you do?"

"I sort of nodded thanks to the guy and sat with her."

"Now, can you see the scene? Put the room and the table in your mind?"

"Sort of."

"What was the lighting like?"

"Very dark."

"What was your reaction when you first saw him?"

"Nothing really." She shook her head slowly. "He was just a man. Or a mark, as Wysper called them."

"A mark? Was Wysper a prostitute?"

"Oh, she always took men for something. Dinner. Clothes. Even cash from time to time. But technically, I don't think you can be considered a hooker unless you put out."

Oscar smiled. "How would you describe this mark?"

"He was older than the regular crowd ... forties or fifties."

"Caucasian?"

"Probably. Definitely not black."

"Hair color?"

"I think it was lighter. Again, not black."

"Color of eyes?"

"I'm sorry. You're asking more than I can give. I only glanced at him for a couple of seconds, and dozens of men like that drift through on an average night."

"But you are sure he was not a regular."

"Well, Wysper didn't know him."

"You think he might live around here?"

"I doubt it. He looked like a businessman."

"From out of town?"

"It'd be my guess from the way he was dressed."

"How was that?"

"You know. Suit and tie. And he had a raincoat."

"Was it raining?"

"No. It was hot and muggy. That's why I remember the coat."

Oscar nodded. "How tall was he?"

"I have no idea. He was sitting down when we came in."

"What about later? Did he say something to you on his way out?"

"I don't think so."

"Did you notice anything unusual about him? Distinctive ring? Toupee? Special eyeglasses?"

"Nothing." She mulled it over. "What about the piano player? He saw the guy up close."

"Gone." Oscar shook his head slowly. "He hung paper all over town and skipped about two weeks ago."

Pamela seemed to be coming around. "I wish I could be more help. I realize you traveled all the way up here to see me."

"You have been most helpful, Miss Drummond." Oscar smiled and laid a card on the table. "If you focus on that night, something may come to mind. Will you call me if it does?"

"Maybe." Her forehead wrinkled. "But why are you interested in that night? And that particular man?"

He hesitated too long. "We're trying to determine if a suspect was in the area."

"How did you know what she was wearing?" Her eyes narrowed. "And how could you possibly know about the check book? Wysper and I were the only ones ..."

Oscar searched for words, realizing that anything he said would amplify her fear.

"Have you arrested him?"

"Not yet."

"Oh, my God!" A look of terror crept across her face. "If that's the man who killed Wysper, he knows I've seen him ... probably thinks I can identify him."

He gazed at her, trying to suppress the anguish he felt. "I wish I could tell you otherwise."

"I've got to get out of here!" She surged up and took two halting paces toward the hallway, stopping in profile with fists clenched and head back, the long matted hair falling across her shoulders. "Will you stay with me? Will you take me to the airport and make sure I get away safe?"

"Yes." He stood up and moved around to face her. "And you won't have to live in fear much longer. We will get this man."

"Thank you." Pamela lunged forward and threw her arms around his neck, sobbing into the lapel of his coat. "You're the first one who's offered to help. I thought nobody cared what happened to me."

Oscar brought his hands up and embraced her tenderly, trying to absorb the pain and despair as he would for his own lost child.

"I care."

Chapter 45

Contemplating the cold coffee in the bottom of his cup, Oscar swore quietly. Two weeks had dragged by since Megan's assault, an endless sea of phone calls and interviews. He scanned his list for the next call, and was reaching for the phone when it went off.

"OSI. Colunga."

"Oscar. This is Harold Gilley from the New London Navy base."

"Yes, Bud. How are you doing?"

"Frankly, I've been better. We're in a flap about hazardous waste at the moment."

"If it isn't one thing, it's another."

"Yeah. Anyway, I thought you'd like to know what I came up with."

"Sure."

"I tracked down some of my buddies from the old days and asked them about those guys in Morocco."

"And?"

"We did come up with one name. Tony Pedilla."

"Spell it." Oscar wrote it in his notebook. "Is that his real name or the one he used for the black market?"

"Sorry. I can't say."

"Well, it's more than I expected. I really appreciate the effort."

"No problem. You come back and see us when you want to play hooky again. We'll have lunch down in Mystic."

"Thanks, Bud. I'll do that." Oscar hefted the receiver, listening to the dull roar of the dial tone. Was it a real name? An alias? Either way, it couldn't be run down in the next ten minutes. He punched in the next number on his list, a scientist recommended by Cruz.

"CIA, Langley."

Oscar stammered, "Central Intelligence Agency?"

"CIA. May I help you?"

"Blake Evans ..."

"One moment, please."

"Damn you, Cruz. You could have warned me." He held the phone out and stared at the small holes in the mouthpiece. "The CIA for Chrissake."

"Hello."

Oscar slapped the receiver to his ear. "Mr. Evans?"

The rigid response took a few heartbeats. "Yes?"

"This is Lieutenant Oscar Colunga of the Connecticut State Police. I was referred to you by a mutual friend, José Cruz." He could hear Evans' voice brighten.

"Ah, yes. What can I do for you, Lieutenant?"

"We're working a serial killer investigation up here, and I need some technical advice."

"Namely?"

Oscar collected his thoughts. "I heard about a device that can absolutely silence victims of a violent criminal. Do you know what it might be?"

"Absolute? No sound whatever?"

"Right."

"Hmm. That would be difficult. We have this movie fiction that a strand of material between the teeth does the job. Of course, a human being can talk quite plainly through such a gag—scream his bloody head off, in fact. Even complete occlusion of the mouth cannot effect total silence, since sound originates in the larynx."

"I agree. Can you think of any way to guarantee silence?"

"Two possibilities. Total restriction of the airway, or inducement of pain in response to sound."

"What's the most probable way to induce such pain?"

"You could stand by with a paddle, but something automatic would probably entail electronics."

"A collar, perhaps?"

"Sounds like a good bet."

"Would it be difficult to make such a device?"

"The concept is simple enough. Trigger an SCR from the microphone amplifier, and dump a charged capacitor through a small transformer to generate a high voltage spike."

"Sounds complicated to me."

"It's pretty basic actually, similar to the old Kettering ignition system on automobiles. I think your biggest problem would be mechanics—arrangement of microphones and contacts, optimum materials, and so on. It would probably require some experimentation to get things right."

"Would the electronics package be very bulky?"

"Roughly the size of a cigarette pack if you built it by hand. Smaller if commercially produced." Evans paused. "Wait! I remember something like this ... a collar to prevent dogs from barking."

After several seconds of silence, Evans spoke up. "Are you there?"

"Yes, I'm here." Oscar remembered to breathe. "Could such a device be designed to shock on demand? Without a sound to trigger it?"

"Like a switch or radio signal?"

"Something like that."

"Certainly. Or, it might be as simple as tapping the microphone."

"Could it burn the skin?"

"You're out of my realm now. I don't have any idea how much energy would be required to do that. But instinct says it would be more likely to cause a burn if the electrode were not in direct contact with the skin ... if it drew an arc, in other words."

"I see."

"You think such a device was actually used to silence victims?"

"Maybe." Oscar paused. "You've been extremely helpful, Mr. Evans. If there's ever anything I can do for you ..."

"Just give my regards to José, and ask him to look me up next time he's in Washington."

"I'll do that."

"Good luck, Lieutenant. Feel free to call if I can help."

"Thanks."

Oscar dropped the phone and surged upward to collect his coat. Still wrestling it on, he stopped in front of Kathy's desk. "Where's the nearest pet shop?"

She looked up in surprise. "Two blocks east. Why?"

"Research." He bolted through the door and down the stairs toward the garage. At the last instant, he lunged through the front doors and turned east along the street, his mind a melee of thought.

Twice he kicked himself for not driving. He had thought the walk would calm him down, but the prospect of a tangible lead spurred him on, and raised a sweat from a mild exertion that he would not have noticed a few years ago.

Finally, he entered the pet shop and glanced around for someone who seemed to be in charge. The young girl at the counter was obviously not the one he needed. He approached her.

"Is the manager or owner in?"

"Yes. Would you like me to get him?"

"Please."

She smiled sweetly and wandered toward the rear of the store.

Oscar stood there trying to remember if he'd ever been in a pet store. As the seconds dragged by, he clasped his hands behind his back and drifted down one of the aisles to see if he could locate the product in question. Suddenly he froze, staring up at a display of collars and leashes. The sight of this mundane equipment assailed his eyes with a tangled glitter. He leaned closer, noting that some of them had links the same size as the bruises on Wysper's wrists.

Slowly, his hand reached out to lift a choke chain from its hook. He fondled the cold metal and tested its strength, noting that the links were welded—light, but strong.

"Help ya?"

Oscar wheeled around in surprise, staring into the craggy face of a compact gray-haired man in his mid-fifties. "Are you the manager?"

"Ayup. Emmett's the name."

Oscar produced his credentials. "Colunga, State Police. I need to know about an electronic device intended to stop dogs from barking. Do you carry it?"

"Ya mean a shock collah?"

"Yes."

"Nope. Used to rent 'em, though ... fairly expensive ta buy if ya only need ta use 'em once."

"Do you have one I could look at?"

"Sorry. Got ridda them all years ago ... not much call hereabouts. 'Round here, somethin's wrong if a dog's not bahkin'."

"Are they still being produced?"

"Ayup. Lotsa companies make 'em. And there's another type that uses ultrasonic. If ya dog's causin' ya problems ..."

"I don't have a dog." He thought for a moment. "Is there a store in the area that might carry this kind of collar?"

"Maybe. There's a big store in that new mall up north."
The man scratched his ear. "Name doesn't come ta mind,
though."

Oscar shook off the temptation to throttle the slow-talk-
ing man. "Would it be possible to locate people who bought a
shock collar?"

"Nope."

"Why not?"

"Ya might find records of people who rented 'em, but
not for those who bought 'em. There weren't no registration
required—like a gun, or dynamite."

Oscar stared at the man in awe. "What did you say?"

"I said, there weren't no registration ..."

"I heard you." Oscar felt the chain cut into his hand.
"Thanks." He turned and headed for the door.

Emmett called out, "Didya want to buy that collah? It's
eight ninety-five."

Oscar tossed a ten on the counter and headed for his
office. He took the stairs two at a time and burst in on the
surprised Kathy.

She looked up at the emotion on his face. "What's the
matter, Oscar?"

"The dynamite!"

"That he used on Megan?"

"Yes." Oscar puffed heavily. "Did you check for purchases
by her known associates?"

Kathy smiled. "One of the first things I did. Nobody
purchased dynamite ... at least, not under their real name."

"I still think there may be a link here." He fondled the
chain in his pocket. "Would you purchase a case, or whatever
dynamite comes in, for one stick?"

She thought it over. "Maybe not. You think he stole it?"

"I'd bet on it."

"So?"

"So, we need to contact all agencies in the area for thefts of dynamite."

"What good would that do?"

"Suppose he stole it close to where he lives."

"I don't know, Oscar." Kathy shook her head. "If I were going to steal dynamite, I wouldn't do it in my backyard."

"But you would be most likely to know where it could be found in your backyard. Maybe it's the mistake we're looking for."

She shook her head. "It sounds like a long shot to me."

"Everything's a long shot, Kathy. How much effort will it cost?"

"Not much."

"Then do it."

Chapter 46

Kathy Huntsinger escorted the handsome man into Oscar's office. Achal Bedi hesitated in the doorway.

"Lieutenant Colunga?"

"Come in, Mr. Bedi. Would you care for a cup of coffee?"

"Cream and sugar, if it wouldn't be too much trouble."

Kathy nodded and ducked out.

"Have a seat." Oscar waited for him to settle in across the desk. "I appreciate your traveling up here. I could have come to New York."

Achal smiled, the white gash of his teeth radiant in the late afternoon sun streaming through the windows. "No problem. I wanted to get out of town."

"Good." Oscar clasped his hands on the desk. "I need to ask you a few questions, some of which may be rather personal. Do you have any objections?"

Achal shook his head. "Anything I can do to help."

"Fine." Oscar smiled. "How long have you known Megan?"

"About six months."

"I understand you were lovers."

"That's not quite accurate. We are in love."

"Then I assume she shared intimate thoughts with you."

"On occasion."

"I want to know about Megan's mental state in the weeks prior to the assault."

Achal reflected. "Chaotic, I would say."

"Why so?"

"There were many business and personal problems that created a lot of tension for her."

"Like?"

"Her grandmother's death. Problems at work. And she was involved with selling her novel."

"Through her agent, Irv Miller."

"That's right."

"What about this book she was reading?"

"The one about the serial killer? Oscar nodded. "It was getting to her."

"Why?"

"I don't know. I read several chapters myself, and I didn't think it was all that scary ... maybe because I'm a man. We aren't usually victims of this type of crime, and our instinctive fears must be different."

"Did she discuss her fears with you?"

"She was afraid it was somehow personally directed at her."

"Did she have any basis for that?"

"I didn't think so at the time, but she was worried ... even asked Irv Miller to check around to see if other editors were receiving it."

"Did he?"

"No."

"Why not?"

"He thought it was an overreaction."

"And you agreed?"

Achal's face showed pain and disgust. "Believe me, Lieutenant, I wish I'd known."

"I'm sure you do." Oscar pondered. "Did she do anything else as a result of this overreaction?"

"She hired a private detective to identify the author. I don't know his name, but I can probably dig it up for you."

"No need. He called me when he read about Megan."

"Then you know he didn't find the man."

"Yes." Oscar held up as Kathy delivered a steaming cup of coffee and took her leave. "Megan never had any idea who the writer was?"

"Not the slightest."

"Do you think he is an established author?"

"He claimed to be in his letter."

Oscar felt the edge of the desk top biting into his wrists. "His letter?"

"Yes. He sent a letter with the first chapter. Didn't you know that?"

"No. Do you think we could get our hands on it?"

"It's probably on file, but I don't think it will do you any good. Megan said there was no address or signature. Nothing to identify him."

"Still, I'd like to see it."

Achal nodded. "I'll see if it's on file."

"Thank you. If you do locate it, please don't handle it. I'll arrange for the FBI to remove it from the file."

"I understand."

"Now, is there anything else you remember about those last days that could point to our killer?"

"I've tried ever since she was attacked, but I can't think of a thing."

"What about something said in the office where you work?"

Achal's eyes widened. "You think it could be someone from the company?"

"We can't rule out any possibility at this point. Whoever attacked Megan knew she was sending me copies of this book." He paused to let it sink in. "Did you know she was doing that?"

Achal blew into the cup and took a sip. "She mentioned it."

"So you knew."

"Yes, but I wouldn't have remembered your name."

"Who else might have known?"

"Irv Miller did, I believe." He thought it over. "Harmon Jarvis knew she was reading the book, but I don't think she would have told him about you. He would have raised questions about ethics."

"But Jarvis would have access to office records, right?"

"Certainly. But then, so did many editors, assistants, readers ... mailroom people and janitors for that matter."

"Is there anyone else, close to her, who might have know about Megan's link with me?"

"The only one who comes to mind is Bernie Yellanik. But he and Meg weren't very close, and he's such a milquetoast. I can't conceive of him as a serial killer."

"Who is he?"

"He was our mystery editor until about a month ago."

"Was? What happened?"

"He was sacked."

"Please spell his name." Oscar wrote it down and looked up. "Is there anything more you can tell me?"

"One thing. I don't know why it sticks in my mind, but I perceive this man to be calculating—rigidly controlled."

"The author?"

"Yes. First person writing tends to be very personal. But even when this guy spills his guts, there is always a measure of control."

"Well, there's one chapter you haven't seen, where I think he lost it."

"How do you know I haven't seen it?"

"It's chapter twenty-three. Did you ever see chapter twenty-three?"

"We only had one through eight. How did you—"

"The bastard sent it to me directly."

Achal stared in amazement. "So he was playing a game with Meg, and you got sucked into it. What a story."

"Beg your pardon?"

"Sorry." Achal dipped his head. "I know it's rather crass under the circumstances, but I had a spasm of professional interest."

"Well, I can't blame you for that. It is one helluva story." Oscar smiled. "Maybe you'll print it someday. In the meantime, call me if you think of anything else that might allow us to complete the plot."

"You know I will."

"Yes, and I appreciate your coming in, Mr. Bedi."

Oscar stood and extended his hand across the desk. Achal reached out to receive it, but sat fast in his chair.

"I'd like to see Megan."

"Sorry."

"Just like that? No qualification? No negotiation?" Oscar shook his head resolutely. "But I have to see her. Maybe love will snap her out of it."

"She didn't snap out of it when you saw her at Fairlawn."

"True, but she's had time to recover. It could be different now."

"I truly am sorry, Mr. Bedi, but we have to keep her location secret from everyone. It's not directed at you personally." Oscar sagged into his chair. "I hope you can understand."

Achal's eyes drifted to the windows. "I'll try."

"Feeling guilty because you aren't by her side?"

"Extremely."

Oscar gazed at him. "When this is all over, you'll have a lifetime to make it up to her."

Chapter 47

It was late September, the time when air conditioning sometimes becomes confused and goes the wrong direction—or no direction at all. Oscar loosened his shirt and tie against the stagnant air, longing to be out in the open.

Kathy sat in front of his desk with her reports balanced on her knee, as she had done so many times in recent days. "May I ask why you wanted background on these particular men?"

"Sure. It has to be someone who was close to Megan—close enough to know that she was sending the manuscript to me. Close enough to know about the house she was looking at up in Pleasant Valley. That means a personal friend or someone in her office who could have inquired of her assistant or leafed through records."

"You asked Heather about that?"

"Yes. She made an entry in her log when she mailed the first eight chapters to me, and Megan's realtor was in her book. Anyone in the office could have looked it up."

"In that case, it could have been the janitor."

"The possibility has been mentioned, but I doubt that a janitor would know enough about Megan's personal life." He rubbed his hands together. "What've you got so far?"

Kathy picked up the first report. "Achal Bedi came to

this country from New Delhi in nineteen seventy-five, to study at the Washington State University in Pullman." She looked up. "They have a good department for communication and media." Her eyes dropped back to the page. "He married a year later and had a child, but his wife divorced him in his senior year. After graduation he took a job with an advertising agency on Madison Avenue and started moonlighting as a reader for publishers. About ten years ago Chester Forrester, then CEO of Gladiator Press, offered him a job as editor."

"No military service? No holes in his background?"

"Not a hint."

Oscar sat for a few seconds. "Even without that, he doesn't seem like a good prospect. He and Megan were already making it. What would he have to gain?"

"Well if he were a psychopath, humiliation and fear might be more important than willing sex."

"Nah. I can't believe it's Achal. Who's next?"

"Harmon Jarvis."

"Her boss."

"Right. Editor-in-Chief, to be exact. Of the four men you had me research, he has the closest thing to a checkered past. Born to wealthy parents in Cleveland, he joined the Army in nineteen sixty-five and served two hitches in Vietnam, some of it with Special Operations Group—run by the CIA as I understand. "After he mustered out, he dropped out of sight for a while and surfaced in nineteen seventy-nine, working for a printer in Hong Kong that did a lot of work for Chartier Press out of Chicago. They liked him and offered him the job of production manager. He came home and filled that position for about a year, then moved into the editorial department where he showed great flare for picking winners. Based on that success, he landed an editor's job with Butterfly Books in New York in 1987, and his combined capabilities in marketing, editing, and production put him in line for his current position."

"How long has he been at Gladiator?"

"Four or five months."

Oscar lit a smoke, glaring at the nearly empty pack. "What about those missing years after Vietnam?"

"Well, it turns out there were quite a few men who hung around Asia after the war, as plantation guards or other form of mercenary."

"How do you find all this stuff?"

Kathy grinned. "From friends or family or former co-workers. People love to talk about their friends—and themselves."

"Does that mean these guys know they're being investigated?"

"Could be. Does that bother you?"

"No. I kinda like it." Oscar took a drag and smiled. "Who's next?"

"Bernie Yellanik, the one who was an editor with Gladiator until about a month ago. Nothing much here. He graduated from Harvard in nineteen eighty-three and went to work for Gladiator as a junior editor. He worked his way up to senior editor about ten years ago, but everyone rates his performance as mediocre at best."

"Any chance he's holding a grudge against Megan?"

"I'll check with Heather. She's been very helpful, so far."

Kathy turned the page. "Irv Miller graduated from Northeastern with a major in journalism and worked as a reporter for the *New York Times* between nineteen seventy-five and nineteen seventy-nine. He must have done some writing on the side. Two of his novels were published in the early 'eighties—only marginally successful. By then he was working for the Smith/Benz Literary Agency and handled some very big clients. He established his own agency in nineteen eighty-six.

How successful he is today, I don't know. None of the financial data are in yet."

Oscar snuffed out the cigarette and stared into space. "So, we do have one man with military service and one published writer who studied journalism. Too bad they aren't the same."

She nodded. "A shame."

Oscar shifted in his chair, jangled by the frigid rush as the sweat cooled his back. "I want you to concentrate on Miller and Jarvis first. Dig deep into their past. Where they lived. Where they worked. Current and former properties. Old flames. Any hint of a criminal record."

"No problem. But you realize we may be comparing everything to a pack of lies."

"Yes." A light came on in his eyes. "Maybe we can turn that to our advantage. As you do your research, don't take anything for granted. If someone says he worked with Irv Miller, ask them to describe him. Verify height, hair color, and so forth. Did he smoke or wear glasses? That kind of thing."

"Why?"

"Well, we assume that anything in the book could be a fabrication. If one of these guys has a background that's also a fabrication, he could be our man."

"I'm with you."

Oscar nodded. "Anything else right now?"

"One more thing." She extracted a fax from her pile and tossed it onto the desk. "I found an incident of dynamite theft in the area—four sticks."

"Really?" Oscar leaned forward with renewed interest. "Where?"

"From an outfit in New Jersey, one of those that razes buildings in downtown areas."

"Where exactly?"

"An old factory not far from the Newark Airport."

"I want you to compute the distance from home for everyone on the associates list."

"All right, but I think it's a waste of time."

"Why?"

"They work in New York. That makes it in easy reach of all of them. And, as I said before, I would not steal something this traceable in my backyard."

"True, but knowing the complexity of law enforcement around here, the thief might assume it would never find its way to the right agency at the right time ... possibly never be reported."

"That would be a good bet." She nodded. "In fact, I think it's somewhat of a miracle that we came across it."

Oscar stared into her dark eyes. "Are we to the point of looking for miracles?"

"I think so."

"Talk to me."

"If this book really parallels his life, we might have a handle on him. But I don't see a strong match with any of these four men. Lots of men were in the military, and journalism majors are not rare. What if it's someone we don't know about?"

Oscar contemplated her. "We have to eliminate these men before opening it up to the entire world."

She collected her papers and stood up. "Okay, but I'm getting discouraged."

"Me too, but we've got to keep plugging away. Megan's life may depend on it."

She turned back at the doorway. "Oh, one more thing. That envelope we sent to the lab?"

He nodded.

"They were able to raise the postmark."

"Where was it mailed?"

"Right here in Hartford."

Chapter 48

Oscar sat at his desk staring at the wall, scarcely aware of the quiet din from the outer office. Nearly three weeks had passed since Megan's traumatic assault. Her condition had not improved, and neither had his. He was no closer to the killer, in spite of Herculean efforts by the FBI, a cadre of detectives from state and local agencies, and his own staff. Based on what they had dug up, he could come just as close by throwing a dart at a map.

The key must be in the manuscript. He was reading it again, trying to relax his body and mind to scan it like a boring novel in hopes that some new insight would spring up. He adjusted his reading glasses and bent over the page to continue where he left off—Chapter Seven.

Have you ever thought, dear reader, how different your life might be if some insignificant variable was different? Wealthier parents. Another name. Some other area of the country. Proclivity for sports or art.

In my case, I felt that my mother was poorer than she actually was. We never went hungry. The house was always heated in the winter. But she had to work long hours to make ends meet. The years wore her down and I don't blame her for marrying Howard, a man from Texas who retained a thick accent. He was a much kinder man than my real father, and he made an honest living as a

house painter. With their combined income, they were able to invest in a couple of rental properties that set them on the road to security.

You might expect this to work to my advantage vis-à-vis college and other opportunities. But in a case of cruel irony, it was the end for me. His family had a tradition. When the children graduated from high school, they were given two gifts–a new set of clothes, and a suitcase. In bitter moments, I still see the pain on my mother's face when he explained this tradition to me.

Being ejected from my own home by this interloper was a crushing blow. I had sacrificed all my life for my family, gratefully accepting clothes for Christmas presents by the time I was five and working from the time I was twelve. Now, on the verge of prosperity, I was flung into the world to seek my fortune. When my scholarship was cancelled, the only option was to join the military.

To this day I dream about smashing in Howard's smug face, but the dream becomes a nightmare because its fulfillment would hurt my beloved mother. These things were, for some reason, on my mind as I processed my most recent procurement.

I sometimes wonder if her stature reminded me of my mother, since I would not have normally been attracted to this girl. The instant I saw her thumbing a ride, I knew it would be a bad scene. She was petite, almost scrawny, the only benefit that her ankles were small enough to take standard handcuffs.

After two days with me, she showed no signs of warming up. Unlike any of those before or since, she seemed to withdraw into herself in a denial of her current condition. All the others had either accepted or fought their fate. But this small young woman dealt with it as a bad dream that would evaporate in the morning.

I lost patience with her. I bound her wrists and ankles and stood her up on a low table I had constructed by setting a square of plywood atop three empty wine bottles in the south end of my secret room.

This is something I have not discussed before. The bed was roughly in the center of the room, with the bathroom in the northwest corner. This left the south

half of the room empty. I had installed a number of devices in this space to make our time together more interesting. One of these was a block and tackle of the type used to change engines. I hooked a chain around her neck and took up the slack.

She gazed at me through dull eyes, clearly not understanding my intent. I explained the words she must say, and she shook her head. I did not know if she understood. The chain would not tighten like a noose, but I was sure it would cut off her breathing if her weight was fully suspended. Death would take several minutes, assuming the hard chain didn't snap her neck.

I sat on the bed to watch her. She struggled at first, but stopped as the small table rocked under her. Only then did she understand the extreme danger of her situation. Still she did not comply.

It seemed like the drive for self-preservation was dead in her. I felt numb. She had destroyed the fun for me. I left without a word and went to bed, knowing that nobody could stand on that precarious platform all night.

In the morning I opened the door and found her staring at me with terror. In a fit of disgust I kicked the wine bottles out from under her and left for the day.

Oscar's head snapped up. "Kathy!" he bellowed, hearing his voice echo from the walls.

She vaulted from her desk and was in the room within two seconds. "What is it, Oscar?"

"I know where to put our effort."

"Where?"

"What did he lie about?"

She blinked. "Almost everything."

"And when did he tell the truth?"

"I don't know."

"What he did to the women. When he talked about that, there was no reason to lie. Only two people would ever know what happened, and one of them would soon be dead. We have to find something concrete in those moments."

Kathy stiffened. "Formaldehyde!"

"What?"

"He said he wanted to keep one woman's head for a while ... that he purchased formaldehyde from a local supplier."

Oscar stared at her. "Could there be records?"

"Maybe. Assuming it was Chesson, we know the date within a few days."

"Give it a shot." Oscar said a silent prayer. When he looked up, Kathy was gone.

Chapter 49

The coffeepot held particular allure this morning. Kathy and Stan Zelinski were working at their desks in the outer office as Oscar made his way to the hot brew. He stirred in extra cream and sugar, and turned toward the protection of his office. Then he noticed something awry.

At the back of Kathy's desk, a small child of two or three sat playing on the floor. Her eyes were bluer than the blanket she sat on, and her long honey hair fell to her shoulders in looping ringlets. She was beautiful beyond belief, and the intelligent eyes assessed him as she wriggled her fingers at him and whispered, "Hi."

He turned to Kathy and smiled. "This must be Leah."

Kathy nodded. "I hope you don't mind me bringing her into the office. My mother had an appointment this morning, but it's just for a couple of hours."

"Not at all. If you'll forgive a man for using the word, she's an adorable child."

Kathy grinned. "Most of the time."

Oscar put his cup on her desk and sat down on the floor. "How are you today, tiny girl?"

She smiled up at him, blue eyes shining. "Okay."

"Do you like coming to Mommy's office?"

"Yeah."

"Do you have enough toys to play with?"

woman until the hostess stepped aside and motioned for him to have a seat in the booth. Then his mouth fell open. Casey had a shoulder-length mane in dark brown, and her smile was a wide gash of the whitest teeth he had ever seen, contrasted against a startling tan on what he knew was biologically fair skin. There was no time to drink in her features or the color of her eyes, or her tailored business suit. The only word that came to mind for Casey Stuart was perfection.

Oscar did what men hate and women love. Had there been a filing cabinet in his path, he would have crashed into it headlong. He stared at her with mouth agape, and mumbled some sort of introduction.

"Good morning to you, Lieutenant. Won't you have a seat?"

"Thanks." He acknowledged the young hostess as he sat down. "And thanks to you."

"You're welcome." She strolled away with an amused grin, leaving the poor man to his fate.

"So, what will I call you? Lieutenant sounds a bit formal, don't you think?"

"It does, and most people call me Oscar."

"Then so shall I." She engineered a disarming smile. "Are you ready to order?"

He noticed that she had already ordered, and was well into her salad, as the very young waitress steamed up to the table and held out a menu.

"Tell you what. Just give me a cup of coffee."

"Are you sure? We have a wonderful special this afternoon."

"Yes, I'm sure."

"Cream and sugar?"

"A lot."

She pivoted efficiently and went away. Oscar felt like he'd put himself at a disadvantage by fumbling around during the introduction. It was embarrassing for a man his age. His primary objective now was escape.

"Sooo, Oscar. You don't have time for lunch?"

"Afraid not. I have several errands to run this afternoon."

"Is that police parlance for investigation?"

"It is."

"Will all your answers to my questions be so abrupt?"

"Could we get on with it?"

"All right." She produced a tape recorder and switched it on. "I have a terrible memory. Do you mind?"

"Shoot."

"I understand you are in charge of this serial killer investigation."

"First of all, we're not sure it is a serial killer. Secondly, I run an office that provides information to the investigating officers."

"I see." She adjusted her skirt. "May I speak frankly?"

"Sure."

"Word on the street is that you are after a serial killer who has been active in this area for a number of years."

"Well, it sounds like the street knows more about this case than we do. Can you shed more light on it?"

Casey looked exasperated. "You aren't going to tell me anything, are you?"

"Look. This is your gig, not mine. Even if I was certain of anything, do you expect me to compromise our efforts by giving inside information to the press?"

"Well then, it looks like this will be a wasted trip." She leaned onto the table and rested her chin in her palm. "Suppose we change tack ... talk about anything except the case?"

"If you turn that damn thing off."

"Agreed." She hit a switch and stowed it in her large leather bag. "I'd like to talk about you."

"That should be a short conversation."

"Too short for you to have a bite?"

He gazed into her sultry eyes, deciding that feasting on her beauty might not be the worst way to pass some time. And he needed food this morning. Turning to the waitress, he said, "I'll have the special."

She sprinted to the table. "Have we changed our mind?"

"We have."

"But I haven't told you what it is."

"I assume that, in a place like this, it won't suck."

She burst out in a high-pitched giggle and ran off toward the kitchen.

Oscar turned back with a start. Casey was removing her coat, and the business façade had fallen away.

"You are Mexican?"

He nodded. "Why do you ask?"

"Because of your blue eyes."

He admired her candor. Most people used euphemisms like Hispanic, or "of Mexican extraction." "My mother and father were both Mexican, so I believe that I am."

She issued a throaty laugh and pushed her plate away to lean onto her elbows, the table supporting her breasts like a shelf. Now he was in deep pizza. But, for the first time in a long while, he was relaxed. And she clearly wanted nothing but company, describing how lonely her travelling way of life was. After an hour of grilling, he did divulge information that he had not intended to—his marital status, and his phone number.

Chapter 50

The front office was empty—somehow dark and foreboding as if he should not violate its space. On any other night of the week Oscar might expect one or two of his staff to be working at six o'clock, but this was Friday. He flipped on the burner under a stale pot of coffee and settled in behind his desk, trying to think of some way to force a breakthrough.

Sensing that he was at the limit of mental and physical stamina, he wasn't sure how much longer he could sustain this level of effort. Yet, what options did he have? To quit? To fail? Unthinkable.

Tonight it would be better. He would be in Rita's arms, and she would comfort him ... console him like a disconsolate child. But here, in this reality, he was lost and alone without a decent idea or positive motivation. Megan was lying on her back, the lustrous woman she had been now reduced to a pathetic heap of living flesh. With bitter irony, he sensed that his daughter was better off. Her pain had lasted less than one day, and she would not live a lifetime of remembering. Even if Megan beat her catatonia, she would carry the scars forever.

He reached for the phone, but pulled back as something in the outer office disturbed his gloom. A man in the uniform of a local cab company stood looking around.

Oscar arose ponderously and moved to the doorway. "May I help you?"

"Gotta package for a Lieutenant Colunga."

"I'm Colunga." He moved forward and reached out for the white business envelope. There was nothing on it but his name and address.

"Who sent this?"

"I dunno. It was taped to the wheel of my hack when I came on."

"You didn't see him?"

"I said that already."

"How did he arrange payment?"

"How d'ya think? It was in a bigger envelope with a twenty."

"Where's the twenty?"

"Where d'ya think? In my wallet."

"I'd like to buy it from you."

"Sure, Mac, I'll pick it out of the five or six in there."

Oscar shook his head. "Smart."

"Yeah, whatever." The cabby rolled his eyes and turned on his heel. "Hope it's good news."

Oscar fell into a near-stupor, hardly noticing the man's departure. He could not recall receiving a hand-delivered message before, and the old jokes about their bad news were a bitter omen now. Especially now.

He tore open the envelope and stared at the three terse lines. Feeling the shaking in his knees, he sagged against a desk and read it again.

> I HAVE YOUR GIRL.
> WILL TRADE FOR MEGAN.
> WILL CALL YOUR OFFICE 10 AM TOMORROW.

"*Hijo de puta!*" Oscar threw his head back and closed his eyes as the room began to swim around him.

He launched himself toward his office and crashed into his chair, lifting the receiver and smashing an auto-dial button on the phone. Two seconds later he heard the sunny voice of the receptionist at Rita's clinic.

"I need to talk to Rita. It's urgent."

"I'm sorry, sir." The fluid response reeked of sweetness. "Dr. Takamura has left for the weekend. Would you like to—"

"No. How long ago did she leave?"

An unending hesitation. "Sir, I don't know if I should give out—"

"Dammit. This is Lieutenant Oscar Colunga of the Connecticut State Police. How long ago did she leave?"

"About an hour, I would say."

"Thanks." Oscar pressed the cradle button and dialed her home.

There was no answer—not even the machine picked up. He slammed the phone down and headed for the garage on a dead run.

The bored officer in the gate house looked up as Oscar approached. "Evening, Lieutenant. Checking out for the weekend?"

"No. I need a patrol car."

"Why?"

"It's an emergency. Do you have one?"

"Well, seven-fourteen's back there." He held out a clipboard and keys. "Sign here." For several seconds he stared in surprise at his empty left hand and the untouched clipboard in his right. He opened the door and stepped into the driveway. "Lieutenant?"

In the shadows, a big V-8 engine roared to life and tires squealed in complaint as the heavy machine surged forward.

"Hey, Lieutenant. You need to sign ..." At the last instant he jumped back onto the curb as the cruiser screamed by, the mirror brushing him like the horn of a bull passing the matador's cape.

Oscar turned on the lights and siren and careened through

the rush hour traffic, heading toward Highway 84 that would carry him southwest to Bristol. He was aware of very little around him, his mind alive with burning memories. Julia was dead. Megan was lying like a zombie in a hideaway. If he failed Rita ...

He floored the big sedan on the entrance ramp, surging onto the broad freeway amidst a cloud of rubber smoke, as the cars ahead ducked left and right to make room. Oscar swore at a driver who failed to yield, either unaware of the law, or deafened by the stereo in the quietized interior.

Oscar jerked the cellular phone from the console and punched in the direct line into José Cruz's office in Manhattan, pounding the steering wheel harder on each ring. "Come on, Cruz. Be a New Yorker. Work late."

"Cruz."

"Joe, this is Oscar. I'm in trouble."

"What is it, *Hijo?*"

"I think the killer we're after has taken my *mujer*, Rita Takamura."

"Why?"

"He wants to trade her for Megan Roarke."

"*Madre de Dios. Que loco!*"

Oscar's face contorted. "I'm on my way to Rita's house in Bristol."

"You want me to arrange backup?"

"I don't know! If the crazy sonofabitch hears a siren ..." Oscar swerved around a car and backed off to miss another. "You call it, Joe."

"How long will it take you to get there?"

"Twenty minutes."

"Give me the address. I have a chopper on the pad."

Oscar shut off the siren and drove the last mile in eerie silence, trailing a plume of dust along rural roads. At last, he coasted to the curb on the street behind Rita's house and reached for the radio.

"Central, this is Lieutenant Colunga."

"Go ahead, Lieutenant."

"Requesting backup at One twenty-four Petra Lane, northeast of Bristol."

"Roger that, Lieutenant. Status?"

"Come in hot and loud. Over."

He loaded his 9MM automatic and charged through the woods, coming to rest behind a tree fifty feet from the rear of the house. The drapes in her study were shut, but a light showed through the small window in the kitchen.

Hunched over, he made his way to the rear wall and flattened out against it, looking left and right for signs of activity at the windows. Finding no threat, he sprang up to look through the kitchen window, gun raised in both hands.

"Oscar!" The word erupted from the open mouth of the startled woman, her eyes wide and color ebbing from her face. "What on earth are you doing?"

He lowered the weapon and snapped on the safety. "I thought ... Are you all right?"

"As long as you don't shoot me."

Oscar holstered the gun. "Let me in. We need to talk."

He drifted toward the kitchen door, hearing the clicks as she undid the locks. He entered sheepishly and took her in his arms.

"What is it, Oscar?"

"I thought you'd been kidnapped."

"Something to do with your work?"

"Yes."

"Damn you, Oscar." She pushed away violently and took two paces. "You said you would keep me out of it."

"I know."

She turned back. "Kidnapped by whom?"

Oscar wanted to retreat. Rita had been the one point of light that held him together these last weeks. "Sorry, my mistake."

"Mistake?" She snapped her head in anger. "I want to know what's going on."

"I received a message that said my girl had been taken."

"Your girl? Oscar, I'm forty-two years old. Who would refer to me as a girl?"

"I—"

"What's more, who would know I was your girl? Has someone been observing us? Have we been followed?"

"No."

"How can you be so certain?"

"I would know if we were being followed."

"I believe that." Her dark eyes gazed up at him. "Who would 'your girl' be?"

"Kathy!" Oscar turned and ran for the den. "I have to call the office."

Rita drifted in and sank onto the couch.

"This is Colunga. I need Kathy's home phone number." He wrote it down on the desk blotter. "Thanks, Susie. And if you hear from her, have her report to the office."

He flashed the cradle switch and dialed. "This is Lieutenant Oscar Colunga. Is Kathy home? ... I see. When did you expect her?" His eyes met Rita's. "Who am I speaking with, please?" He made another note on the blotter. "Listen, Kathy may be in great danger. I want you to make every effort to locate her. If you find her, tell her to go to the office and stay there. And, miss, if you hear anything at all, call me at this number or leave word at my office ... That's right. Lieutenant Colunga." Oscar fed her the numbers. "It is urgent! Do you understand?" He hung up and turned to Rita. "I'm sorry. Things have gotten ..." The sound of helicopter blades ruptured the evening silence.

Rita's head dropped forward in a gesture of despair. "What now?"

"It's Cruz."

"Cruz?"

"An old friend ... with the FBI."

"The FBI? Coming here?"

With great trepidation he watched her head come up, expecting to hear words that would end the best thing in ten years. There was a deep gurgling sound in her throat. Then her head flew back and the rumble cascaded into raucous laughter.

"What next? Is John Wayne's ghost going to hitch his horsey to my fence post?"

Oscar cocked his head as approaching sirens permeated the room. "I don't know what's going to happen, but I have to make sure you're safe. I want you to spend the night at your mother's."

"Oh, Oscar."

"No arguments." He pivoted to the front windows. "There's a state trooper out front. He'll take you over there."

Chapter 51

José Cruz turned to Colunga as the patrol car pulled away from the curb. "I am relieved to know your *mujer* is safe, *Hijo*, but who has been kidnapped?"

"I think it's that young data analyst who works for me. Kathy Huntsinger."

"You're not sure?"

"No, but she's overdue at home."

"So what should we do?"

Oscar thought. "Let's work out of my office."

"Lead on." José turned toward the waiting craft. "How did he contact you?"

"He sent a message by cab. Says he'll call me tomorrow morning at ten."

"Crazy." José hauled himself into the shotgun seat and barked their destination to Paul Jones. "Who would think we could turn over a woman to a loco?"

In the rear seat, Oscar shook his head. "Only a loco."

"He must be getting desperate. Does he have any reason to believe you are closing in on him?"

Oscar raised his voice over the beating of the blades as they took to the air. "Kathy did say that the men we were investigating might be aware of it."

"Why?"

"Because she's contacted relatives and friends."

"So it could be more than taking someone close to you." José's jaw set hard. "He may also intend to eliminate a valuable resource directed against him."

"You could be right."

"Either way, she doesn't stand a chance if he has her. Our only hope is to find them before he kills her. What are the odds?"

Oscar bowed his head. "Zero, based on what we know now."

"So, what's your plan?"

"To look at Kathy's latest research."

"Do you know how to access her files?"

"No. Can you patch me through to a local number?"

"Sure."

"The man's name is Stan Zelinski. He lives in Windsor."

José turned and spoke into the radio. Two minutes later he handed the headset over.

"Stan?"

"Yes, Lieutenant."

"I need your help at the office."

"Tonight? I have a house full of relatives over here."

"Kathy may have been kidnapped."

A stony silence. "What do you need?"

"I want you to look up some files on her computer. If you leave now, we should arrive about the same time."

"Right. See you there."

Oscar leaned heavily on the back of José's seat. "Don't you guys have any leads yet?"

"We have a lot of resources on this case, but I wouldn't hope for a break in the next few hours."

Oscar's head drooped. "Then it's up to us." He lapsed into a moody silence until the chopper was nearly over his building.

Paul Jones glanced over his shoulder. "Do you have a landing pad?"

"No. There's a small park one block west."

Two minutes later, José and Oscar sprinted through the glass doors and pulled up at the front desk.

"Any news?"

"Why yes, Lieutenant. Kathy's roommate phoned to say that she can't find her."

"Is Stan in yet?"

"I haven't seen him."

"We'll be in my office."

"Yes, sir." She gazed at them as they mounted the stairs.

Oscar pushed the door open and recoiled at the stench of burning coffee. He quickly stepped over and turned off the switch, pulling the pot off the hot burner and setting it on top.

José wrinkled his nose. "Aye *Hijo*, that smells awful."

Oscar nodded. "Reminds me of the coffee you used to make when we were camping."

"At least that was intentional."

Oscar led the way into his office. "Have a seat, Joe. I don't think there's anything we can do until Stan gets here." He rummaged in the drawer for a pack of cigarettes.

"You're smoking again?"

"Yeah. I've been under a lot of pressure these last few weeks."

"Not a good excuse." José eyed him. "Do you and Kathy have a close relationship?"

"Not really. She works for me."

"Come on, Oscar. This isn't some gringo you're talking to. I know how you care about people." José's head fell back and he stared into another time. "I've seen you try to fix a hawk's broken wing. I saw you stick a branch into a pool of water to rescue a bee that had fallen in."

"Not anymore."

"Why not?"

"Because the hawk died, and the bee would sting me the next time without the slightest hesitation."

"So you don't care about this young woman?"

"I didn't say that ..." Oscar's deep voice trailed off.

"It's Julia, isn't it? You're afraid to let yourself care again."

Oscar's face seemed sad and haggard. "If you let yourself care, you get hurt. It changes a man."

"But not forever. You have a light in you, Oscar. I want it back."

"So do I." Oscar paused to collect his thoughts, but the response of that moment died forever. A heavy, treading noise pervaded the silence, and they rushed to the outer office as Stan Zelinski burst through the door.

"Stan, this is José Cruz of the FBI. He's backing us up on this thing."

Stan gave a brief nod. "Has Kathy really been kidnapped?"

"We aren't certain, but it looks that way."

"God. What can I do?"

"You know how to access her computer files?"

"Sure. What are you looking for?"

"Recent entries—say the last two or three days."

Zelinski moved to her desk and turned on the computer as he sank into the chair. He ran his fingers through a thick mop of brown hair and muttered obscenities under his breath while the computer stepped through its self tests. At last, he leaned forward to the keyboard.

"Here they are. But the only records accessed in the past few days are these two—Miller and Jarvis." Zelinski looked up. "Where do you want to start?"

"Miller."

He brought up the file. "That it?"

Oscar put on his reading glasses. "Yes. But I've seen all this before. Page forward."

Several screens later, he touched Stan's shoulder. "Stop. This is new stuff." He straightened up. "Financial data?"

"Yes. He owns a house in Fort Lee, New Jersey—owns it free and clear by the way. Checking account balance, twenty-one hundred. CDs and savings total twenty-four thousand. No information on stocks, annuities, or other investments. And there's one last note. He raises pedigreed dogs."

Remembering the vision of tangled chains in the pet store, Oscar felt like he'd been hit between the eyes. "Give me his address."

While the paper bumped forward in the printer, José studied Oscar's face.

"What is it, *Hijo?*"

"Our man used dog chains for bonds, and a silencer on his victims that may have been a shock collar to prevent barking."

"Could that be the link we're looking for?"

"I don't know. What's the flying time to Fort Lee?"

"Roughly twenty minutes."

"Then it won't take us long to check it out." He headed toward the door. "Stan, you coordinate things from here. Make sure we have all the latest entries, and try to find Kathy."

Zelinski nodded and reached for the phone.

Chapter 52

The relentless beat of the rotors assaulted Oscar's mind, adding to the already unbearable tension. He perched on the edge of the rear seat, staring at the grid pattern to the left of Paul Jones.

"How far is it now?"

"About two miles."

"That blip on the screen?"

"Yes. It's a satellite navigation system that'll put us down within fifty feet."

"Good." Oscar turned to gaze out the side window at the sea of lights that was Manhattan, now becoming visible against the darkening sky. Was it possible that the trail would end here—a murderer undetected for more than a decade, run to Earth in New Jersey?

Paul hunched over to peer through the Plexiglas. "I see a grassy clearing down there, but I can't make out if it's a park or private property."

José followed his line of sight. "I don't give a damn. Put her down!" He tossed off his seat belt. "Where is it from here?"

"About a half block east, I would say."

José and Oscar hit the ground at the same instant, angling to the sidewalk and walking briskly eastward. Oscar pulled out the address and verified the descending numbers on the houses they passed. The fourth one matched. They turned onto the front walk and pulled up in surprise. A man stood on the porch with hands on hips, watching their progress.

José called out. "Mr. Miller?"

"What the hell is going on? You got permission to land that thing in this area?"

They closed the gap and José held out his ID card. "José Cruz, FBI. And this is Lieutenant Oscar Colunga with the Connecticut State Police. May we have a word with you?"

Miller's wrath dissolved into a puzzled expression. "Gentlemen, this is not a good time. I have dinner guests. Business, you understand. Could we talk tomorrow?"

"Sorry. This won't wait."

"Well, what is it you want?"

Oscar glanced around. Several curious neighbors had come out onto their porches or lawns.

"Perhaps it would be better if we spoke inside."

Miller looked down the street and nodded. "All right. Come in." He led them along the central hallway, pulling up at the dining room door.

"I have some unexpected visitors. Please enjoy yourselves. I'll only be a few minutes."

An attractive brunette arose and strode to the door. "What is it, Irv?"

"Nothing, Lisa. Just keep them entertained until I get back."

He closed the double doors on the pouting face and motioned to follow, guiding them into a lavish den on the northeast corner. Behind the mahogany desk, gracious windows looked out onto the backyard and the interior walls were lined with oak book cases, shelves stuffed top to bottom. He closed the door and took up a position in front of the desk, declining to offer them a seat.

"Now, what's this all about?"

Cruz cleared his throat. "We are investigating a kidnapping."

"Oh? Someone I know?"

"A Connecticut police officer."

"Well, what has that to do with me?"

"She was investigating Megan Roarke's assault."

Miller took a step back and sagged against the desk. "God, there's no end to it."

"Not so far."

His eyes seemed to focus on Oscar for the first time. "I know who you are. I saw you at the hospital when I went up to visit Meg."

Oscar nodded. "Did she ever mention my name to you before this happened?"

"I think so."

"Why?"

"She sent a partial manuscript to a police officer in Connecticut. I assume it was you?"

"Yes."

"I don't understand any of this." He turned back to José. "What do you want from me?"

"We'd like to look around your house."

"Oh, come now. You think I've done something wrong ... that I'm involved in kidnapping or murder?" His face held the look of betrayal. "Do you have a warrant?"

"I hope that won't be necessary."

Miller shook his head sadly. "All right. I have nothing to hide."

He led them through the ground- and second-floor rooms in a matter of minutes, opening every door and closet for inspection, then into the cramped basement, just large enough for the furnace and water heater. "Watch your head on these pipes."

The coal furnace had been replaced by an oil burning model, but some of the old pipes still swung from the ceiling. Oscar moved along the periphery, running his hands across the dank, moldy concrete walls in search of some fissure that could be a secret doorway. Even in the dim light, he was satisfied that none existed.

Miller watched him with keen curiosity.

"Nothing here." Oscar brushed his hands off. "Do you have a garage?"

"Out back." He headed for the stairs with a look of annoyance.

The garage was a separate structure to the rear of the house. Except for the sleek sedan, a few garden tools, and an abundance of dust and cobwebs, it was barren and clearly not used for some secret purpose.

As they returned to the house, Oscar paused to survey the caged dog run. "I understand you breed dogs."

Miller smiled for the first time. "I used to, but I gave it up a few years ago. I have one old bloodhound bitch left."

"Where is she?"

"At kennel, because of my dinner party."

Oscar turned to him. "Perhaps you could tell me something. I heard about this shock collar that prevents dogs from barking."

No flinch or strain showed in Miller's face. "What about it?"

"I'd like to see what they look like. Do you have one?"

His head wagged back and forth. "We rely on obedience training. You'll notice dogs seldom bark at shows, unless directed to."

"So you've never used one."

"Never had the need for it." He glanced at José. "If you gentlemen have seen everything, I must get back to my guests. Publishing is tricky business nowadays, and I have a little sucking up to do."

José smiled up at him. "Thank you, Mr Miller. You have been most cooperative."

"Sorry I couldn't have been more help." He'd regained some of his natural charm. "I hope your officer is all right." The back door slammed as Oscar and José skirted around the house and made their way to the helicopter, past several pairs of inquiring eyes.

In deference to the neighborhood, Paul Jones had killed the engine. He watched them scramble into their seats. "Anything?"

José sighed. "No joy. What did you think, Oscar?"

"He came off like Mary Poppins ... not a thing out of place."

"Yeah. And if you were going to pull off a kidnapping that involved blackmailing the police, would you organize a big dinner party for that night?"

"No. But I'm not crazy. If he stashed her somewhere else, he has a perfect alibi. And Miller is our best candidate. He was close enough to feed on Megan's fear. He lied to her about things. He knew she sent the manuscript to me. And he used to live in northwest Connecticut."

"Did you check out his house up there?"

"Yes. It's nothing like the one in the book, a single-story ranch."

"Then I'd say we've used up all avenues of investigation, *Hijo*."

"I'm afraid you're right." Oscar rubbed the stubble on his jaw. "Maybe Stan's come up with something by now. Do you have a phone?"

Paul passed it back and glanced around. "I think we should get out of here before the zombies attack."

"Go." Oscar dialed as the blades began to wind up. "Stan?"

"Yes, Oscar. How'd it go?"

"I think we drew a blank here. Any news of Kathy?"

"It doesn't look good. Apparently she didn't make it back from lunch."

"Damn!" Oscar thought for a moment. "Does Miller have property anywhere else?"

"No indication of that."

"What about Jarvis?"

"Earlier data is fairly routine, but these new entries indicate some hidden assets, including a cabin near Winsted."

"Where's that?"

"North of Torrington."

Oscar swallowed hard. "In the northwest quadrant?"

"Yes, sir."

"Why did it take so long to uncover this house?"

"It's in his mother's name."

"Does she live there?"

The pause lasted an aeon. "It looks like she lives in Atlanta."

"When was that entry made?"

"Yesterday."

"Do you have addresses and phone numbers for the houses?" Oscar took out his notebook and printed them carefully. "Good work, Stan. Did you find anything else?"

"Well, you told me to look for all recent entries ..."

"Yes?"

"There was one other file accessed today."

"What's in it?"

"A very short entry. Two gallons of formaldehyde sold by Channel Chemicals of Hartford to a Mr. J. Harmon. Cash. Invoice to be faxed."

"Did the invoice come in?"

"I found it on the machine."

"What's the invoice date?" He listened intently. "Stay there. I'll get back to you."

In a cold sweat, Oscar dropped the phone into his lap.

"It's Harmon Jarvis."

Cruz spun around. "Her boss?"

"Yes."

"You sure he's the guy?"

"Positive."

"What now?"

"He has two places—a house on Long Island and a cabin in northern Connecticut. If we pick the wrong one, it could mean the difference between life and death."

"How about we call him?"

"What? A mysterious call might spook him."

"Trust me. We have people who do these things. We'll try Long Island first." He reached back. "You have the numbers?"

"Yeah." Oscar dropped the phone and his notebook into José's hand, then closed his eyes. If he hadn't gone to lunch with that damned reporter ...

José turned to him. "They got an answering machine. Want to call the cabin?"

"No. If it's a secret place, any call would panic him. We have to go in and take a look."

José nodded. "I agree. Get us up, Paul."

"Roger." He brought the chopper up to cruising altitude and dialed in their course, then glanced over his shoulder. "I think your plan has one flaw, Lieutenant."

"What's that?"

"I don't think we can land anywhere near this guy. If he so much as hears a rotor, he'll break and run. I have a feeling that's what scared him off last time. I just realized that we flew right over the Pleasant Valley house on our way to the realty office."

"You could be right. What do you suggest?"

"I think we should go the last few miles by car."

Oscar shook his head. "How can we get a car there in the next twenty minutes?"

José turned to him. "I could radio our office in Hartford to bring one up."

"No. It would take too long."

"Oscar, we may have to wait for it. I think Paul's right."

"Damn." Oscar twisted his head away. "Wait! Hank Oliphant lives in Torrington. He could get there before we do, if we can reach him."

Chapter 53

The helicopter settled onto the baseball diamond infield, raising a sandstorm that swirled in the landing lights. Hank Oliphant stood on the bleachers and waved.

"I'm coming with you."

José put his hand on the big man's shoulder. "No. If things go wrong, we may need your chopper. Stand by here."

Paul sat back, disappointed. "You guys watch your ass up there."

"Count on it."

José bailed out with Oscar close behind. They ducked under the settling blades and followed Oliphant to the un-marked car behind the backstop. Oscar jumped into the shotgun seat as José' climbed into the back.

"Hank, this is José Cruz with the FBI."

Oliphant flipped a signal of acknowledgement and fired up the engine, taking the tarmac in a cloud of dust. Several blocks later, he turned north onto Highway 8.

"I scoped the place out on a map. I know right where it is ... may have seen it before."

"Good. How far is it?"

"Oh, a few minutes to Winsted. Then maybe another five or ten to find the place and plan an approach." Oliphant glanced over. "You guys armed?"

Oscar drew his 9MM automatic and loaded the chamber.

He tossed his head toward the back. "Cruz?"

"I use a .357."

"Well, I brought along some extra firepower in case the bastard wants to shoot it out." Oliphant shifted his weight. "Now, what's this all about, Oscar? You say this guy grabbed Kathy?"

"Yeah. I got a message saying he would trade Kathy for Megan."

"He must be running scared."

"I'm not so sure."

"What?"

"Listen, Hank. He knows we can't make that exchange. No one would give us the authority, even if we wanted to."

"So why did he grab her?"

"My guess is, we're getting too close. A final act of vengeance."

"How could he have known about Kathy?"

"I have a suspicion he's been dogging us ever since he found out Megan was sending his book to me ... studying the opposition. Or someone may have told him Kathy was making inquiries. All they had to do was remember her name."

Oliphant pressed the accelerator a little harder. "I don't know Kathy very well, but she's one of ours. If I get the bastard in my sights ..."

"Easy, Hank. This is no vendetta."

They drove in troubled silence for several miles. As Hank turned onto Highway 44 and passed through the town of Winsted, he glanced over at Oscar. "You know, this is only a stone's throw from where Megan was assaulted."

Oscar's head snapped around. "Don't tell me it's the same house!"

"No. We're going in the opposite direction."

"Could it be that he knew the realtor he killed?"

"I'd say it's a good bet."

"Hmm. That might explain how he was able to get her alone in the house."

Oliphant pulled over at a stop sign and turned on the interior light to check the map. "After we make this turn, it will be on the right about a half mile. Take a good look as we pass. Then we'll swing up on this road and approach from the rear."

He switched the light off and turned westward, rolling slowly along the dark road. Subtle noises from bearings, wind, and engine seemed amplified, and the crackling of sand and gravel under the tires raged into the still night air.

Oscar rolled down his window. The moon had risen, partially obscured by a high layer of thin clouds, and the black shape stood well up the hill at the end of a long driveway, its upper floors looming over a wide garage on the ground level. Zelinski's use of the word cabin was misleading—an enormous place in the style of a Swiss chalet. There was no light or hint of movement. No car in front.

When they had passed, Oliphant whispered to Oscar. "Well?"

"Looks abandoned. Did you see anything, Joe?"

"*Nada.* What do you want to do?"

"I think we should go with Hank's idea ... approach from the rear."

They turned north onto the dirt road and pulled off a hundred yards in. Doors opened and closed stealthily as Oliphant slipped around to the trunk. He held out a thirty-ought-six rifle with scope.

Oscar whispered, "Joe's a better shot."

Hank handed the rifle to José and extracted a twelve gauge shotgun and canvas bag. "Ready?"

They headed into the woods, placing their feet carefully among the dried needles and twigs. Each crack sounded loud enough to echo as they moved like dark wraiths toward an uncertain destiny. Finally, they crouched down at the edge of the clearing behind the house.

Hank pulled a night vision scope from the bag and scanned the rear windows, then bent close to the others. "Looks clear. What's the game plan?"

Oscar replied, "I think we should see if there's a car in the garage."

"I'll go." José slipped out of his shoes. "You have a flashlight in your bag of tricks, Hank?"

He nodded and fished one out.

"I'm going to circle around through the trees, down there on the left side of the house. Give me ten minutes."

Oscar said a silent prayer as José padded down the hill. He subconsciously counted the seconds and was ready to follow when he saw the compact shadow returning. José knelt down close to their faces.

"There's a red Mercedes behind one of the doors."

Oscar frowned. "One of the doors? How big is this thing?"

"Looks like a four-car garage."

"Four car?" Oscar felt his brain go numb. "Was the back wall lined with shelves?"

"Yeah, but they were nearly empty."

"How could you see all that? Did you use the flashlight?"

"Didn't have to. There was light coming under a door between the shelves."

Truth settled like a shroud. Because of the steep slope, the rear of the house was underground—just as the book described. Oscar had come to believe that the killer's nest was a fantasy, but there it sat in front of him. Now he cringed at the realization that Kathy was inside this vile room where so many had suffered before.

José examined his face. "What's wrong, *Hijo?*"

"That's the house in his book. Don't you remember?"

"*Dios!*" José blanched and turned to Oliphant. "Can we get in from the back?"

"The place is a damn fortress. Steel door and barred windows."

"It's the same round front. We'll have to call in an assault team."

"No!" Oscar shook his head violently. "There isn't time."

"I'll have them here in thirty minutes."

"And what if he kills her while we're waiting around? Can you live with that?"

"Sorry, Oscar. We can't handle this."

"Fuck we can't!" He turned to Oliphant. "Gimme the keys."

"Why?"

"I'm going to ram the garage door."

Oliphant shook his head. "It's too risky."

"Risky? That's Kathy down there, Hank. You think she's safer on the business end of a SWAT team's automatic rifles?"

"But we're not sure. What if she isn't in there?"

"Then, I'll have to take out a loan."

Oliphant dipped into his pocket for the keys. "We'll need five minutes to get into position."

"Which side is the car on, Joe?"

"Left. The right door is clear."

Oscar turned and scrambled up the hill.

José retied his shoes and loaded the chamber of the high-powered rifle, then he and Oliphant started down the slope toward the house. After a few steps, Cruz laid his hand on the big man's shoulder and stopped dead in his tracks.

"Listen." He turned his head, straining to interpret the sounds and light patterns from the road, then stared in horror as headlights appeared at the driveway's entrance. "Son of a bitch! Oscar's not going to wait for us."

The car came on fast, trailing a cloud of dust and gravel in its wake. Oscar hit the door at thirty, locking the brakes when the bumper penetrated the lower panels, and slid to a stop against the splintering shelves as headlights shattered and wisps of smoke erupted from dying filaments.

He drew his gun and bolted from the seat, stumbling over broken lumber. The heavy door gave way under his weight and swung inward, slamming against the concrete wall at the end of its long arc.

In an instant, he assessed the room with a feeling of *déjà-vu*. Torture devices on the left, desk and bathroom to the right ... the bed directly in front of him. But there was no sign of human life. He turned and glanced up at three monitors on the wall over the door, cringing as he realized that one of them was a view of the house from the foot of the driveway. Jarvis had seen him coming.

He returned to the garage as Cruz and Oliphant surged though the shattered door, weapons at the ready. "They're gone!"

José's eyes first widened in disbelief, then settled on a stairway in the northwest corner. "Upstairs!"

Oscar sprang up the stairs with the others on his heels. At the top, he noticed that the steel bolt on the heavy back door was pulled open but, knowing Jarvis, he couldn't be sure the killer had taken Kathy from the house. He whispered, "Check the place out, and be careful."

They nodded and turned to their assignment as Oscar slipped through the door. Because he had been too long in the bright light of the interior, his eyes were useless. Recognizing the danger of his position, he crouched down and closed them tight, putting all his concentration into listening. It was eerily quiet. There was no sound, even from the house where Cruz and Oliphant were stealthily making their way through the rooms.

Then a branch snapped. It was distant ... well up the hill to his right. He opened his eyes and headed in that direction, scrambling over the uneven ground in a squatting, serpentine run. Oscar sensed true physical fear. As he stumbled along in the dark, his footsteps in the dry loam on the ground reverberated like a circus parade. Anyone up there would know he was coming, and he had no idea what Jarvis was armed with. He crashed down behind a fallen log, and held his breath to listen. Dead silence. His eyes were adjusting to the dark, and he peered over the downed tree, looking for any sign of movement. Seeing and hearing nothing, he considered his options. Then a woman screamed.

Oscar focused on the probable location and saw a hint of movement. As the high cloud cover briefly relented, he could clearly make out the figure of a man on the far side of a large tree trunk thirty feet away. Big as it was, it was not enough to block out the wide shoulders and torso of the man who backed against it for cover, especially since he was battling something that made him rock violently back and forth.

Oscar checked his 9MM and skirted the fallen log to stand near the protection of another large tree. "Give it up, Jarvis!"

The figure tensed as if preparing for action. Then Jarvis turned and stepped out to face him, virtually carrying the naked form of Kathy Huntsinger in front of him with a large black butcher knife at her throat.

"Give what up?" he bellowed. "I'm holding all the aces."

Oscar assessed the situation. Her wrists shackled in front with silver handcuffs, she was virtually dangling in the strong man's embrace, a thin trickle of red from the sharp blade cutting into her skin. The full moon now bright, Oscar stood frozen, staring into the eyes of the killer.

Jarvis seemed to be delighted. "So, Lieutenant, we meet at last ... our game of cat-and-mouse at an end."

"Yes, and I'm afraid you lose."

"On the contrary. I offer you a trade—my freedom for this young lady's life."

"You know I can't let you go on to kill others."

"And so, the moment of truth. You denied me my time with Megan. You have driven me from this special place. You have destroyed my very way of life ... cost me dearly, Lieutenant. Do you have any doubt that I would kill this girl as an act of retribution?"

Kathy squirmed and Oscar focused on the terror in her eyes. "Let her go, or as God is my witness ..."

Jarvis eyed him like a mother dismissing her pouting child. "How very grand of you, my dear fellow. But you see?" He slid the knife an inch across her throat, deepening the cut. His face twisted into a mask of malevolence. "You know I won't hesitate to kill her."

Kathy's lips moved in a silent plea for help.

Jarvis sneered, seeming to sense that time was running out. "That's a mighty impressive piece you have there. What's it hold? Fourteen or fifteen rounds?"

Oscar nodded, dumbfounded by the question.

"Tell you what. How about an old-fashioned gunfight for all the marbles?"

"What?"

Jarvis twisted sideways so that Oscar could see a heavy revolver in a low-slung holster on his right hip. "I'll put Kathy down, and we'll shoot it out. Like an old-fashioned gunfight. Chivalry and all that. What do you say?"

"I say you really are crazy. I'm not going to holster my weapon."

"Didn't ask you to. Just lower it to your side. I'll release the girl, and you can fire when ready. Deal?"

Oscar regarded the terrified girl. "Deal." He dropped his hand to his side.

"Fair enough." Jarvis threw down the knife and pushed Kathy to the ground at his feet. "But I have to warn you, I've fired single action revolvers in competition, so don't think you have to cut me any slack."

Fear clutched at Oscar's mind again. Had he allowed the madman to lure him into a fight that he might lose? Or was it just another lie, designed to gain an edge? Oscar fought his anger and listened. Behind him was stony silence. Cruz and Oliphant must have finished their search, and would undoubtedly follow. Was Jarvis aware of the other men? Were they in position to back him up?

"Any time you're ready, Lieutenant."

Oscar made sure his grip was optimum and mentally practiced firing the gun. An instant before his mind triggered the attack, Kathy moaned and came to her knees.

Jarvis reacted with a startled jerk, and then Kathy arched her back and whipped her shackled hands around with animal strength, striking him squarely below the belt. He slapped her hard, sending her flying backward where she rolled into a quivering heap.

"Bitch!" Face contorted with searing pain, Jarvis fell to his knees, leering at her with hatred and rage, while both hands rested where she hit him.

Oscar stood transfixed, viewing the scene with no idea what to do. Then Jarvis made a fatal mistake.

He spat through clenched teeth, "I should have taken care of you before this!" His hand moved with lightning speed to the gun on his hip.

Colunga reacted on instinct. He had no idea how many times his gun spoke, but he didn't stop firing until the murderer toppled backward onto the dank ground. He closed his eyes as a strange yellow fog drifted across his mind, sensing that he was about to pass out for the first time in his life. Then someone eased the gun out of his hand.

"Are you all right, *Hijo*?"

The voice of an old friend drifted from a far place. He sucked in great gasps of air and the yellow fog began to dissipate. Finding it impossible to move, he tried speech.

"I'll live. How's Kathy?"

Oliphant shouted, "She'll be okay."

Colunga felt his feet moving. He removed his coat to cover the sobbing young woman, as she threw her arms around his neck and buried her face in his chest.

His tears mingled with hers. "I'm so sorry I let this happen to you."

She jerked her head back and fixed him with a stern gaze. "Oscar, it's the risk we take when we decide to become cops. You can't blame yourself for this one."

Somehow, through his anguish, he knew she was right. He turned his head to Cruz, who was kneeling over the body. "What about Jarvis?"

"You put a half dozen rounds into his chest, *Hijo*. I don't think he's going to make it."

Oscar nodded. "He won't be missed."

"Yeah." José turned his head with a puzzled look. "But there's one thing I don't understand."

"What's that?"

"Who buried this butcher knife in his groin?"

Chapter 54

The black sedan moved silently up the driveway at Fairlawn Medical Center. A formation of Canadian geese honked noisily overhead in their northward flight, and the tall poplars lining the road were starting to leaf under the relentless pressure of spring. Oscar Colunga turned his face to the afternoon sun, at peace for the first time in his recent memory.

He left the car and ascended the broad stone stairs, then walked down the long corridor for what he knew would be the last time. Regardless of the outcome for Megan, he would no longer be a part of her life, nor she a part of his. There was no mutual debt. He had done his job ... saved her body. Now it was up to those who had the power to treat her mind.

Oscar pushed the door open reverently. Megan was just as he had last seen her, eyes half open and the covers over her heart moving in shallow stuttered breaths. He moved forward slowly and was startled by a movement across the bed.

Achal Bedi lowered his magazine and leaned into view. "Afternoon, Lieutenant."

Colunga nodded and pulled up at bedside. "How's our girl?"

"No change, I'm sorry to say." Achal stood up to face him. "She's been like this for six months. Can't they do something for her?"

"I'm sorry, Achal. It's beyond my understanding."

"Mine, too." He shook his head. "It seems so unfair."

"Yes, she certainly didn't deserve this. But I need to talk to her. Could we have a minute alone?"

"Of course." Achal edged toward the door. "I'll be right outside."

Oscar pulled up a chair and took her limp hand in his. For some time he stared at the beautiful lifeless face.

"It's Oscar Colunga. Do you remember me?" He scanned her for some sign. "I'm leaving Connecticut. It's time for me to go home."

He searched for words, staring at her tortured isolation.

"There's something I have to tell you. They wanted me to wait until you were well, but we've run out of time." Tears welled up and his voice ran hoarse. "The man who did this to you ..."

He stammered to a halt and dropped his face to her hand. "Harmon Jarvis is dead. I killed him for you, Meg. Now I want you to come back for me."

Horror rose in his throat. The slight pressure on his fingers was like a blow from a skeletal hand. At dream speed, his head came up. He gazed at the staring eyes for some time before admitting that hope had deluded his senses.

"*A Dios.*" He tucked her hand under the blanket and blindly lunged for the door, calling out in passing, "Take care of her, Achal."

He gazed at the imposing building one last time as the engine caught. "Goodbye, Megan." Strong urges tugged at him, calling him back to finish what he could not control. Oscar wiped his eyes and slammed the gearshift lever down.

In the sterile white room, Achal Bedi stood by Megan's bed, staring with wonder. The blanket across her breast rose and fell with the power and rhythm of an ocean wave. Tears traced tracks into her rosewood hair, and her great green eyes slowly closed.